Praise for the wri

"This was an incredibly hot read. Ms. Harte creates captivating characters that will steal your heart."

-- Astraea, *Enchanted Ramblings*

"The sex scenes are hot enough to fry eggs and left me breathless."

-- Susan White, *Coffee Time Romance*

Stay

"This book will leave you hot, sweaty, and looking for your significant other."

-- *Two Lips Reviews*

"*Stay* drew me in from the first word to the last..."

-- Maura, *Joyfully Reviewed*

Home

"With non stopping drama and succulent passion, one will be thoroughly entertained by this romantic yet compelling story of love."

-- Jasmina Vallombrosa, *TCM Reviews*

"The sex is sweaty, steamy hot. It will bring out the animal in any reader, just like it does in the characters."

-- Brigit Aine, *Just Erotic Romance Reviews*

LooseId®

ISBN 978-1-59632-509-8
ALPHA
Copyright © 2007 by Treva Harte

Cover Art by April Martinez

Publisher acknowledges the author and copyright holder of the individual works, as follows:

ALPHA 1: STAY
Copyright © February 2006 by Treva Harte
ALPHA 2: WALK AWAY
Copyright © September 2006 by Treva Harte
ALPHA 3: HOME
Copyright © January 2007 by Treva Harte

All rights reserved. Except for use of brief quotations in any review or critical article, the reproduction or utilization of this work in whole or in part in any form by any electronic, mechanical or other means, now known or hereafter invented, including xerography, photocopying and recording, or in any information storage or retrieval is forbidden without the prior written permission of Loose Id LLC, 1802 N Carson Street, Suite 212-2924, Carson City NV 89701-1215. www.loose-id.com

This book is an original publication of Loose Id®. Each individual story herein was previously published in e-book format by Loose Id®, and is a work of fiction. Any similarity to actual persons, events or existing locations is entirely coincidental.

Printed in the U.S.A. by
Lightning Source, Inc.
1246 Heil Quaker Blvd
La Vergne TN 37086
www.lightningsource.com

Contents

Walk Away
1

Stay
103

Home
205

WALK AWAY

Chapter One

"He's gay."

"He's not."

"They're all gay."

"You're going to make me cry."

"Who is gay?" Leila broke into the chatter between the two waitresses as she peered through the little bar's murky light.

"They're *not*. God couldn't be that cruel." Sasha stared off to the left and jerked her chin instead of pointing. "We're talking about *Them*. Three of the most gorgeous men that have ever stepped into this place."

"They stick close to each other, they don't look at women, and they're way too good-looking. Gay, gay, gay." Thea hissed the words to them both.

"Indoor voices, girls." Leila looked where Sasha was still staring. "Oh!"

"You see?" Both of the waitresses chorused together.

"They are gorgeous." Leila automatically smoothed her chestnut hair, even though they weren't looking back. "Drop-dead, finger-licking gorgeous."

"If they were interested, it wouldn't be my finger I'd want licked. Or theirs." Thea pursed her lips. "Yum yum."

The tallest one in the group, the one with the rich brown hair that fell to his shoulders, suddenly looked their way. Leila gulped. Intense blue eyes seared her for a moment. Then he turned his face away and spoke to the other two. Two dark heads bent close to his. He didn't look back up.

"He's so not interested in women." Thea shrugged. "We lose again, ladies. But I win my bet, Sasha. Pay up, girl."

"He might not be interested in me -- us. But he's not gay." Leila held on to the counter, trying to settle her stomach. It was as if he'd hit her. Not that he ever had. Not physically.

"How do you know?" Sasha asked. "Did he try to wrestle you to the floor and have his way with you one dark night?"

"He must have been about twelve. He doesn't look all that old, and Leila hasn't gone out with a guy in years." Thea giggled.

"Actually, that's exactly what Dek did." Leila let go of the counter, very carefully. "If he asks, tell Jeff I'm taking my break early. No. Tell him I'm leaving early."

"*What?*" Leila knew she never took breaks, much less left before she was supposed to. She never changed routine. She worked her job from start to finish, like a good little girl.

That's what she was now. A Good Girl. She'd worked her ass off to get that reputation, and she hadn't messed up in years. Five and a half fucking years, almost exactly. Not since Dek walked out of her life. He'd grown up -- gotten harder and muscular and even more masculine. She'd thought he was devastating before; now he was overwhelming. At least she was overwhelmed.

She ignored the other two gaping women and walked away, one step after the other, balancing her weight as if she were drunk. When she got to the employee exit, she rested her head for a moment against the splintered wood barrier that lay between her and escape. She wasn't sure she had the strength for this. Not again.

She thought she heard noise behind her. Dek?

Leila pushed the door open and ran into the night.

If he did follow her, she was dead meat. He could catch her. She heard her footsteps slapping against the pavement and the hitch in her breath. He could outrun her easily. If he did follow her. If he wanted to.

She turned the corner sharply. Paused a moment. She didn't hear anything behind her. In the distance a car's horn honked. The wind rattled a trash can. They were all normal sounds. Safe sounds.

Dek wasn't normal. Wasn't safe.

The first time she'd met him, she'd known. Of course, he had made it pretty obvious when he tried to kill her stepfather.

"I tell you, I saw the little b -- booger turn. I'm bleeding from where he attacked me. Damn it, he's dangerous." Rod's red face turned even redder in the silence that met his words. He swung toward her. "You were there! Tell the cop! Go on, girl."

She swallowed. She hated his sweaty face. Hated the piggish eyes that glared at her right now. They might be under the same roof, but that didn't mean she had to like pretending he was kin. She didn't have to enjoy living with him, listening to him...obeying him.

"Damn you, girl, if you don't talk up, I swear --"

She took a half-step back. The policeman put his hand on her shoulder, and she tried not to flinch. The eyes under the police cap were all right. They were searching her up and down, but they were human eyes. They might even be kind. She took a deep breath.

"Tell me what you saw...Leila, is it? Don't be afraid."

"Yes, sir. That's me. I-I didn't see anything. I mean, I came in and I saw Rod -- I mean, my stepdad -- screaming and swearing and bleeding. I didn't really look at anything else."

"How the hell did you miss what was going on, you stupid sl -- child?" Fascinated, Leila watched his red face slowly turn purple. She waited for her stepfather's head to blow off. Instead he whirled and pointed at the one person left in the room who hadn't said anything. "I tell you, he went for my throat. You think something human went for me like this?"

Leila stared at the bleeding wounds.

"He tried to jump me." Dek's voice was whisper-soft. "Rape me. I fought back. What else could I do?"

"You see any of that, Leila?" The policeman sounded safe. But he wasn't. No one was safe. Leila knew that.

What should she do?

"I -- No, sir." Her voice firmed. "Nothing."

"Your stepdad ever try to hurt you the way the boy here said?" The cop's voice hardened.

Jesus. He was smarter than she'd expected. Or else Rod had what he was like written all over him. Written so clear that anyone could see. Except Mom. Mom always believed Rod.

Leila gazed down.

"No, sir." But she let her voice get more Southern and liquid. Let her lips tremble as she said that final word. She knew what it sounded like with that little catch over the syllable.

The cop's breath audibly hissed.

"I'm the one who is bleeding here!" Rod's voice rose. "Arrest that mongrel bastard."

"I'll have the authorities take him back to the County. I'm taking you in for questioning." The policeman didn't take his eyes off Rod. "Step outside for a minute with me, Mr. Voss."

"What the f-- hell!"

His voice faded a little as he got outside. Leila shut her eyes, tried to pretend she was alone and everything was all right. She'd made a decision, and now she'd have to live with whatever happened next.

"I owe you." Dek's whispery voice cut through her self-protective shell, and she opened her eyes.

She stared at the slight teenager who was maybe a year or two older than her. Her stepdad had brought home a stray kid to abuse and bully, like he did now and then. But this time he'd brought home something that took him on. Who would have thought it?

"You don't owe me anything, Big Bad Wolf." Leila crossed her arms. "It was my pleasure. Wish you'd ripped his liver out."

"I wish I had, too." Dek smiled, all pointy, big teeth.

"But for now you'd better run out the back door while Rod is keeping the cop busy out there."

"I already had that in mind." He hesitated. "What about you?"

"What about me? You're not concerned about me."

"You're wrong. I am."

"Well, you can't do anything for me, so you might as well do something for yourself. Go on."

"Come with me."

"What?" Leila blinked. She'd planned to escape the second she hit eighteen and no one could drag her back. Three months, one week, and four days from now.

"You heard me."

Or she could go now. Even if he did get out of trouble with the police, Rod wouldn't be chasing this particular stray.

"That's a hell of a big decision to make. Why should I trust you?"

Dek flashed that big smile, looking as trustworthy as any wolf in sheep's clothing. He didn't look like just a kid. Why did that make the back of her neck tingle with nerves and…and something else? He was dangerous. But dangerous wasn't all bad, was it? "You can find out why on the way out of here, kid."

Leila almost smiled at the memory. Rod Voss had been a nasty pig, but just for once, he hadn't been lying to the authorities. She'd been the liar. She'd never forget the first time she'd seen Dek turn. One minute he'd been another victim for Rod to pick on, and the next he was a big bad wolf who'd almost gobbled down the little piggie. Too bad she'd walked in before he'd finished the job.

Then again, her timing with Dek always sucked.

"Little Red Riding Hood, did you think taking a shortcut would save you?"

Leila jumped. She'd slowed down, getting lost in the past. He hadn't gotten lost, though. He'd honed right in on her because there he was, leaning up against her apartment building, looking too casual and too beautiful to be believed. Damn it. Not only could he follow her physically, he was already back to walking into her brain and picking up her thoughts.

Busted. There was no way to escape Dek once he was on the hunt.

"I should have known." She was proud that her voice didn't shake. Then again, she never let anyone see what she really felt. Not even Dek. *Especially* not Dek. "So, Big Bad Wolf, you're back again."

"Yeah. And this time you're finally all grown up, Little Red." The wide, predatory smile was still the same, even after all these years.

"I'm grown up enough to know I'm not interested in a quickie this time." So what if she lied while her legs shook and her pussy clenched with need? The important thing was to get rid of Deklin Kinkaid.

He reached out for her arm. She tensed, prepared to fight if he pulled her close. Instead he turned her wrist over and gently traced the veins under her skin with one roughened fingertip. His finger tickled. It aroused.

"Your wrists are still tiny. Damn, you're so dainty." His voice roughened almost to a growl. Then he bent his head and licked the pressure point where her wrist beat wildly. His rough tongue scraped against her vulnerable pulse. He looked up at her, those blue eyes impossibly hot. "I'm interested in something that would take a long, long time, Leila."

Oh, Jesus. She was toast.

But before she grabbed him, she remembered. It wasn't just her. She had someone else to watch over.

Good girl. She was a good girl now.

"I'm not interested. At all." She enunciated clearly and pulled her arm away.

"Really?"

"Really."

"You smell interested. All hot and spicy."

Leila cursed those hot, spicy feelings that were running through her, filling up the air. Damn pheromones. The way she felt, she probably reeked of sex to him.

"So I'm interested in sex. What of it? That doesn't mean I'm really interested in you. Maybe I just like a guy who can do it doggy-style. Any guy." Leila edged toward the street.

Much more of this conversation, and she'd be underneath Dek with her clothes ripped off. She'd been there before.

God, she wanted to be there again.

"Call me shallow. I can live with that, as long as I'm the guy on top of you, making you howl." Dek's voice was impossibly low, incredibly sexy. "I can do that, Leila. Remember?"

"Listen. I said no. You left last time. You'll leave again whether I say yes or no. It's going to end the same way, so can't you just accept my answer and this time go before we have the sex?" Leila crossed her arms tight against herself, refusing to let the need overwhelm her. She was stronger and smarter and had more to lose now. She could fight this lust.

What was wrong with her? She wanted him. She wanted sex. Every millimeter of his body was in tune to what she was screaming for. He tasted it, smelled it...he just couldn't see it. Even though his eyesight was blurring a little from the haze of raw desire coursing through him, he saw her crossed arms, that rigid stance. He had learned to read human body language, and Leila's body was sending up the message like a big flare in the night sky.

No. Not now. Not ever.

Damn it, *why?*

The animal in him wanted to fuck the "no" out of her. It wouldn't take much to have her whimpering under him, writhing, wanting him again. She loved him being inside her. He remembered those scratches and bites she gave him when they fucked, the cries to keep going, to go faster, harder. He could hear *Pleeease, Dek* like she was groaning it in his ear right now. Her ass grinding against him, her breasts jiggling, demanding his hands all over them... Dek forced himself to stop the crackling-hot replay in his head. But, dear God, sometimes he'd thought he really had met his mate after a bout with her. He'd never met anyone else who came close.

But she wasn't. She was a human, and humans went by different rules. Ridiculous rules.

But he had to -- Dek took a deep breath -- play by those rules. For now. He had to try to think like them. Well, at least he had to think like Leila. She wasn't like most humans.

Sudden insight hit. "Is it because I left before?"

"Naw. Why would I be upset because you came after me like I was prey, couldn't seem to get enough of me for a month, and then -- disappeared? No calls, no note, nothing. Asshole wolf." He thought her eyes glittered, but he wasn't sure if it was with tears or anger. With Leila it could be either. "I was younger then. Stupider. I thought something had happened to you and I'd never know what."

She didn't understand. She probably never would. Dek circled closer to her, and she backed up a half-step.

"I'm a were. You're not. We weren't supposed to stay together. I have to stay with my own. My pack."

"I bet you aren't supposed to fuck with non-weres, then, either, but you did. If you can break one rule, why not another?"

Dek winced. He had broken the rules to be with Leila. Others did it, too, but he'd learned breaking those particular rules wasn't smart. He was older, understood more than when they were teenagers together. He struggled for the right words to explain. "I found my first packmate in Del Rio, in an alley near where you worked, after I'd walked you to your job."

"You always did walk me to work. Said it wasn't safe for me alone." Her voice softened for a moment. "Once you said...the real reason was you wanted to spend every minute with me that you could."

"Yeah. Well..." Dek swallowed. "It wasn't safe to be alone, as Grey discovered. He'd turned, and the humans had turned on him. My packmate was beaten, left for dead. I had to get him out of town fast."

"You couldn't have told me?"

It would have killed him to hear her voice again, knowing he couldn't go back. Back then he truly had meant it about wanting to spend every minute with her. He'd followed her everywhere. Damn it, had he ever been that desperate? Dek looked at her, at those pert breasts and that firm chin. He licked his lips. Oh, hell yeah. He had been just that desperate.

"No. I couldn't tell anyone from the outside. Grey...Grey is one of mine. We're family."

"Family? You could have had --" Leila stopped short. "Fine. Understood. You left me for your *family*."

She spit the last word out. Dek growled a little, deep in his throat, then caught himself. She wasn't a were. She didn't know what she was saying. And he wanted her, no matter what she said. Screw what he should do. He was as dumb as he'd been at a randy nineteen, just as willing to break the rules to have her again.

To have her, he had to placate her. It had been a while since it mattered, but he tried to remember more of the human rules. The courting, mating rules. *Show an interest.* Human women liked that.

"You're still waitressing. Did you ever take those college classes like you wanted?"

Damn. Now he *was* interested. What had happened to her? She'd been planning to go to school, take two or three classes and waitress at night. She'd been ambitious when he met her at seventeen. Young, driven, determined. She couldn't be so different now from back when she was younger and had lied for him. Hell, she'd been right about how he couldn't get enough of her then. The seventeen-year-old Leila had been sexy. Smart, sexy, and going places.

Of course, he'd have taken notice of Leila today even if he hadn't known her before. They didn't need a past for that. After all, she was still sexy. Still smart. So why was she still standing in an alley in yet another town in Texas, waiting for him to steal a second bite of the apple?

"You remembered about the classes. I'm surprised." Leila didn't take her eyes off him while she spoke. She was waiting for him to pounce. Oh, yeah, she was still really smart.

"I remember everything."

She smiled, a tight little smile. "No, I never did go. I wanted to, but after you left...things got difficult. No time, no money. You know. Life stepped in and changed my plans."

"I'm surprised anything made you change your plans. You got out of Del Rio, though." He didn't want to talk. He wanted to sink his teeth into her, to mark her. To sink into *her.* He smelled her arousal, and it kept teasing his nostrils, making him edgy and hungry and damned hard.

How long did they have to keep talking before he could finally scoop her up and get her on her knees the way they both wanted?

"Yeah. There wasn't anything for me there. It just took longer than I'd expected. I guess El Paso is a step up." She shrugged. "Well, nice talking old times with you. I have to go."

She was leaving?

Leila made it to the building's entrance before he got over the stunned outrage that froze him. With a bound he was next to her.

"Not so fast, Little Red. We're both going together."

Chapter Two

"You can go now." She pushed on the door to close it against him, but it didn't budge. Neither did he. Of course not. Who was she trying to fool? He wasn't a stray poodle she could shoo away.

"I don't think so."

He barely remembered how to say the words. He was close, so close. He wasn't leaving now. She knew him. She had to realize what would happen next.

"Fine. Might as well get this over with." The words sounded impatient, but when she relaxed her hand against the door, her eyes were wide and dazed. They stared at each other. A fixed gaze was a direct challenge to a were. Was she trying to get him to attack? He didn't want to do that to her. He would win, but that wasn't the right way. She was going to have to agree, not just succumb.

Of course, he was going to be right here until she did. Dek rested his body against the door frame, keeping his hands close to his thighs, afraid he might disgrace himself if he so much as twitched. He stared her down. When her gaze shifted down, submissively, like a were's would, his cock twitched eagerly.

Soon. Were, no were, she was accepting his mastery.

"You might as well come in. You will anyway." Leila stepped back, allowing him in a little further. Those were meant to be tough words, but the last few trembled a little when she said them, as if she was afraid. Truth or lie? He remembered back when she let herself sound vulnerable to the police just that way. She'd been a teenager then. She'd had even more time to practice her technique.

"Not until you ask me nicely." Dek bit each word off.

There was a long silence.

"Please." Now the tone was resentful.

Dek bared all his teeth. "Ask nicer."

She was going to have to do this right, even if it killed them both. No lies or tricks. Complete submission.

As if she read his mind, she pulled off her shirt and unhooked her bra almost before he had time to kick the door closed. With that chore done, he backed up against the wall to watch. Sweat gathered at the base of his spine at the sight of her.

There were marks near her breasts where the bra had pressed indentations. He wanted to lick the redness away, soothing any hurt they caused. Her nipples were already tight and waiting for his mouth. He wanted to bite them until they were red with hurtful pleasure.

"There. Is that nice enough?" Her hands shook as she kicked off her shoes, ripped her pants down her legs. Hell, if he let go of the wall, his hands would shake, too. She was so damn beautiful.

Even better than he remembered. Bigger-breasted, thinner at the waist. Long legs, ones he needed wrapped around him. She was perfect. His throat ached at the sight of her standing there with her chin up, wisps of hair in her face, wearing nothing but thin black panties and a scowl. He could have cried at the vision of her naked. He'd thought he'd never see her again, and here she was. *Thank you, God.*

"Come on, Wolf Boy. This is what you want. Do me."

Instead of tears, his hand moved to his aching cock.

"Shit." He ought to ask for more. She should have asked for more. But she was right. He did have to do her. Now. He'd waited too long.

It took half a second to rip those black panties away from her crotch. Another instant to have her flat on her back, legs apart. He liked the look of that submissive pose. He liked hearing the catch in her breath when he nuzzled her pubic hair. Wet. Very wet.

He buried his nose in the folds of her labia. *Leila.* The smell and feel of her arousal was too much. He moved his face so he could lap her up. This was his. He'd made her this way. Every drop inside her was his. The noises she'd begun to make in the back of her throat -- they were his, too. The were-need began to wash over him, the clawing desire ripping out of his tight control. He was almost too painfully pleasured by the woman beneath him. He used his teeth, just sharp enough to make her pain real. Her cry rose a little higher, a little sweeter. He licked her again.

When her howl stopped in mid-note, he looked up. She was arched high, quivering, her fist stuffed in her mouth.

"What the hell?" Dek moved his body, positioned himself so his chest brushed against her nipples. "Ashamed of being noisy, Red? You know you're going to scream for me for hours. You always did. Why fight it?"

"The neighbors. The walls. They're so thin --" Bright spots of color burned in up from her neck to her cheeks. "Everyone will know."

So? He wanted everyone to know. His balls were aching with the need to come inside her and mark her again as his. Let them envy him!

But she was different. Damn human rules.

"All right, then. We can try to be quiet." He would have sulked if her hand hadn't slipped over his cock just then and given it a short, hard squeeze.

He muffled his yelp against her shoulder.

"It's just...I have a rep around here. Screaming for wolf men isn't part of it." Her words didn't make sense as the head of his penis slid against her tight, wet little slit. Nothing made sense but the sensation of female against his cock. He was close...really close. He rested himself just outside her entrance, and her breath tickled his ear as she whispered again, "I won't do it; I can't do it -- but you can try to make me howl."

She bit his chest when he slid all the way in, fast. Wet, moist, tight. Oh, yeah, that was -- that was --

"*Fuck!*" He remembered to yell the word close against her neck. He might be the one howling soon.

"Oh, yeah, Dek. Fuck me." She bucked up, squirming even closer

Her words were too much. He fastened his teeth, hard, into her hair, forcing himself not to go for more sensitive flesh. He pulled back, listening to her soft, muffled whimper of protest, and slammed inside her. Her sheath gripped him, milked him, and he lost it.

Were. Scent, sight, sound changed, heightened, and time suddenly teetered. The scent of Leila filled him. His slow-motion vision stretched out as his perception of time changed, and he watched Leila's mouth fall open as he began to turn.

Werewolf. That shouldn't get her so crazy, so needy. But even as Dek's hair grew shaggy and his face turned feral, she could feel her climax rising up, shooting through her body as the adrenaline smashed through her system. She couldn't breathe as need grabbed her by the throat. Instead she clutched at his furry pelt and sobbed, trying to force her vaginal walls to accept all of him.

The best sex they ever had was when he lost control and turned. It had been five and a half years since she'd had a were to fuck. Five and a half years since they'd had incredible sex. There was nothing like a beast. There was nothing like Dek.

She was starving. She wanted to be eaten up in quick, hungry bites. Thank God, Dek was just the were to do it. To do her. He growled as he pulled at her hair with a sharp tug of his teeth. Leila shuddered. She wanted that. Teeth, growls, ferocity. She wanted everything.

She spread her legs and accepted the first shock of hard cock probing at her needy flesh. He didn't waste time plunging inside her. She whimpered, trying to learn to accept his hungry thrusts again. He wasn't going to wait, and God, she didn't want to wait, either. But it had been a long time and -- Oh, yes. Oh, yeees. That was it. Pain shifted almost too rapidly to pleasure as Dek's cock cunningly scraped against every sensitive spot her clitoris had. Yes! His erection seemed to grow and lengthen with each stroke, filling her.

The world spun. Her head lolled back as the fireworks began to warm up, ready to release. She wanted to feel them roar, ricocheting and exploding, spreading from her cunt up through her legs and arms and chest. She clawed at Dek's back, lifted her legs up higher to get every last millimeter of his cock. The heat ripped at her as she snarled.

Everything. She wanted --

"*Ahhhh!*" She couldn't see through the intensity of her impending climax, as the orgasm she'd been waiting for teetered, then crashed into her, skittering through her body.

"You screamed." Dek's voice was lazy with satisfaction.

Dear God. She'd passed out for a few moments. She had to have. She knew why she felt so sticky and sore, but she couldn't remember the details. She'd meant to talk about protection. She wasn't sure how to protect herself from were-sperm, but she'd never had the chance to try.

Too late to worry now. She didn't have the strength to worry. She felt way too good to worry.

"I got rug burn, too." Leila shifted under his weight. "Are you sure I screamed?"

"Like a banshee."

"I'd kill you, but your cock was too nice to waste --"

Bang!

Only one person smashed her fist into the door just that way. Energy flowed back into her, fueled by sheer terror. Leila shoved him aside and struggled to sit up.

"What?" Dek lay back on his elbows and raised an eyebrow.

"Go to the other room."

"What?"

At least he wasn't still furry. Sex tended to calm Dek down. He was, however, naked.

Very naked.

"Go. To. The. Other. Room." She wiggled into her pants almost as fast as she'd gotten them off, kicked the shredded panties under the chair, and grabbed for her shirt, pushing her thick hair back from her face. "It's the vice squad."

He snorted, but got up, still very naked and very fine, and strolled into the other room. She'd deal with the fallout from that later. She still had to figure out --

She pulled open the door, thanking fate that her visitor hadn't tested the doorknob before knocking. Dek hadn't bothered to lock the door.

"Mrs. Stiller."

"It's past time." The older woman should have looked like a grandma, all dimpled chins and white hair. But on Mrs. Stiller the chins and hair looked more like the most dreaded elementary school teacher you ever had, the one who had been there forever and knew every sin you could ever commit there.

"I'm sorry. I -- I lost track of the time."

"I didn't. Heard you come in, and I waited. And waited. You owe extra." She turned, propelling a small flurry of ruffles through the door. "I'll expect the money in the morning. If you do it again, you can find yourself someone new."

"Right. Right." Leila shielded the sleepy child with her arms and struggled to lift her. "Thanks."

What an idiot she was. She'd forgotten. After all this, she'd forgotten why she'd been trying to keep Deklin Kinkaid away.

"What's going on?" Dek was back in the room the second Mrs. Stiller left, of course.

"Nothing much." Leila kept the child's face covered. The gesture was stupid, and way too late now, but then, she'd been stupid all night. "Listen, you've had your sex. Can't you just go now? Let me live my life?"

Dek's head tilted. She could almost see him scenting, discovering more than she wanted about the new person in the room.

"Who is that?"

"Lin."

"*Who* is that?"

"My daughter, Lin. Go away before you scare her. She's just a baby who has had a tough night. She ought to be asleep."

"Leila, tell me." He began to circle again, like she was prey. Like she and Lin both were.

"Fine." The postponing was over. She'd tried and failed. On to the next plan -- whatever it was. "You know that thing you told me back when we were together? About how

I was safe? How weres could mate but couldn't breed with humans?"

His breath hissed in. "What do you mean?"

"I mean you were wrong."

"She's mine? I mean -- she smells like mine, but...that can't be."

"You're right about that. She's not yours. She's mine."

"Mommy?" Tired and whiney, Lin spoke up. "Who is he?"

"No one, baby. He's leaving soon."

His eyes glowed. Leila took a step back, then edged toward the bedroom. As she put her already half-asleep baby back to bed, she wasn't surprised to find Dek had followed her, staring down at the little girl.

Lin whimpered just a little as she burrowed her head into the pillow. She was so beautiful. Maybe she was biased, but Leila had always thought Lin was the most beautiful child she'd ever seen.

"Mine." Dek sounded as if he was trying to absorb the idea. But he also sounded possessive. She knew about Dek and possessive. It wasn't good, at least not if you intended to keep something he wanted. And, damn it, who wouldn't want Lin once they saw her?

"Not yours. Mine." Leila braced herself for an argument.

"Leila." His voice wasn't angry. But she could hear the rumbling of a warning nonetheless.

"What?"

"Stop. Just stop. Don't you see how this changes everything?"

"No. You're still your same wandering self. I still have Lin. We can just go on the way we've been for the past four years and forget --"

Dek stared at her as if she had lost her mind. His fists clenched, and she braced herself for yelling. She could handle Dek's anger. She could handle anything he could dish out. It didn't matter. He wasn't getting Lin!

To her shock, though, he calmed himself. His hands unclenched, and he relaxed his shoulders. That did focus her. A calm, dangerous Dek -- a Dek able to keep control of his emotions -- was a real threat.

"Leila, you need to understand. She's part of me. Don't you realize how dangerous that is?"

Chapter Three

Lowell sucked in with his eyes half-shut, thinking about the small, leggy brunette he'd seen at the bus stop this morning. She'd smiled at him; he was sure of it. He liked females. He liked men, too, couldn't help that, but females were interesting. Different. Not that he'd mention that interest to Grey. That would just be stupid.

Especially not when he was crouched over Grey, swallowing down the head of his cock. You needed to concentrate on Grey when you were with him. You never knew what he'd want next when --

The door opened with a crash.

"*Grey!*"

Lowell jumped and then cowered to the floor, hoping not to be noticed. Being bottom man in the pack meant staying out of harm's way whenever possible. When Dek yelled like that, it was easy to figure out there was trouble.

"What the hell?" Grey headed for the next room at a run, zipping up his fly.

Grey wasn't afraid of trouble or Dek. Lowell admired that about him. Lowell was afraid of both men -- respected the hell out of them, but knew exactly what either of them could do to a teen his size.

But since he wasn't in trouble yet, it was time to go see the show. Lowell stood and trotted to the living room just in time to see Dek pounce on Grey, who staggered back for a moment. Lowell's own mouth dropped open. Those two never fought -- not physically. But right now Dek was on top of Grey, forcing him down to the ground. It sure as hell looked like a fight -- or rough sex.

Lowell's mouth went dry as he saw Grey's muscles straining, the sweat shining on Dek's face. Whatever it was, this wasn't play. Grey finally lay flat on the ground. The panting breaths of both men filled the room.

"Who's master here, Grey?"

"What's wrong with you, boss?" Grey struggled underneath him, even though Dek had his arm pinned back.

"Who is the fucking top dog?" Dek forced the words out from bared teeth.

Lowell quivered. Something was wrong. Dek never demanded to know who was alpha. All of them knew.

"Damn it, Dek! Ow. Fuck you." Grey struggled.

Lowell crept out from behind the chair and crouched down, just in case.

"Tell me, Grey." Dek turned his head and spotted Lowell. "You, boy. Who is top dog?"

Shit. Noticed. That was bad.

"You are, Dek. You're boss." Lowell was proud of himself for not stuttering.

"Grey? Who is boss?"

"You are, asshole."

Dek stood up, suddenly completely calm. Grey lay on the floor for a minute more before he pulled himself up to his knees. He stared up at Dek, chest still heaving.

"What was that all about?"

"Stay right there. Both of you." Dek's voice got deadly quiet.

Grey froze in place, just the way Lowell had already. For all his yelling, Grey knew when to obey orders.

"Leila, come here." Dek's voice changed from commanding to gentle as he called outside. Damn, he sounded almost pleading. Lowell tilted his head to one side. *What now?*

He could hear footsteps moving slowly, reluctantly, to the door.

"Leila, this is my family. Grey, Lowell, this is my mate." Dek pulled forward a woman.

Lowell's breath caught. Jesus, that wasn't just any woman. Trust Dek to bring home a special treat. She was beautiful. Her hair was long and mussed. She looked angry. Gorgeous and wild, but furious. Lowell decided it was smarter to stay on his knees and properly respectful.

"Gentlemen, this is Leila."

"Aw, shit." Grey's voice was rough, but he stayed crouched, too. "You've gone and done it now, Dek."

"You're insane. All three of you." This Leila hugged a small child close to her legs. "Why are you doing this, Dek?"

"She's a human, Dek." When Grey spoke up, he sounded angry and -- and frightened? If Grey was afraid, Lowell didn't understand anything. The world had just rotated and left everything upside down, and he didn't get it. "How the hell can she be the one for you?"

"She has to be, Grey. And something inside that human hide of hers is were. Has to be. She birthed my daughter."

"A daughter?" Grey yelped.

"Gentlemen, this is Lin."

Lowell sniffed. There was woman scent in the air and more. The girl...Lowell gave a small chuff of surprise. A small face peered at him, with Dek's color eyes and a wary look in them.

"Lin is mine, just like Leila is. You'll obey Leila; you'll care for Lin. Law of the pack."

Leila knew her palms were sweaty. When Dek said they were going to his house, she hadn't expected any of this. The isolated ranch, the rest of Dek's "family." Like the big Hispanic-looking guy had said, she was human. She wasn't one of these -- these pack animals! What was she supposed to say or do now?

Whatever it was, she knew it was important.

"Stand there, Leila. You too, sweetheart." Dek's voice changed, grew tender, as he spoke to the little girl. "Just stand. We'll take care of everything from there."

Take care of what? Leila kept a grip on Lin.

"It's all right, baby. They aren't going to hurt you." It was fortunate Lin was so tired, or she'd have a sobbing little girl on her hands. God knows she felt a little like sobbing herself.

Dek motioned to the other men. "Grey."

"Aw, shit."

"Grey." Dek's voice snapped.

Leila wanted to shrink back as the large stranger came closer to her. He looked a little scruffy, a lot mean. She could see a scar on one cheek. Dek had said he'd been beaten...

"Hold out your hand." Grey's voice was gravelly, as rough as his face.

"W-why?"

"Because it's the most polite place I can think of to do this." For a moment it looked like a smile would almost touch his thinned lips, but then it disappeared. "Uh -- please."

She held out her hand, proud that it wasn't trembling. She yelped a little when Grey's nose rubbed against it. Yewww! But she held still as he sniffed it thoroughly. Didn't even blink when he lifted Lin's hand and did the same. The little girl giggled.

"Tickles, Mommy."

"Hush, Lin. This is important." Why it was important didn't matter. Apparently it had to be done. But Dek sure as hell better explain a lot, very soon now.

The young one of the group came next, in a half-crouch. She almost expected him to crawl over on all fours. He sniffed, looked up at her face, and gave her a shy smile. Almost a reverent one.

Lin held up her hand like a princess when he turned to her. He bent over it like a courtier. When he was done, he backed away.

"Now."

At Dek's word, the two men actually bent down, on their knees. Heads went to the floor.

Oh, my God. What had she stepped into here? Well, she hadn't stepped exactly. Dek had more or less dragged her. But what was going on? She knew Dek was different and that meant his "family" was different. But no one had told her the rules.

"Leila is my mate. That means she has my authority and my protection." He turned to her. "Leila, meet the pack, Grey and Lowell."

"Gentlemen." Leila nodded at the still bowed heads. She felt like an idiot. What do you do in a situation like this? Miss Manners hadn't ever discussed this kind of scenario. "Will you please get up?"

They glanced over at Dek and then stood, still shooting uneasy glances over at their fearless leader. Wonderful. Apparently they weren't into obeying her the way they did the top dog in the room. Dek ran his hand down her shoulder.

"Take Lin to the far bedroom down the hall and let her sleep. We're not done yet."

She stared down at Lin, who was already closing her eyes. It had been too long a day for the poor baby to worry about a strange bed. Hell, so many strange things had happened, what difference did the bed make?

Was she really going to throw away everything to follow Dek around? He might not leave her this time -- she was almost sure of that. But she was sure it was because of Lin, not because of her. Lin was family, and Dek didn't leave family.

Leila wasn't family. Dek liked her body just fine, but he'd never said he loved her. Maybe that wasn't a were thing.

Leila stared at her daughter's mouth, relaxed in sleep, the wild tangle of hair that no one could quite tame. Those eyes, just as intense and hot as her father's, were hidden behind closed eyelids, but they were there. Dek's eyes and maybe Dek's way of seeing the world. Dek said having his baby changed everything. God knows Lin had changed her life, but he hadn't meant that. He meant things she couldn't even begin to imagine.

Leila bent closer. She couldn't see any traces of were in her baby, but it was early days. Deklin told her once that he first found out he could change in puberty, but every were was different.

Different.

Her baby was different. Leila knew that, but she chose to forget most of the time. This whole bizarre evening had reminded her. Lin was going to grow up and face things Leila knew nothing about. Things only her father could teach her.

For that alone, Leila knew she had to stay. Not because Dek told her she must. Not because of the great sex.

"Not that great sex can't be a real nice bonus." Leila heard herself say the words out loud and almost grinned.

She wasn't going to let Dek think he could have everything his way. If she was sticking around, there were some rules to lay down right off. Men, especially werewolf men, needed rules.

Grey tried not to twitch as they waited for her to come back. He didn't want her to come back. If he could, he would have erased the whole past hour. He surely didn't want to deal with what came next.

He'd never wanted a woman. They were all right, he supposed, but they meant nothing to him. They all heard her footsteps coming back to the living room. Blackness gnawed inside his gut. Inside his heart. He might not need women, but his alpha was different. Dek had a new mate and a woman.

Dek. Ah, damn it. He'd known this would happen eventually, but he'd hoped it would take much longer.

When he'd first met Dek, back when his leader found him in that stinking hole, Grey had looked up and thought he saw an angel. A dark angel, perhaps, but still someone unearthly…precious. They'd left hell together. Dek had carried him, washed him, fed him, cleaned up after him. They were a family, a pack, together and united. Lowell's presence hadn't changed that.

But this woman would. A woman and a child. Wolves mated for life. The pack took care of its own, most especially its children. That was the point of the whole damn stupid show they were going to go through now.

Fuck this. Not only did he have to give up Dek, then watch Dek with some woman, but he had to devote his life to Dek's human woman and child. Law of the damned stupid were-pack.

He watched Dek hold out his hand as his new mate returned. Like it or not, life was about to change.

"I'm here." Here and ready to stand up for herself.

It didn't matter that somehow Dek oozed sex pheromones just standing in the center of the room. It didn't matter that she was the only woman in the group and very far from civilization…if you could call El Paso civilized. The point was that things had gone way off course this evening, and she was going to get them straight.

"Good." Dek's voice was low and way too sexy. It was also much too bossy for her peace of mind. Why did she want to respond to both the sex and the command wrapped around his word?

"We'll see just how good it is once you explain what's going on here."

"This might seem a little different than what you're used to, Leila --"

"No lie, buddy."

"-- but it's necessary, especially because you look and act so damn human. No, don't try to smart ass me on that, lady. You're were now. Some trace of you has to be, or you'd never have had my baby. But we need to make sure the whole pack and any stray who comes by knows you're were and you're mine."

Were? She'd never considered that. Damn, she didn't have time to consider it, not with Dek prowling toward her. Leila fought taking a backward step as Deklin moved in.

Instead she poked a finger in his chest as soon as he got close enough.

"I'm thinking you don't mean you're giving me your class ring."

His teeth showed in that damn grin, and his hands went to his belt buckle. "Not exactly. I'm going to give you something, though. I'm going to mark you."

Leila shuddered. She couldn't help it. For just a minute, the old, bad memories of Rod came back. He'd marked her backside often enough with a belt.

"No, baby. Not that." Dek touched her chin, smoothed her hair. "You know I wouldn't ever do that."

Damn mind reader. She hated his ability to do that almost as much as she hated showing weakness.

"What do you plan to do, then? How are you going to mar -- Oh, no." Leila grabbed the hand with the belt. "No way."

"It's the only way. It's not like our marking won't wash off if you really want it to."

Leila stared at the man in front of her, the sexy one with the half-undone fly. She could almost reach out to touch the avid interest from the other men who stood silently, waiting. What the hell would the rest of them do if Deklin insisted? Would they hold her down? Maybe that's what they wanted to happen.

For a moment she toyed with the idea of those jeans falling to completely reveal that enormous cock...the belt wrapped around her wrists...those other men watching...and, by God, her breath quickened. So much for all that work at being a good girl. Oh, damn, why could

Deklin get her secret fantasies so stirred to life by just looking at her?

Then she remembered just how every dog she knew marked his territory.

Oh, no, he wasn't. Nononononono. Not this woman. That was definitely not one of her fantasies.

For a second, red-heated anger really did film over her vision, just like the books said. Leila growled. She could hear it herself, over the noise of adrenaline-pumped blood hissing up through her ears.

"Listen, you. I've put up with being fucked on my floor, manhandled out of my house, and having me and my daughter sniffed by two very strange men. If y'all think you're going to pee on me after that, I'm taking every last one of you to the pound and getting you fixed. We're doing things my way now. Civilized human style. You can start by talking instead of lifting your leg."

Dek couldn't stop the strangled sound that came out of his mouth. Jesus, he'd forgotten how Leila made him laugh at the worst possible times.

"You have about ten seconds to start talking, Rin Tin Tin." Leila's chin jutted out.

"The explanation can come later."

"The freaking explanations can come right this minute." She was smaller than he was, but for a moment he wondered if she really could take him on.

Oh, shit, who were they both kidding? Of course she could. And his cock was already so hard against the fabric of his pants, he was going to have to keep unbuttoning his fly, or explanations weren't the only thing that would be coming in a minute. Even her glare got him going, damn it.

"We won't make this too bad for you, Leila."

Her eyes narrowed. "You better make this real good for me, bucko."

Oh, hell. He could feel the heat of his seed, the pressure inside his balls, wanting to spill. This wasn't the time to suddenly wonder what happened if he didn't make things good. What did he do if she wanted to run afterward?

Run her down. Keep her. The wolf in him rose at just the thought of the hunt.

He fought the change this time, fought the sensation of time-changing motion as he turned. Leila seemed to like his wolf form, which was a big plus, but he didn't think she wanted three wolves in front of her, all waiting to --

"Oh, my God, Dek."

Or maybe she did. He could tell she was as fascinated as she was afraid. The scent of her aroused musk was beginning to fill his nostrils. Shit. Maybe the problem was that he didn't want to see her in the circle with all his packmates. She was *his*.

Before he could think anymore, he pulled his hard cock out of his pants. That head didn't want to think. It wanted Leila. She licked her lips, her eyes widening. She didn't say anything else, and the blood pounded in Dek's ears. If Leila wasn't talking, that meant...that meant...

He didn't care what it meant. He gripped the material of her shirt, ripping it open so it gaped wantonly, baring shoulders and showing off her pretty lace bra. Leila's erect nipples scraped against the bra's sheer fabric, straining against that slight constraint. He lunged, and somehow he was on the floor, on top of her. She whimpered when he nipped her shoulder. Her back arched up, fitting her more closely to him. When he reached down, she had already loosened her pants. The panties had been discarded back when they'd fucked at her apartment, so the only thing left was -- he took a handful of that sweet muff and savored the wet invitation at the V between her thighs. Yeah, she wanted him. Almost as bad as he did her.

"Who do you belong to, Leila?"

She opened her eyes, looking dazed and delighted and mad all at once. There. That was his Leila. He tickled the folds of her labia, and she whimpered again. Then he waited.

"Who, Leila? Say it out loud."

"N-no." She whispered, arching up again.

Stupid human inhibitions. If she wouldn't say it, he'd have to make her. Because right now, like it or not, they went by were rules. He'd never wanted to be human before, but just now -- Hell. That was just being stupid. Instead he growled, "Who? Come on, woman. Talk."

She looked at him again, a small bit of awareness stirring in all that confusion and pleasure. He slid one finger just a millimeter inside her and let her clench before he ripped it away. That was all she was getting until --

"You, Dek."

Just vaguely he heard the guttural growls of the pack behind him. He was too far gone to wonder what anyone else was doing after her hoarse cry of submission. He thrust his finger up hard and high inside her sheath, just once. She jerked, bucking against his hand, and moaned.

That was it for him. Still fingering her, he squeezed his cock with the other hand. Once, twice. Then he spurted hard, freeing the come inside him and letting it spill in a hot, fierce gush between her breasts.

She writhed, and he flicked her swollen little clit before he worked a second finger up into her. Leila moaned again. Dear heaven, he was getting hard all over again, looking at her. It didn't matter if the others were watching.

The others. Dek reminded himself of just why they were doing this.

"Go on." Dek turned to the rest and forced the words out.

They stood there, looking -- well, damn it, like a pack of wolves, waiting to jump on a bone. Part of him wanted to slap them down for staring at his mate like that. Part of him wanted to taunt them with what he had.

What happened next wouldn't be so bad. Not with his fingers working Leila, making her wetter and hotter with every second that passed. He was in charge; he was the one making her want, even if --

Lowell broke first, giving a long howl, his fist clenched on his cock. Dek watched Lowell's semen mingle with his, splashing on Leila's skin in a long stream. Leila panted now, staring up at Lowell in disbelief, but letting it happen. Dek stroked her thighs to quiet her. Possessiveness, anger, satisfaction, pure heat spread over Dek as he watched Lowell mark his mate.

"Grey. Damn it, go ahead!" Dek wasn't sure how much longer he could allow the ritual to continue.

"Omigod, omigod, omi --" Leila's voice, strained but undeniably aroused, broke on the words as Grey bent over the two of them.

"Fuck it." Grey glared at Dek, crouched between Leila's knees, and Grey's teeth bared. "Only for you, you alpha bastard." He groaned, as if he were in pain, and Grey's semen added to the rest.

The men all stared down at the residue, and Dek added a third finger, stretching and shoving into Leila's channel, not letting her think about what was happening. Instinct. They both needed to go on instinct here. He probed and explored the passage that belonged to him. She shuddered. She wasn't quite ready yet? Dek snarled out a laugh and pinched her clit. Leila howled, brokenly, and for a moment he thought her canine teeth lengthened, turned wolfish. The thought of her biting him made the breath catch in his throat.

Her hands scrabbled on the floor as if to find a place to rest while he worked his fingers fast and hard up deep within her body. Red-hot lust and jealousy clouded Dek's vision for a moment. He could smell the other men -- all of them -- on her, mingled with her sex and his, and the mixture triggered something too complicated and too fierce to be borne.

That was when Leila came. Beyond shame or fear or thought, she ground her cunt against him and let everything go. Weeping, shaking, she thrashed her head back and forth and rode his hand until she gave one last, pitiful moan and collapsed.

Done. Dek swallowed, fighting the need to cover her…with a blanket, with his body. Instead he let her legs relax, left them spread for the others to look. Almost finished now. He gritted his teeth.

Dek pulled out his hand, wet with her juices, and stuck his fingers into the pool between her breasts. He lifted his hand to his nose and then stretched the hand out, fingers shaking, to the other men. They bent, sniffed.

Lowell did more than scent. He licked Dek's hand, growling deep in his throat. Dek snarled, snatching his hand away. For the first time, Lowell stared back at Dek, still growling, not giving up.

"Are you ready to try something, pup?" Dek let just a tenth of the anger and confusion out with those words. Lowell shriveled back to his old self.

"N-no. No, boss." Lowell flattened himself back down on the ground.

"Good enough." Dek took a deep breath, trying for calm. Then he placed his hand under Leila's nose.

"It's done. You're one of us now." Dek let her take a long whiff of what their mingled scent was like. Her eyes flickered open, and she stared at him. There was no threat there, though. She looked almost frightened. Dek understood. He knew what the smell of it was like to her and him both. Arousing. Disturbing. He sensed her guilty pleasure mingled with regret. He knew all those emotions because they mirrored his own.

Dek stood, fastening his pants, looking down at the rest while he did. "And that's as close as you'll get to any of my packmates again. You're one of us, but above everything, you're mine. Does everyone understand that?"

"Yes, sir." If there was something new, some faint menace in Lowell's tone, it was well concealed with prompt deference.

"Understood." Grey bit off the words.

Dek turned to Leila, who sat up, still looking a little weak.

"Leila?"

She got to her knees, swayed a little. Dek pulled her the rest of the way up, letting her rest against his body. God, she felt so good like that. They stood together, just that way, for a long moment, Dek shielding her from the rest.

"Yes." She whispered her acceptance, just loud enough for everyone to hear.

Dek relaxed against her. It was done. The toughest thing he'd ever had to do was finished, and it had worked out the way it was meant to. He buried his face in the nape of her neck. It was the two of them now, just the two of them. He lost himself in the softness, the warmth of her.

Then she pulled away from him.

"Just everything I understand is better said away from the rest of this pack." Leila's voice was getting back under control. Her chin firmed, and Dek almost snickered as his world righted itself. "You can come to the next room with me, Mr. Top Dog, while we discuss a few important details."

She turned on her heel and, still mussed and tumbled, stalked away from their audience like an offended queen, refusing to give any of them another look.

"Dear heaven, she's made to be an alpha b --" Lowell hastily stopped his babble when Dek turned to glare at him.

"Show is over, boys." Dek straightened his shoulders, getting ready for battle. "Button up and back to work."

Chapter Four

Leila took the washcloth Dek held out to her. She knew where he expected her to wash, but she took it and buried her face in it first, savoring the coolness and buying herself a little time. She didn't want to look at him and explain...well, how did you explain what happened?

What did you say once you'd come so hard and so noisy that your insides nearly shot out of your mouth while you screamed? And you came that way in front of three werewolves...because of all three werewolves. She was still shaking inside, still trying to curb the animal that had run a little too free in the last hour or so.

"So much for the good-girl image. I gave it a really good try." Leila slipped the washcloth between her breasts at last, letting a trickle of water run down her stomach as she wondered how long it would take to wash the memory from her mind. "I don't have anything to wear. You ruined my shirt, and the rest are all home...are all at my apartment."

Dek's mouth was hot on her neck, his tongue nuzzling her fine hairs.

"Who cares about your image?" He bit her neck for good measure. "You look damn sexy like that."

"Don't tell me you're a vampire, too." Leila swatted halfheartedly at him. "And *I* care about my image."

"You've traded it in for a new one. A much better one. You're the alpha bitch now, baby. Whatever you want, the pack will do their damnedest to take care of it. You want shirts? I'll send Lowell to fetch your clothes and things from the apartment."

"Huh. Alpha bitch." Leila blinked at her image in the mirror. "Well, who would've thought?"

"I'm ready to explain now. If you want to listen." He looked more interested in the water still trickling down her skin. In fact, he still looked aroused and dangerous and angry. He looked ready for anything except calm conversation.

Was she ready? Could Dek really make sense of everything that had happened to her -- to them all? Leila put the cloth down, very carefully, on the sink and braced her arms on the countertop. "All right. Try."

They stared at each other. She knew how he hated that. But damn, he did look tasty. How could you blame a woman for looking at that rumpled hair and those pretty eyes? The body was damn good, too. All those muscles and power...She licked her lips, and his eyes sparked.

"I -- shit, it will have to wait." He pinned her to the wall smoothly and removed her pants. He nudged her legs apart while his fingers fumbled at his waistband. "I thought I could last after jerking off, but I can't. You reek of sex and I want you."

"What a smooth talker -- Oh, damn it, Dek!" He slid into her with one sure thrust, she was up against the wall, and everything inside her melted.

Neither of them should have needed sex quite this badly, but they did. Watching Dek throw his head back, face contorted in desire, always flicked her switch. Leila gripped his shoulders with her hands, his waist with her legs, and hung on.

He was sweaty and she was damp from her quick washing, and their bodies, slick and hot, slapped against each other with hard, smacking noises. She thumped against the wall and briefly realized the rest of the adults in the house could hear them, before she lost track of sense and sound and everything but Dek.

Dear, sweet God. *Dek.*

Years of learning to do without him, and in one night he'd come roaring back, changed her careful life and -- Leila let her fingernails dig into his skin, not sure if the gesture was a punishment or a reward for the way he made her feel as his hard body slapped against her once again.

"That's right, baby. Let me feel your claws." He panted the words in her ear. "Just like that. When you do that, you get tighter around my cock...God, yes, milk it."

She shuddered, desire coiling up inside her until she could hardly breathe. When Dek talked dirty to her, she always came.

"Yeah. Moan for me. You know you want to make noise when I have my cock inside you. Squeeze me. Tighter. You're always so wet for me, so good."

He filled her, then reached to tweak her clit. That was the match that set her primed body on fire. Heat licked over her body as she jerked against him. My God, it was too much…

"Dek!" She heard herself scream as if she were far away from her own body, for a moment lost in some other world of pleasure and need.

He groaned, and she came as sensation rushed back into her body, sweeping over her with blinding force.

She opened her eyes, grateful the wall was supporting her now aching back. Her legs slowly gave way, letting her slither more or less gently onto the floor.

"Whew." She stared at her lover, who looked only slightly less shell-shocked.

He shook his head and then took the washcloth to wipe himself. She wondered how he had the energy. She was a blissful, exhausted pool of goo.

"Well, now that you don't have the strength to jaw at me, I guess I can talk."

Leila watched Dek pull his jeans back on for what had to be the tenth time that day, too sexually sated to even protest that comment.

She watched him pace back and forth as he began, admiring his tight butt more than concentrating on the words at first. "Above everything, whatever we do is about the pack. You wanted to kill me before, when I told you family was the most important. But that's how it is with weres. The pack comes first. Has to. Once I took on Grey, I had a pack and I had responsibilities to him." Dek eyed her and took a half-step away.

"I'm not going to hit you. I was mad because you already had a family started when you took off for another." Leila took a deep breath and watched Dek's gaze flicker down to her still half-naked body. To his credit, he looked right back up into her face. She saw the regret there. She was pretty sure the emotion was for his past actions, not because he had to stop ogling. "Some of that was my fault. I didn't say anything to you. Then again, I was young and I didn't know anything. Not even that I was pregnant."

"I'm sorry, though. I should have been with you."

"Well, sorry isn't going to change anything. You might as well keep talking."

"No matter what happened before, I made you family tonight. Each of us, not just me, knows you're one of the pack. That's how we do things. Given that you seem so human, doing this the right way is important."

"You're telling me that's how you welcomed Grey and Lowell to the family?"

"No. Well, not exactly. We -- They --" Was Dek actually turning red? "It's different for weres than humans. Lower-ranking wolves don't mate. They concentrate on taking care of the alphas and their kids. We all have to care for the kids. That's why I'm so sorry to have left Lin."

Strength from outrage poured back into her.

"Sorry to have left Lin and not me. I see. All right, buddy, we can talk about that later." She struggled to her feet and raised her hand when Dek opened his mouth. "You just finish up explaining everything else first."

"I'm in a lot of trouble, aren't I?" He ran his hand under the edge of her torn shirt and felt her shiver at his touch. "But you're right. Some things need to be talked over, like it or not. Grey and Lowell, they can't mate. But we agreed -- pack rules -- they can have other men. That's the way Grey likes it anyhow. And Lowell? Well, Lowell is our omega, so I don't know what he likes, and it doesn't make much difference. He doesn't complain about the arrangement, anyhow."

"Dek?"

"Yeah?"

"Grey didn't have just Lowell before this, did he? I saw how he looked at you."

Dek swallowed. "*I* had Grey. Lowell, too, when I wanted. Mostly during a full moon. Things get -- ah -- crazy then. You have to have heard some of the stories. Hell, you've seen me during a full moon."

Leila shivered. Oh, yes, she remembered those nights.

"I'm the alpha. Whatever happens in the pack is what I say happens. I'm not denying it." Dek shifted his feet. "But that's just a were thing, Leila. Mostly it was to quiet them down. I'm not gay. Not the way you'd understand it. I'm top dog, and that's how things work sometimes. You have to show them who is alpha."

She could almost wrap her mind around that. Especially after tonight. Dek was sex. Walking, breathing sex. She'd always seen that. Now she'd seen how the others responded to him. Hell, she responded pretty close to the same way.

Shoot, he'd screwed her silly a few minutes ago, made her mad enough to rip him apart after that, and she was getting turned on all over again. At least she hadn't taken to bowing before him.

"I'm going to have a lot of problems keeping you in line, aren't I?" Leila touched his chin, feeling the stubble. She wondered if it was normal beard or incipient werewolf. "Don't think you can go running to the other boys for help whenever I give you trouble."

Dek's smile was all wolf. "I wouldn't dream of it. But don't you think you can run to them, either. We're bonded now, sweetie. It's you and me, one on one."

"So that was sort of the were version of a wedding? Huh." Leila tapped him on the chin. "I want a legal ceremony, too, if we're in this for life. But we're not having the best men grab for my garter."

"Hell, no. There'll be no more grabbing by anyone except me. Wolves mate for life, but if you want some damned human wedding to make yourself feel better, I guess we can manage that. I might have to fake the blood test, though. My blood type doesn't exactly fit the standard."

Dek bent his head and kissed her. He was gentle at first, tenderly drawing out the kiss and bringing her near to tears. Gradually the kiss turned more fierce, with his teeth grazing the tender underside of her lip, promising more.

"So, are we done explaining? Can you kiss me again?" Leila could have smacked herself in the head the minute she asked that. Never show a man you're more interested in him than in having him grovel. Those were basic human rules. He was already throwing her off stride. She'd had him right where she wanted him -- promising a wedding and a lifetime together -- and then she'd changed the subject. Dek sighed and reluctantly moved his hands from her shoulders.

"I'd love to. But -- well, there are more things you need to know right off." He ran his hand through his hair. "You and Lin -- you're the women."

"I figured that part out."

"I wasn't kidding when I said it was dangerous to be were. It's most dangerous for Lin, because she's so young. But it's dangerous for you, too. You need to be a lot more careful than you've been up to now."

"I'm not planning on going to bars to get beat up like Grey."

"You damn well aren't going to any bar. But that's not what I meant. It's not just humans we need to worry about. It's other packs."

"Other packs? How many weres are there in West Texas?"

"Not so many. Female weres are scarce. That's one reason packs are so anxious to raid other packs and get a few. But if they can't get the females for their own, then they'll take or kill the other pack's women and children. If they can't survive, the other pack can't, either."

"You're kidding. And if you're saying I have to spend the rest of my life not able to go where I want, you'd really best be kidding."

Dek's stare turned lethal rather than sexy. He reached into his back pocket and pulled out a billfold. He rummaged for a moment and then handed her a yellowed, folded newspaper article.

"Read it."

"You don't have to give me orders, Dek. I --" Leila gasped as she read. "My God! That's awful!"

"That was my mother, Leila."

"She died from a wolf attack? In her own home?"

"That's just the way humans told it because they didn't know any better. It wasn't wolves that killed her. It was weres. She was driven from her own pack, and when she was left alone, another pack attacked her. She didn't have a chance."

Leila read a little more and realization hit. "My God, Dek! The little boy left alone in the house for days before someone arrived...that was *you?*"

Leila held him close, felt the tightness in his body. After all these years, it was still almost too much for Dek. He still had to brace himself. No wonder. She couldn't imagine a toddler, alone and traumatized, with the body of his mother still there.

"Yeah. That's how I discovered I was part of the were. It was kind of a tough welcome to the neighborhood."

"Don't try to joke," Leila whispered against his neck, trying to absorb some of his lingering pain with her embrace.

"Right. Bad joke anyhow. Well...I remember Mother hiding me under the bed, saying not to make a sound when she heard them start to break in. I don't remember everything else. Not entirely."

Except in his nightmares. Leila remembered certain nights. Remembered Dek crying out, struggling, and then getting up to roam for hours.

"I'm so sorry, darling."

"It's nothing to do with you, Leila. I'm just telling you because I know what would happen if I didn't. You'd nag and poke at me --"

"I would not! And you were the one doing all the poking just a few minutes ago, mister."

His smile flickered on and off again. "All right. No nagging. You'd persist until I told you anyhow. You never just take orders."

"Well, that part is true enough."

"But that's why I'm telling you to stay near the ranch and close to the pack. I can't let that happen to you or our baby."

"I understand now you've explained and didn't order." Leila stroked his back, trying to silently show how sorry she was for that little boy and his mother. "And I understand the rules better now."

"Well, then --"

She could hear the rasp in his voice, the one she was starting to think of as the alpha tone. She even knew what he wanted her to promise. Well, she wasn't stupid and she was going to stay safe, but she couldn't promise to never leave this isolated ranch or to have weres as her permanent bodyguards. Promises like that were just meant to be broken. It was probably time to change the subject before he got all dominant and made her want to jump him…for sex or for murder, depending on the situation.

"One thing you need to tell the others, though." Leila smiled up at him, sweetly. "Anyone dares call me 'alpha bitch' to my face, and I'm gonna take his tail and rip it right off. I'm not anyone's bitch."

"But --" Dek smiled a real smile at her. "Sure, honey. Whatever you want. The name doesn't matter. You have the attitude."

Chapter Five

Leila pushed back a little from the computer and tapped her fingernails thoughtfully on the desk. *Click, click, click.*

She stared down at those nails. It was the first time in her adult life she could afford to have nails. Waitressing wasn't a job that allowed for them. She didn't have to do that anymore. In the other room she heard the sound of the washing machine and dryer running. Lowell was doing the wash. She didn't have to do that any longer, either.

She had leisure time. Now that was something she hadn't had since…well, she couldn't remember when. She had time to have long bouts of sex with her favorite alpha. Time to play with Lin and bake her cookies when she got home from kindergarten. Time to hang out on the computer and read up on wolves. Time.

Too much time. It was driving her crazy. She kept thinking about the damnedest things. Like what she'd just pulled up online: *Alpha wolves remain leaders until successfully challenged by another member of the pack. Alpha females are particularly prone to being challenged.*

Dek hadn't told her mating for life meant someone else might kill her for the chance to mate. Not that anyone around here was challenging her. Grey might want her to drop off the face of the earth, but...And she wouldn't have had the least worry about him or anyone else here if she had something else to do.

She wasn't a '50s sitcom mom...not that she could remember a '50s family quite like the one she'd fallen into here. But there were definite similarities. Dek disappeared every day into his home office and didn't emerge until evening. Lowell did all the shopping and cooking and cleaning. He even dropped Lin off at school and picked her up. It was only because she glared at him that she got to bake those damn cookies for Lin. Grey roamed around outside, fixing up the ranch house -- and while the main part of the building was more than adequate, the damn place was huge and rundown. All the men had plenty to do.

What activities did she have to occupy herself? Baking cookies and having sex. Was her life a cliché or what? Who would have thought life with wolfmen meant turning into a girly female?

Almost as if he were tracking her thoughts, Lowell switched on a soap opera on the TV in the kitchen.

Leila pushed the chair back and stood up fast. She was *not* going to spend her afternoons listening to that. Pretty soon she'd be asking to have the walls painted pink or something.

She stalked into the large kitchen, ready to snarl. But Lowell had switched to a channel that played country videos.

He had his back to the picture window that faced out to the corrals. The view to the outdoors was always beautiful. Lowell wasn't looking. He was ironing, humming to himself with the music, oblivious to her presence. His dark hair was a little mussed, and he hadn't shaved that morning.

It was a hot day to iron, even with the air conditioning on. Of course, he had the advantage of being able to take his shirt off. Leila blinked. The view indoors was pretty damn nice, too.

He had a delicious body. It was lean, with beautiful bronzed skin and muscles rippling just under that skin. He was built like a swimmer, not a bodybuilder. You might call him pretty, but there were a few bruises around his shoulder, a scratch on his chest -- sort of like the marks Leila left on Dek after sex. Lowell's jeans slipped just a little lower when he bent over the iron, and she got just the tiniest glimpse of a really nice, tight butt.

Leila blushed.

She wasn't supposed to be ogling him. She wasn't supposed to be thinking about -- not that she was thinking --

Lowell looked up at her, focused on her, and then smiled.

He didn't do that a lot. He always looked ready to jump when she was around. Damn. Lowell had a gorgeous smile.

"Can I get you anything, Mistress?"

She hated that title. But this afternoon it felt sort of naughty. Dangerous. Alphas were fun, but a nice submissive change of pace could be...

Whoa, girl. She had more than enough male on her hands -- and everywhere else on her body. What was *wrong* with her?

"I was going to yell at you, but it's too late. You did what I wanted before I asked." She smiled back at him as he stared blankly.

"Did I do something wrong?" Tension was seeping back into him.

"No. Nothing."

He relaxed, just a little, but kept eyeing her as if she was going to take a bite out of him. Hmm. Now that was a thought...

A bad thought. Bad alpha girl. The poor guy would jump if she so much as reached out to touch his shoulder.

She touched it anyhow. He was warm and smooth under her fingertips. And he didn't jump. For a moment he tensed; then he smiled at her again. Was that a brief glint of interest in those dark eyes?

"Are you sure you don't need anything?"

That wasn't a come-on. They both knew Dek would rip him apart if it was a come-on. But her skin prickled as if it had been the most suggestive innuendo she'd ever heard at the bar. Except she usually ignored the comments there, and here -- here she was staring at him like she wanted to taste some boy candy.

"Mommy, can I have some juice?" Lin called from the other room.

The weird energy in the room went poof! Lowell put the iron up.

"I'll get her some, Mistress."

He turned to the refrigerator and poured juice into a small plastic cup. Then he walked out to where Lin was undoubtedly enthroned on the living room sofa. Damn. The perfectly trained houseboy. There definitely was something seductive about that idea.

When he came back, he poured himself a glass of water, and she watched him tip his head back, the muscles of his throat working as he swallowed thirstily. When he put the cup down, he hesitated, glanced over at her, then turned back to the iron.

"Why are you ironing on such a hot day anyhow?" Leila pulled up a high stool from under the kitchen counter and plunked herself down.

"They're Dek's business shirts. He needs them for next week."

"Oh?" Dek hadn't said anything to her about shirts or next week or business, for that matter. She could play it cool and wait for Dek to tell her. She didn't have to lower herself to pump their omega for information.

"It's for a consult in Houston. One of the oil companies is flying him in." Lowell sounded almost as proud as if he had been the one summoned.

It didn't count if the omega started talking all by himself, did it?

"That happen a lot?"

"Some. Mostly he works from here, though. Dek said he can do just as well online with his own computers usually, and he doesn't want to leave the ranch much now that he bought it for us." Lowell wet his finger and tested the heat of the iron. "I bet he'll leave even less now that you're here."

"He must be pretty important, then."

"Yeah." Lowell beamed. "He's one of the best."

The best what? And why hadn't she ever wondered how this huge old ranch had been acquired by the pack? Even if they'd just rented the place -- which she'd assumed up to now -- that required money. Apparently Dek provided all of it, supported all of them in fine style on his own.

Maybe she should put all that leisure time toward thinking some useful thoughts and getting some real information. She really was a '50s woman, just calmly expecting men to provide for her without a thought as to how.

"I think I'll go pay Dek a visit." Leila stood up again.

"He doesn't like to be bothered -- I mean, whatever you think, Mistress." Lowell held up the crisply ironed shirt and carefully put it on a hanger. "I'm sure he'd make an exception for you."

She watched those muscles ripple again as he stretched over to put the shirt on a rack by the washing machine. Yeah, a trip to visit Dek *right now* was in order.

Leila paused before she left. Sure, Lowell was the pack's omega, but that didn't mean he didn't deserve some common courtesy. Why hadn't she ever offered him some before this? Where had she been for the last two weeks? Maybe Dek had sucked her brain away when he'd whisked her away to his den.

"And Lowell -- thanks."

"For what?" He looked startled.

"For everything. You keep this place spotless; you take care of stuff before I even think of needing it; and you're just a generally useful guy. Those are pretty difficult to find." Leila decided to make a joke of that slightly uncomfortable moment they'd had. "And you're not bad-looking without a shirt, either. Nice eye candy."

He blushed and dropped his gaze.

"Uh...well...thank you for the compliments. Mostly that's all just part of my job."

"Well, you do it well, then." She patted his shoulder -- just to reassure, and definitely not because she wanted to touch that pretty flesh again -- and headed for the office.

She woke up, thinking she'd heard something. But all she heard now was the hum of insects and the coo of quail in the early morning. Leila reached out and realized maybe it was too quiet.

Dek wasn't by her side.

"Why didn't you tell me what you do all day?"

"Because I didn't think you'd be interested."

"Am I stupid? Self-absorbed? Why wouldn't I be interested in what my guy does to keep us all in kibbles?"

"Stop with the dog jokes." Dek clicked the computer off and stood up. Leila clenched her fists. He might think the discussion was over, but he was very wrong.

"Stop with the 'no trespassing' signs." Leila deliberately stepped closer, invading his space.

"Fine. I consult with companies that are either corporate raiders or afraid they're about to be involved in a corporate takeover. My corporation is called Predators. I'm good at figuring out strategies to take over unsuspecting companies." Dek brushed past her and began to pace. *"Satisfied?"*

"No." Leila swallowed. He looked up at her, and heat damn near sent a flaming arc between the two of them.

"No? What more do you need, baby?"

"I need -- I need to do something for myself. To contribute something around here besides being your breeder. Don't even try to fool me by saying you mean me to be anything else. I've read enough and see how you act around me. You want me around to have more kids."

"I'd like more kids. Sure. We all want that." Dek moved closer to her this time, very close. Another half-inch, and his crotch would be rubbing against her just where she wanted it. "But that's not the only reason I fuck you, Leila. You know how much I enjoy it."

"Gee, overwhelm me with charm."

"You don't want charm right now, Leila."

"My, no, but I want something. I -- I'm restless, Dek. Bored. Itchy. If I don't have something real to do soon, I'll explode."

"It's almost the full moon, babe. We all feel that way. Restless. Itchy." He was close enough now, close enough to rub against. She almost cried with the need that rippled through her when she felt his hard length.

"Do me, then, Big Bad Wolf. But I have to have something else to do, too." Thoughts of Lowell flashed in and out of her mind. No. She didn't mean that. She meant --

He flipped her over so that she was bent over his desk. His zipper slid down with an impatient hiss.

"If you promise to stay in the hotel room while I'm in Houston, I'll take you with me. There will be just the two of us at night. I'll take you -- anywhere --"He plunged inside her, and she cried out, sharply. "Anywhere you want to go."

She couldn't think now. All she wanted was the change in his breathing that signaled his transformation, the weight on top on her that meant she was fucking a wolf, not a man. The slide over the edge to the beast that she was able to create in him.

His howl sent her into the first shiver of climax.

But he wasn't here right now, making those urgent noises. Instead she heard a sudden, broken-off yip in the distance, more a cry of distress than the howl of a mating wolf. It made her sit up in the bed.

Was that a real wolf, or one of the pack? She heard a thud out near the corral.

No matter who or what it was, it was on their land. Then she heard a yell. Dek's voice.

Trouble. Wide awake now, Leila pulled open the nightstand and pulled out the gun, loading it with fingers she willed not to tremble. She didn't like using guns, but some trouble called for them.

No one in her family was going to fight alone and unprotected if she could help.

"Where the hell have you been?" Dek's voice was dangerous as he dangled Lowell in the air.

"Does it matter?" For the first time ever, Lowell didn't hunch over and try to pretend he didn't exist. For the first time, the kid dared to stare at him, to challenge him. "You've got your piece of ass tucked away in your bed. Why don't you leave me alone while I look for some of my own?"

"Listen, pup --" Dek could feel the adrenaline rising. He tried to temper it, to remind himself this was just an adolescent under the influence of the moon. This was family, not a real enemy.

But even family could threaten, if they wanted to take over the pack.

"I'm not a pup, even if you do treat me like one."

"I'm not the one who stayed out when he was supposed to be on guard. We don't have just us to think about anymore --"

"I know. We have a woman and kid. I think about them!"

"He thinks about the woman too much. That's probably why he was bar-hopping tonight. Get any, kid?" Grey loomed up on Lowell's other side.

Dek sniffed. "He sure as hell got something that made him come tonight. But I don't smell any pussy."

"You whoring around again with cowboys, kid?" Grey cuffed Lowell on the side of his face. "Thought we broke you of that habit when we took you in."

"So now all I do is whore for the two of you for free? Fuck you both."

Dek looked over at Grey. Full moon or not, some things couldn't be tolerated.

It was a wonder she didn't shoot when she saw three men thrashing around in the front yard. But the bright rays of the moon soon made her pause. She knew those men, and that wasn't a fight.

She damn near pulled the trigger again from the shock, once she realized just exactly what was going on. Instead she carefully put on the safety and slipped the weapon in the desk by the hall. A nice girl would have gone away and tried to wipe the sight from her mind. That was why Leila ventured out onto the porch for an even better look. She'd done pretending to be nice.

Once she did, she put her freed hands to her mouth, willing herself not to make a sound. She sure as hell didn't want to be caught. But the men weren't thinking about the almost soundless squeak of the porch door right now. They had more than enough to do.

Lowell was sprawled on the ground, kneeling, ass up high. He was struggling, cursing, spitting, in a way she'd never seen Lowell do. Dek had the omega's arms pinned back.

"You think you're tough enough to be top dog, pup?" Dek snarled the words.

"Maybe he's tough enough to take it in the ass without lube." Grey jerked Lowell's head up. "What do you think, kid?"

"You can make me do this. You can't make me like it." Lowell twisted and cursed again.

"Aw, kid. You love bottoming. You were born for it." Grey tossed something small and white at Dek. "Here you go, boss. Even though he doesn't deserve it."

Leila's throat dried. Dek wasn't going to -- The sound of liquid spitting out of a tube was unmistakable. He *was*.

Grey already had his pants down to his boots, and Lowell audibly swallowed at the sight of Grey's erection. The noise made Leila shift her feet. Should she do...something? Grey shoved his cock into Lowell's mouth, and the younger man's lips closed over him without any more words.

"Let's see if we can fuck the sass out of you, pup." Dek's voice was almost gentle, yet the words held just enough threat to make Leila wonder.

But Lowell didn't seem worried. The moan he gave as Dek thrust from behind wasn't from pain or fear. Leila knew just what that sound was because she'd made it often enough when Dek fucked her. Lowell writhed again, but this time both men over him grunted with satisfaction.

Dear heavenly wonder from above. Leila had seen things in bars and outside them, but she'd never...she'd never...

It was beautiful. Frightening and strange, but beautiful. The three of them rocked together in as intimate an embrace as any trio could have, a mix of force and anger and pure sex.

And tenderness. As they moved together, she could see all of that in how Lowell tilted his head back for Grey. How Grey clutched the omega's hair. How Lowell sighed when Dek moved inside him. How, in turn, that sigh against Grey's cock made Grey cry out with pleasure. She stared as they paused. The tableau shifted from moonlight to shadow, skin gleaming bright and then hidden again, teasing her with a glimpse of the male mating dance.

Leila realized her hand was still over her mouth and she was biting it to keep from shouting out with them. Her other arm was wrapped tightly around her waist, the way she wished she was being held.

Oh, God. Oh, God. Oh, God. Grey was moving again, rapidly, pumping in and out of Lowell's mouth.

"Swallow the whole fucking thing, pup," Grey rasped out. "Take my come like it was candy."

She could feel a wet trickle run down her leg when Grey moaned his delight with Lowell's response. His fists dug into Lowell's back for a moment, then slowly relaxed. Lowell dropped his head down once Grey was done and hid his face in his hands, working his ass harder, grinding it against Dek.

"Got the spot, didn't I?" Dek sounded like he was speaking through gritted teeth. "Not so unhappy about me pounding into your ass now, are you?"

"God, no."

"You don't want me to stop, then?"

"Jesus, don't stop now, Boss. I'm so...fucking...close..."

A half-second later, Lowell's howl rose up, uncertainly at first, then stronger. He bucked, almost as if to dislodge Dek, and then stiffened in place. Dek stepped back, and Lowell dropped to the ground, panting.

"Who is top dog, pup?"

"You are."

"Fucking right. Don't forget that."

"You didn't come." Lowell turned to look at Dek. "Do you want me to --"

"I have my piece of ass in bed, just like you said. She'll take care of me."

Leila managed to make her legs work then. She stepped back into the shadows of the porch, creeping back for the door. For a moment she thought she saw Lowell glance her way, but he sank back to the ground without acknowledging her movement or staring in her direction again.

She ought to smack Dek for that remark. But the way she felt right now, it was use him, or wear out the vibrator. She guessed she'd best start with him.

He passed by her as she huddled in the bed, her heart thumping, her pussy wet and aching. Passed by her with barely a sound to let her know he had returned. The sound of water hit the shower stall in their bathroom.

Theirs. Leila clenched her fists, letting the bite of pain as her nails worked into her flesh compensate for the sensations she wanted to feel. That was a lie. Everything on this ranch was *his*. The bathroom, the bedroom, the people. Her.

Leila stood and unbuttoned her nightie. Wearing even the thin cotton fabric was too much. She was too hot. The fabric scraped against her tight nipples as she pulled it over her head. She threw it on the floor and walked after him.

He had soaped himself up by the time she opened the shower curtain. The water rose in steamy rivulets around him.

And he was still hard. Impressively erect and ready. She watched the droplets of water slide over his penis and wanted to lick them off.

"You decided to make me wait?" she asked.

"Hell, no. At least, I sure don't want to wait. But I was a little...dirty." He reached out, fished her into the shower and under the warm spray.

"You have the damnedest ears and nose. And most times you seem to know exactly what I'm thinking the second I think it. So once I stopped to figure it out, I knew you had to be aware of what I'd been doing." Leila wondered why she'd imagined she could hide from him.

"Just like you know what I've been up to." He bent, sucked one sensitive nipple, and allowed just the hint of teeth to rest against the tip. Leila choked back a cry. "How are you feeling about that, woman?"

"Hot. Bothered." She spread her legs to allow his hand better access. He immediately took advantage.

"Not just plain bothered?"

"Some. I guess. Ahh, Dek, right there." She shifted and he chuckled. She just wasn't sure if he was amused or not.

"Guess the full moon gets to you, too. Right?"

"You get to me. Always have." Leila shifted back as he pressed against her, moving her toward the shower wall.

"Then you won't mind if we --" He lifted her up without so much as a deep breath to show effort, and she curled her legs around his waist. He slid into her without finishing the sentence.

At least you won't mind for now. Leila opened her eyes, which had squinted shut to keep the water off. She stared up at her lover's face. She'd heard him, but he hadn't said anything out loud. He hadn't taken to talking to her inside her brain, had he? If he was going to say something nasty to her, he better say it out loud.

He moved, a long, sweet pull within her, and she forgot to talk. There was something else, though, something important -- and then he bit her shoulder, growled into her ear. "I can't wait, Leila. I can't. I need you too much."

She'd have melted then and there if she hadn't been melting already. For an answer she hitched her legs up just a notch higher and kissed him.

Their teeth scraped against each other, harsh and greedy. She wanted blood now. Wanted to feel a little pain. Wanted to feel his need and hers.

He filled her, and the water turned cold, but his body was still hot. She gulped and let herself go under, shuddering as her climax triggered his.

"You look so tired, Dek."

"Been a tiring night. You can wear a man out." He tried to smile. But she was right. He was tired, down to his bones.

Her eyes narrowed, but she didn't say anything. He wondered if that would really be the end of it. Most women would ask. Leila wasn't a peaceful kind of woman. It probably meant something that she was keeping quiet now. What was she thinking?

She smiled as if she could hear him. "I was thinking before how you owned everything and everyone on this ranch, body and soul." Leila traced an imaginary line down his face. "But seems like everything and everyone owns you, too."

"I'm alpha. I'm responsible for it all." He knew he hadn't explained it to her very well. Weres never needed to explain such a fundamental idea.

She nodded. "You do all kinds of things as the alpha. Some you like; some you don't."

Maybe that's why she hadn't asked. She'd managed to reach inside him and find out for herself.

"Yeah." Dek wondered if they could stop talking now so he could kiss her. His mate. She was perfect. They were in harmony like they were meant to be.

"But what part of tonight did you like, and what part didn't you?"

Ow. The question he hadn't wanted, and she sneaked it right in. He stared down at the pillow. Leila looked mussed and flushed and worn out. She should have been too exhausted to talk. He'd done his best to make her that way. Damn. The woman was tougher than you'd think.

He stroked her wild reddish curls. Leila was such a tiny thing -- she almost looked like a kid, except for the woman's build on her. Ah, she was tiny maybe, but she packed a mean sucker-punch. She could also wait forever until he coughed up an answer.

"I liked fucking you silly. I always have. Soon as we get to Houston -- damn, we have to leave in just a few hours now -- I'll do it again." He pulled her close against him and shut his eyes, hoping to shut off the questions.

He knew he hadn't really answered her and she was still awake, but he was damn tired. So long as she was here and safe and with him, he'd let everything turn off for now. But as he drifted to sleep, he wondered why her silence made him even more uneasy than her words.

Chapter Six

The hardest thing about being isolated on the ranch -- at least, if you didn't count the enforced leisure -- was the lack of women. Leila wasn't the most social creature on earth, but she'd gotten used to being with Sasha and Thea at work, listening to gossip, commiserating on small disappointments, and celebrating small triumphs. Just being with someone who knew what she was about.

It was bad enough being the only human. She was the only grown-up female within miles -- not that she could talk about Dek or what was bothering her. A girl had some pride. You couldn't talk about not being sure why your man was keeping you or how much he really cared. Maybe it was better Sasha and Thea didn't visit.

Leila stared down at the paintbrush. Grey had grudgingly allowed her to paint one of the smaller rooms for a study. The dingy off-white walls were being transformed into a much more cheerful pale, pale yellow. She'd move one of the dozens of computers in the house there and...and what? What did she need a study for?

"Damn it." Leila carefully shut the paint can and dumped the brush in a jar to soak. "I just have way too much time to think."

The boys -- she'd begun to think of everyone but Dek as the boys -- had gone to the city for the weekend. In her opinion, they hit the bars in El Paso a little too much for people who were supposed to be worried about safety.

She scowled as she began to scrub her hands in the guest bath off the hall. Maybe it was just her staying home everyone was worried about. Things just weren't fair. She wasn't supposed to wander off, but no one else was around, either. Dek was in his office, Lin was taking a nap before dinner, and here she was with nothing to do again. Lowell had even left them some enchiladas for her to heat up while he was gone. She could whip up a dinner by herself now and then. She used to be able to take care of herself quite well not so long ago.

She stared in the mirror. Shoot, she'd managed to sprinkle yellow paint all over her T-shirt. Hissing with annoyance, she pulled it off. It was just her painting shirt, but since she was done painting for the day, she saw no reason to traipse around smearing paint over everything else.

Maybe she'd go take a shower before they ate. Or wander over to show Dek her new topless look. Or take a shower and show off her naked look to Dek. Giggling, she shucked off her bra, jeans, and panties.

The bathroom door opened.

"You should knock before --" Leila blinked. "Oh. Oh, *shit!*" A few humming seconds of shock froze her before she whirled, snatched a towel, and twisted it around her. Damn it for being one of those skimpy ones you used to show off for guests. Why did they have such small towels anyhow? There were never any guests to impress. "What are you doing here?"

"I live here." Lowell looked more stunned than she felt. "I -- I didn't know. Sorry."

His gaze had already taken a good, leisurely trip from her toes right on up, with plenty of stops along the way. But he didn't stop staring. Leila shifted her feet. Whoa, that boy was bigger than you'd think at first. The tiny bathroom wasn't made to hold two people. She began to feel crowded and -- if she stepped back, there was nothing but wall behind her.

Back? What was she thinking? She was the alpha here.

"Damn it, Lowell!" She snatched up her clothes from the floor. "Get those eyes rolled back into your head. It's a wonder they haven't popped onto the floor by now. While you get yourself together, I'm going to get rid of these dirty things and take a bath. Since you seem to have forgotten your manners, at least try to act like you're housebroken and go away."

He shook his head just slightly, blinked, and then dropped his gaze down to his feet.

"Ye-yes, Mistress." Lowell took the bundle from her hands without looking at her again. "I can take care of that for you. When you're finished, dinner will be ready."

The words were right, but the tone was just a little off. There was just a little too much awareness of her underneath the quick obedience.

"I can fix my own dinner, thanks so much!" She glared at him until he got out of her way. Then she walked, rather than scurried, down the hall to the bedroom, refusing to let herself turn bright red.

If she wanted to stroll around the house naked in front of all of them, it was her right. Certainly some pup, one barely old enough to sneak into bars, couldn't say boo to whatever she chose to do.

Maybe she did take a little longer with her shower than she had to. That didn't mean she was trying to avoid anything. And maybe she dressed in a black shirt and skirt, even though it was foolish to wear black in such heat, because it just looked more authoritative and adult. But she had to admit the truth when she put on her shoes. Leila stared down at her high-heeled sandals and shook her head. When she took to trying to add a few inches to her height just to show she was boss, she was embarrassed.

She hoped Lowell didn't know how much he'd shaken her.

That was just stupid. They all lived together. Sometimes they'd see each other in ways and places civilized humans didn't expect. Leila swallowed. All right. So they weren't all civilized humans. Some of them were werewolves.

She took a breath, firmed her chin, and opened the door.

That didn't mean they had to act like heathens!

When she sailed into the kitchen, ready to tell Lowell just what for, she was ridiculously deflated when she realized he'd taken her at her word. He wasn't in the kitchen, hastily heating up dinner and setting the table. The laundry wasn't even started.

Had he turned tail and run away for the weekend the way he had planned originally?

She wasn't actually missing him, was she? Leila went to the kitchen window to see if his battered truck was still in the driveway. As she peered out, she heard a soft sound behind her.

She whirled. There was more silence. The kitchen clock chimed, and she jumped. Then she heard the odd, stifled sound again.

A groan?

Leila slipped a carving knife from the rack. Probably it was nothing. But it was a big house, and security systems had been known to fail...She headed toward the noise --

And realized it came from the half-open door of Lowell's bedroom, right near the kitchen. She hesitated, her fingers on the doorknob.

Hell, he'd come barging in on her, hadn't he?

She threw open the door.

"*Fuck!*" They both said it at the same time.

Maybe she should have realized -- but there must still be some naïve little girl left in her after all. She'd thought of a lot of scenarios when she heard those noises, but she'd never imagined she'd see Lowell, his neck stretched back and his face as strained as if he were being tortured, both legs spread wide with his knees hooked over the arms of an easy chair, jerking off.

"With my panties!" Leila yelped. "You're using my panties."

"Jesus, Leila! Have some mercy here! It's not like I'm not embarrassed enough!" He dropped her clothing to the floor.

Leila noticed nothing else dropped. Dear sweet heaven, if anything, his cock was getting bigger.

"I -- I --" She stuttered, looking at this very aware, very aroused Lowell. His eyes were hot and focused directly on her.

She'd glimpsed what he could be like before, with the other men, when he was getting his brains fucked out...but suddenly she realized she was closer to the real Lowell than she'd been in all the weeks he'd been carefully tending to her.

Wolves were freaking dangerous. Even the ones in sheep's clothing. And especially one who had her underwear wrapped around his cock when he masturbated.

What the hell were you supposed to do in a situation like *this?*

Be alpha.

Images of three bodies in the moonlight danced in her mind.

She put her knife down on the dresser. "I guess I won't need to cut off your cock with this, even if you are waving it around like a flag."

Then she looked him over, just as carefully as he had her a half-hour before. He sat, frozen, and let her get a good eyeful. Damn. It wasn't anything she'd tell him, but he didn't have anything to be ashamed of if he did want to show off. She fought the urge to lick her lips.

She looked at his hand, still resting on a hairy thigh, close to his balls. "Looks like you still want to jack off, don't you?"

The head of his cock turned redder. Bobbed up as if to agree.

She circled him. "And maybe you wanted to jack off in front of me, or you wouldn't have left that door open, would you?"

He made a soft noise in the back of his throat as if to argue. She put her hand over his mouth and shook her head. "Don't."

"Jack off?" He whispered around her palm, his lips soft and tickling against her skin.

"Don't talk. Don't think. Don't do anything except what I tell you. Understand?"

He swallowed and nodded.

"Don't you think you need to be punished for being insolent?"

He nodded again.

Leila smiled, suddenly giddy as the rush of lust and naughtiness and power mixed inside her. She took her hand away from that warm mouth and let one nail scrape against his thigh, up higher and higher, almost to his swollen balls. Lowell shut his eyes and groaned.

"Open those eyes. And be silent." Leila touched the liquid pooling on his cockhead, and he jumped. "You're already damn near ready to come, and all I'm doing is telling you what an insolent, dirty boy you are. Ordering you to obey me. I can see your punishment will have to be harsher than I thought. You might enjoy it too much otherwise."

He shuddered, and another few drops trickled from his cock.

"How dare you sit in front of me? Get off that chair and get on your knees."

He scrambled off the chair and down, crouched before her in a wolfish subservient pose. None of them had ever done that for her yet, even if she was considered the alpha b -- female.

Another dollop of excitement twisted inside her as she looked at that tight ass in front of her. Being alpha was damn fun.

Leila sat in the chair. It was still warm from the heat of Lowell's body. She could smell him on it. Smell his sexuality. She looked down to where he was crouched. Yes, there was definitely the scent of his obedience and desire mixed. Why did that make her so excited?

She hooked her legs open, slowly and deliberately, in the same position he'd been moments before. Another stifled groan -- or was that a growl this time? -- came from the crouching omega. Someone was peeking. Leila chuckled.

"So show me you can pleasure a woman and not just imagine what it's like, Lowell. Push up my skirt."

His hands were shaking as he reached for the material. She lifted her hips almost to his face and made sure he could get a good look.

"You can use your tongue. Just your tongue. Don't so much as twitch with anything else."

He looked up at her. Dear Lord. There were tears swimming in his eyes.

"I've never --"

"And if you make one more sound, I'll blindfold you so you can't see yourself doing it." Because suddenly she had an urge to cry, too, which was all wrong for an alpha. She needed to stay the boss because...because it felt like she was shoving him into doing something powerful, something she might not be able to control if she let him free. That would never do.

The feeling fled as he jumped forward. The boy didn't need any more urging to crane his neck forward. At the first touch of that eager, lapping tongue, she almost screamed. She fought the urge to stroke his back, the need to ease the tension in the tendons of his jaw as he worked it against her flesh.

"Higher and deeper." She was stunned at how coolly she rapped the words out, even though she was damn near choking. "And *harder.*"

When he blew against her clit, she clutched the arms of the chair as if she were on a bucking horse. In the silence she could hear the rasp of his tongue against her, the short, indrawn breath he took when she got wetter still.

"You're humping the chair, Lowell. I didn't allow that, did I?"

"Shit. I can't -- mercy, Mistress. I can't hold on much longer. You smell too good. You feel like..."

"Did I tell you to talk?" If he kept talking, she was going to fall apart in front of him. "Get away from me."

He shivered, hesitated, and backed away.

"I guess pleasuring me is too much for you. You're forgetting what I ordered." He looked like he wanted to protest, but he kept his mouth shut. Leila continued. "You wanted to masturbate for me? Stand up and do it now."

He pulled himself up, legs shaking. For a moment he stood, looking down at her, his face unreadable. She smiled and put her hands behind her head, pretending to be relaxed, and let her breasts thrust forward under the thin shirt.

"Do your best, Lowell. Make it good and make it last, or I won't let you finish me off. You want to do that, don't you? It sounded like I tasted pretty good to you. I can still see my juices on your face. Lick them off first."

He licked, carefully erasing all traces of her from his chin and cheeks. When he was done, he cupped his balls as if he was offering them to her. She chuckled. In a way, he was. Clever boy. She nodded, signaling him to start the show.

He had good hands. Strong. Eager. His fingers held his shaft tight while his other hand began to pump. Leila reached forward and squeezed his heavy balls just a little. Lowell's eyes shut, and his teeth bit hard into the front of his bottom lip to keep from crying out. A small drop of sweat ran from his forehead, and she smiled again.

"Go on." She stretched out her foot, slid it between his opened legs, and let the tip of her tall, pointed shoe heel rest between his ass cheeks.

A thin line of come dropped onto her leg. He stopped his steady jerks and stared at her as she pulled her leg slowly back. He panted, shivering all over.

He was waiting for permission. The knot of excitement in her gut, in her pussy, tightened up another notch.

"Touch your nipples first. You ought to have them pierced. We'd both like that." She saw them turn bright red as he tweaked them impatiently, his balls pulled tight against him, his cock erect and tall. "Now your balls." He pulled at them harder than she'd dare, rolled them in his hand.

"Now. You may come for me." He arched back, running both fisted hands up and down his shaft, letting her see every inch. His breath rasped in his throat. It took about two strokes before he began to shudder, as if fire was licking through his body, or a whip's lash was tickling his ass. At last he came, the thick white liquid erupting from his body in spurts as if it would never stop.

"Fuck. Oh, fuck. Oh, fuck."

Lowell sang out the words on a howl that sounded like pain and pleasure both. Then he sank back down to his knees and rested his head on her lap, covered in sweat. Leila trembled as if she had come herself -- and she damn near had at the sight.

"You came on my leg." She cleared her throat, made her voice rasp with authority, rather than need. "Disgusting. Lick it off. All of it."

He lifted his head as if it were almost too heavy to move. His eyes were glazed, staring. Then, blindly, eyes shut, he slid his tongue down to her calf and licked. He got on all fours and stroked her leg with his mouth, slipped her foot out of her shoe and bathed that with his tongue. He teased the arch of her foot, tickling the sensitive nerves bundled there.

God, he was young. Young and strong. He was already getting hard again when she pulled him back up in front of her, between her thighs.

"Are you ready to finish pleasing me?"

"I never want to stop pleasing you." His erection stirred against her mons.

"Now you may use your hands and your mouth."

"Thank you." He bent, spread open her pussy, and placed his mouth against it, teeth pulling on her clit, then suckling it.

Leila tried, but she couldn't help breathing hard -- breathing as hard as Lowell was. She looked at his cock, pointing out at her as he attended to her. Jesus, the boy learned fast -- almost as fast as his recovery time. He paused when she stilled, moved harder and faster when she shivered. He moaned against her clit, and she gasped.

He put one finger inside her, moving tentatively, deliciously up. She wriggled against that finger, clenched hard around it. Without any words needed, he used a second and then a third. Suckling, then thrusting up with all three digits, he pushed her closer to the edge.

"You're so beautiful." She thought she heard him mutter it even while his mouth was busy doing other things.

"Ahhhh." She ground her pussy against his hand and let the ripples of a climax clutch her, one too intense for her to breathe.

Spots flickered in front of her eyes before she managed to get her lungs working. Jesus. He was still there, mouth and fingers pressed against her, feeling every jolt of the earthquake he'd stirred up.

"Stop. You can stop now."

He looked up, as intent as if he were on a hunt and close to his prey. "Let me wash you off."

Wash. Oh, my God. What if Dek smelled -- realized -- *Dek*.

It wasn't much more than he'd had them all do when they first met. Not too very much more. Somehow she knew

Dek wouldn't see it that way, though. Leila rubbed her face. Stupid were rules.

Damn. What she'd done probably didn't work under any rules. What had she been thinking?

"I'll wash up myself."

"I could do it better...Mistress."

She'd been thinking of how she'd felt when she saw Dek with the other men. The shock and the interest, the anger and the lust. Or maybe she hadn't been thinking at all. She'd been an idiot.

"Lowell, what we did -- It didn't really mean anything --" And just what did that comment make her sound like? Leila shut her mouth. *Never apologize; never explain* sounded like a good motto right now.

"I'm sure glad you think so, Leila." A third voice spoke up.

Oh, shit! He knew. Idiot. Of course he would know. That damned alpha knew everything and could sneak through closed doors if he wanted. How long had he been watching? Quite long enough, she was sure. Leila stared at the scuffed work boots and slowly up the familiar jeans that seemed to fit him like a second skin. She stopped at the belt buckle. His erection was pushing hard against the fabric of his jeans. That was reassuring, but Leila wasn't sure she really wanted to see Dek's face right now.

"It's not -- we didn't --" Lowell started to stammer words out and then realized the virtue of closing his mouth a few vital moments after she did. In silence, he jackknifed up off the floor and pulled his pants on.

Leila lifted her chin and refused to hurry. She wasn't some damned omega. Instead she smoothed down her skirt and crossed her legs. She darned well knew he was taking a good peek. "Did you enjoy the show, Dek?"

She got her courage together and looked up. When she met his eyes, she was stunned to see something that looked like amusement.

"Sure did. Didn't you?" He beckoned to her, and slowly, still refusing to hurry, she stood up and inched a little closer. He didn't sound like he was ready to fight, but she wasn't letting her guard down yet.

"Yes. And did you have anything more you wanted to say about it, Mr. Deklin Kinkaid?"

"Just don't forget that was mostly all show, baby." He leaned forward and kissed her forehead. As if she were maybe Lin's age!

Leila tried to talk then, but something garbled and choked came out. She was torn between wanting to smack him and weep with relief.

"Now, bend over the chair and spread your legs." His big, pointy-toothed smile was back. That was the grin she didn't trust for a second, but could never resist. "Pup, get closer and take a good look. While you're at it, hold on to your cock, because we're going to show you how sex is really done."

Chapter Seven

"You're twisted." Leila knew her resistance was token. He did, too, because even while she said the words, she leaned over and let him push her legs a little further apart. She didn't even squawk when his hands moved high up on her thighs.

"You're nice and wet, babe. I like you that way."

Leila gasped when Dek entered her without any more warning or ceremony. She was still sensitive, and it hurt a little. Dek bit her neck as he touched her clit. She bucked, realizing that Dek had known the pain would almost immediately translate to pleasure. Damn it, she was still aroused. How many times could a female come in an hour?

Guess she was going to find out.

"I liked that little alpha bitch display of yours," Dek whispered in her ear. His nail scraped her clit lightly, and she moaned. "You're definitely becoming were, baby."

Another groan echoed the sounds she was making. Lowell. Dear heaven, she'd almost forgotten they had an audience.

"Pup, crawl on over and soothe her while I'm busy."

"You are...too twisted --" Leila gasped and shut her eyes. That didn't help. She was still able to listen to the sounds of Lowell placing himself before her again, feel the wetness of his tongue against her. Why was she the one who had to make the objections around here? "He's licking me *and* you!"

There was something unbearably kinky -- and arousing -- about the tickle of Lowell's tongue against her and Dek.

"Well, Lowell has a first-class mouth. He can do a lot of things with it all at one time," Dek said absently as he abruptly pulled out of her.

"Now what?" Leila was afraid to even try to imagine.

She heard the smack against her butt a split second before she felt the sting of his hand.

"There. That's to make you feel better."

"Ow!" The second smack stung even more. When she jumped, Lowell buried his tongue even deeper inside. Pain...pleasure...pain...*Jesus.* "Ow! Ow! How is that supposed to make me feel better, you -- *ow!*"

But the flicks of fire were suddenly making her claw at Lowell's shoulders and shout out with more than just anger or agony. She couldn't think straight, didn't even want to. She teetered on the edge of cutting pleasure.

"Because now when you think about tonight, you aren't going to feel guilty, Leila. Instead, the first thing you'll think of is how that bastard alpha Dek made sure you couldn't sit down for a week. You might get mad and you might want more, but that's what you'll be thinking about." She heard his chuckle through a welling passion. Hot damn, he was probably right. The way she felt right now left no room for guilt. "Lowell, you have some of that lube handy?"

That helped focus her scattered thoughts in a hurry.

"*What?*" Leila gulped. "Now listen here, Deklin. I didn't sign on for what it sounds like you have planned."

But she stayed still, and Lowell didn't pause with his rhythmic strokes. She was being pulled into something dark and fearful and…exciting. Dek was behind her, holding her because she was trembling so hard. God, she wanted to stay this way forever…caressed and cherished. Dek always made her feel so damned safe, even in the middle of his frightening promises.

When she leaned over again, knowing her ass was up high and inviting, they all knew she was going to accept.

"Hell, baby, before we're done, you're going to beg for more," Dek echoed her thoughts again as his finger pressed against her anus.

"*Dek!*" Grey's voice echoed down the hall. It didn't take long before the three of them heard the sound of his footsteps coming toward the kitchen.

"Dear heavenly mercy, why didn't anyone stay out when they said they were going out?" Leila mumbled, and Dek laughed.

Leila shoved her shirt and shoes into place at nearly the same moment, some leftover adrenaline giving her speed.

"Dek, damn it, there's danger!" Grey roared. "Where the hell are you?"

Amusement gone, Dek sprinted out the bedroom door. Lowell growled, almost under his breath, and got up from his knees. He whirled around, grabbed the knife she'd left, and then opened the bureau drawer.

"What are you doing?" Leila had almost grabbed his wrist before he pulled out a revolver. She backed up a step. You didn't play with things like that, and you didn't get too close to someone who looked like Lowell when he had a weapon.

When Lowell bared his teeth in a threat face, Leila forgot he was just the omega.

"Where are you going?" Grey bellowed from the other room. "Dek, stop running like a damned jackrabbit and let me tell you what's going on!"

Leila stepped into the kitchen a split second before Dek arrived there, with Grey at his heels. She had to wonder if Dek hadn't planned it just that way. At least she didn't have to think about explaining or apologizing to Grey.

Dek had scooped up Lin, who was clinging to her father's neck. Leila opened her arms, but Lin shook her head, burrowing her face against Dek. Thank God Dek's first instinct had been to grab their baby if there was danger. Grey was still talking, his face looking grimmer than ever.

"What happened exactly?" Dek touched his little girl's hair lightly, absently patting her shoulder while he paced. "And how many of them are there?"

"I'm not sure." Grey locked the kitchen window. "Two of them stopped me at the bar."

"You hurt?" Dek asked.

"Two what?" Leila asked at the same time.

"Weres." Grey barked the word at Leila and then turned back to Dek. "Naw. They'd need more than those curs to take me. They knew that. In fact, they acted real nice. Bought me a drink. They offered --" Grey looked over at Leila and then went on. "They offered to take Leila off our hands if I'd help them."

"What the hell --" Leila stopped and thought about it. It was the perfect bribe for Grey. She'd be gone, and there was Dek, back again with Grey for company. Damn. Whoever it was, they knew how this pack worked.

"They offered to take Dek out if I'd help." Lowell skidded into the kitchen, still barefoot.

Dek gave a long, considering glance at Lowell, then Leila. Her stomach knotted, but he didn't say anything. He just handed Lin over to her and stepped away. Had all that unconcerned amusement of his been just for show?

It's not like that at all, really. Honestly, Dek. I let some kind of weird brew of jealousy and curiosity take over for a minute. That's all.

Why the hell didn't she know he was reading her mind now when she desperately wanted him to?

"Why didn't you say something right off, boy? They must've talked to you first," Grey demanded. "You ran home before I did."

"I meant to. I --" Lowell flushed. "Aw, shit."

"Thought you might take them up on their offer, did you?" Dek sounded as calm as he had in Lowell's bedroom.

Much too calm for Leila's taste. Didn't anything bother him? Didn't it *matter?*

"It wasn't like that." The omega made a helpless, hopeless gesture with his hands and then let them fall to his sides. "Not really. I started thinking about what it would be like if things were different in the pack. If I were different. But it's not, and I'm not. Anyhow, I told you now."

"You damned idiot." Grey shook his head.

"Will they come for us right off?" Leila interrupted, thinking longingly of her own .38. Fool that she was, she'd left it in the hallway all this time and never thought to pick it back up.

"Most likely not." Grey kept his eyes on the picture window -- that huge picture window that was suddenly more liability than asset. "They're looking for a weakness and haven't found one yet."

"We'll be all right, Mommy." Lin smiled at her. Patted her hand. Leila smiled back and watched her other hand curl into a fist. Leila needed to make sure they were all right.

Dek leaned over and slid her revolver into her hand. *Thank you, Jesus.* It couldn't all be a show, because he was back to reading her thoughts without a problem, knowing what she needed the second she did, or even long before. Maybe things were all right after all.

As all right as you could be with a pack of werewolves after you. Inconveniently, she remembered in vivid detail everything Dek's old clipping had said about what might happen. Dek had lost his mother, but he'd survived somehow. Not everyone was that lucky. If there was an attack, what might happen to her own baby? She hadn't wanted to think about it, but now bloody, frightening images crowded in.

"I think I'm feeling a little dizzy." Leila heard her surprised voice a long, fuzzy way away from her body.

Chapter Eight

"Leila. Baby. Are you listening? Are you able to hear me? Leila, will you fucking open your eyes?" That was Dek's voice, damn near screaming in her ear. She wanted to respond to the urgency in his tone -- and shut up the shouting -- but she was so tired. He could wait just a little longer, surely, until she got the gray mist cleared out of her brain.

There was something she had to ask, though. Something that couldn't wait. She licked her lips, forced the word through. "Lin?"

The voice immediately lowered down to a more soothing rumble. "Oh, baby. I wondered there...Lin is fine. Grey has her outside, until we got you moving again. You scared her half to death."

"I didn't faint. I never faint."

"Right. Well, you decided to sit down and take a rest on the kitchen floor for a little too long."

Leila blushed. "I'll go see Lin and reassure her."

"I'll carry you."

"Stupid."

"Stupid yourself. I don't trust you to stand right now. You'd fall over and hit your fool head," her lover said tenderly, and then she was pulled up, left dangling in the air, with her head spinning all over again. She hung on to Dek's shoulders and let him carry her away.

It was quiet outside as the sun disappeared slowly from the sky. So quiet. She wondered if it was safe to be outside, but she figured the he-men around her, particularly Mr. Head He-Man, who was hauling her around at the moment, would laugh if she mentioned her concern.

"She's over there." Grey was propped against the porch. He pointed to where Lin was dangling from a pecan tree limb. "Lin's fine. How about *her?* She doesn't look so good."

He never called her by name if he could help it, but if she strained a little, she thought there might be some faint concern in Grey's voice.

"Better." Leila cleared her throat, embarrassed at the squeak in it.

"She need the ER? We could get her in without anyone knowing about us. She's human." The usual scorn in that word was muted just a little maybe.

"Better to keep away from them if we can," Dek said. "Besides, she's coming to."

"I hate hospitals." Leila was pleased to realize she sounded much firmer this time.

"I'm keeping an eye on her." Dek's finger lightly traced what must have been a bruise on her cheek. Leila winced. She must have fallen. "The minute she looks like there's a problem that some time won't take care of, I'll get her checked."

"Whatever." Grey shrugged. "You're the boss."

"Damn straight." Dek kept his hand on her, circling her back in slow, light movements. As if he was checking to see she was all right. As if he wanted to keep being sure of it.

She stared over at Lin, who was running around and around a tree. "You know, why are you growing pecans anyhow? That doesn't go with your macho image, cowboys."

"She's feeling better, boss."

"Yeah." Dek squeezed her shoulder a little. "She's back to being nosy and demanding. Go ahead and answer the lady's question, Grey."

"We can't raise animals. They get too skittish around us. And, well, you never know what might happen --"

"During a full moon. Gotcha." She pushed away from Dek. "I'm starting to feel fine now. Really."

"You still look a little ragged." Lowell's voice behind her made her jump. "Maybe you should rest some."

"Maybe you worry about me too much."

The dark jealousy was still there, lurking underneath. The wash of possession, the mix of joy and pure showing-off when he fucked Leila in front of his packmate, was gone. But above all that was something more, something worrisome.

Dek didn't like it.

That damned mostly human female. If Leila ever knew what a hold she had on his balls, he'd be dead meat. He'd chosen to treat that little escapade of hers with Lowell as an experiment. Fun and games. It was, mostly. Alpha females did things like it all the time in their packs, showing their own dominance. Leila was learning to be an alpha bitch, like it or not.

But what if she didn't like what she had to become? She wanted him. She still did. He could feel it whenever she got wet, see it on her face when she looked at him. Hell, he could touch and taste and smell her wanting whenever they got in the same room. But he didn't think she wanted everything that came with him. Was her slap and tickle with Lowell the start of her trying to pull away from the pack?

That would be a damned shame.

Something was off tonight. Not just the threats and the fainting, but something else. Grey tilted his head, trying to figure it out.

"Daddy, look!" Lin called from the distance.

"Yeah, sweetie," Dek called to her, but he looked at Leila instead. Grey scowled. There was something…he caught the whiff of her scent mingled with…

"Maybe you do worry about her too much." Grey stared, eyes narrowed, at Lowell. The kid shifted his feet.

"I have something to tell all of you." Lowell spoke abruptly, a little too loudly. He didn't look at Dek directly, not even for permission to speak.

No one answered for a long moment. Damn it, all of them knew exactly what was up except him. Grey hated that.

"What's up, pup?" Fine. He was willing to be the one to ask. Obviously he wasn't going to find out anything if he waited for the rest to speak up.

"I care about all of you. I thought I should say that first. And -- and I'll miss you when I leave." Lowell's voice was more confident, more certain than Grey ever remembered it being. "This is good-bye."

Grey stared at the omega. Lowell looked different, just as he sounded different. His head was up, and his shoulders weren't hunched over in that deferential slouch. Damn. The pup seemed more determined. More adult.

"No need for that." No matter what had happened.

"Yeah. Yeah there is."

"You've thought this out, Lowell?" Dek asked. Grey wondered if he'd ever called the kid by his proper name before. If any of them had. But Dek seemed to know now was the right time for it. "Because we want you to stay."

"I've been doing nothing but think about it," Lowell said. "And about...well, about a mate. I've been thinking too much about what that would be like to be satisfied here."

Dek looked at *her*. "What about you, Red?"

"What about me?" Leila sounded like the village idiot, but then, Grey wasn't so sure he wasn't gaping at them as if he were a second one.

"Are you staying?"

"You don't want me to? You'd rather I went with Lowell?"

Grey gave her credit. She sounded almost as hurt as he would be if Dek had said that to him. But none of this added up. He could live without Lowell or the woman in the pack.

But Dek? When the hell did he let go of family? Of this woman? It was unimaginable. He didn't understand anything that was going on. Even stranger, somehow Grey found himself being the one who gripped their alpha bitch's elbow, holding her steady. She looked like she might just pitch over again if he didn't. Her damned mate was still standing a little away from her, hands shoved in his back pockets. What the hell was with Dek? He never had a problem talking.

Dek spoke to her -- to them all -- much too calmly. "It's your choice, Leila. Mostly members of the pack have none. I'm bound -- maybe more bound than anyone else -- to the pack. But I've been thinking. An alpha doesn't have to be challenged before leaving. She can go before then, when she's no longer useful to the pack. Or, like Lowell, when he decides to find a new pack or a mate. You can stay, of course. You might be safer with more weres to guard you rather than just one. I'd offer you the choice to do whatever else you want, if it were possible, but it isn't. You and Lin are in too much danger alone."

"You're giving me any choice? Alphas never give choices." It sounded like she was finally getting the idea, human though she was. Grey almost relaxed. Damn. He hadn't even realized he was as tense as the couple in front of him.

"I'll always be alpha. But you're a human. Well, mostly human. You need different rules. It doesn't matter what I think about what you should do."

"I see. You could give me up, but not the pack."

Idiot woman. She had missed everything important. Why did non-weres misunderstand the most basic ideas? And Dek wasn't saying a damn thing. He just stood there with his fists balled up, staring at the human. Good God, if everyone stayed silent, she might really leave.

No women around. Everything back to normal. Grey stole a look over at his boss. Everything and everyone would be the same but Dek.

Oh, hell. Someone was going to have to step in, and why the fuck did it have to be him?

"You're a fool, and you have it all wrong." Grey told her, almost pleasantly. "Don't you see the alpha bastard is doing this for you? He and Lowell both are tearing themselves up inside so you can have things any way you want. They both want you that badly. Real weres never get chances like that. He's letting you leave if you don't want to be part of the pack. You can have him with us, but you can't have him without. What he really ought to do is take you by the scruff and shake sense into you until you can't leave."

He'd asked her to leave. Was the giant pain in her chest from her fall, a wound she hadn't felt before, or was it just from his words? The hurt clawed into her as if it were physical. Leila gasped for air.

Doing this for her? Grey's vinegary tone had cut the panic and pain long enough for her to think. Dek had said he wanted her to have a choice. That had to be some kind of first in were history, but she needed to know why.

"You can shut up now, Grey. And you, Dek --" He looked over at her, his expression polite and remote and totally unDek-like. She opened her mouth and decided words weren't enough. If she was going to have to be honest no matter what, she was going to make it count. And he wasn't allowed to be distant from her.

Leila walked over and grabbed Dek's shoulders, shaking him with every other word. "I love you. I love all of the pack, but I *love* you. That's not a were emotion, I suppose. You don't love me. I'm your mate or your responsibility or whatever it is females are to you, but it's different for me. So if you're doing this to make it easy on me or to punish me or -- Don't."

Oh, hell. She was crying and her nose was clogging up and her voice was getting all quivery. This was not the way to make a forceful statement. Leila let go of him to wipe her eyes and tried to come up with the right words. But all she could manage was "Just -- just tell me what you want, Dek."

"Were you really afraid I'd leave you?" Dek's low rasp in her ear and his tight embrace made her cunt tighten even before the words' meaning hit her brain. "Are you trying to get yourself fucked silly in front of the entire pack?"

He sounded like they did when they had sex. He was as hard against her as he was when they did, too. God, it was just like when he was so crazy for her he couldn't stand it anymore. But if she had no intention of making public sex a mainstay of their relationship, she'd better start talking and stop bawling. She could do that. She was strong.

"I wouldn't mind." Leila gulped and blinked the last of the tears away. "So long as you were doing it."

Well, that didn't come out the way it should have. Dek's eyes got even hotter and more intense. Whoa, baby, she was going to melt.

"Me, either. Except for Lin." Dek straightened and spoke louder. "I take it that means you don't want to go?"

"I don't want to, really. Not unless you leave. But what it really means is that I'll go wherever you do, boss." She almost giggled at the way his eyes narrowed when she called him that last word. He could look as fierce as he wanted, but she knew he liked it. "But there are going to be some changes around here. I'm going back to school, like it or not. And we're going to see that Lin has plenty of opportunities to do what she wants…and…"

"Mommy? Did you see me?" Lin ran up to pull at her elbow just then.

With an effort, Leila got her mind off being fucked silly. "Yes, honey. I did. You're getting very big."

"Pretty soon I'll be big enough to fight the bad guys, too, and not just hide." Lin looked at her nails thoughtfully. "I'll need some claws, though."

She stretched her hands out to Lowell and smiled.

"You'll have huge claws when you grow, princess. You can decorate them when you aren't going into battle." Lowell squatted down to Lin's eye level. "I wanted to be sure to tell you what I just told everyone else. I'm leaving today. I'll miss you."

Lin stared at him, slack-jawed for a moment. Then she glanced at everyone else to see their reactions. Finally she scowled and crossed her arms. "No! You *belong* to us. Who will get me at school? Who will clean up after everyone? Who will Grey yell at? You have to stay."

"Another stray'll come by to do all that soon enough, princess. I have to go find another place for myself." Lowell straightened and backed away. "Shit. Somebody take her before she cries."

"Lowell, she's right. What she and I both told you. You belong here as much as any of us do." Dek kept his hand on Leila, but his voice was calm.

"I don't want to challenge you, Dek, bad as I want your mate. Besides, I couldn't do it now and win, even if I wanted to. Neither of us wants me to spend years waiting for you to show a weakness, getting ready to fight you. But I can't stay here as I am." Lowell shrugged. "So I'll take my chances on leading some other pack. Finding a mate of my own."

"*Adios*, then, Lowell." Grey cuffed him lightly on the head. "Be careful."

"No fun in that." Lowell grinned, a little uncertainly. "Good-bye."

* * *

"I was told I had to come and give you this." The teenaged kid's lower lip was stuck out in the biggest pout Dek had seen since his five-year-old was told she couldn't have dessert. But the catch in the kid's throat sounded like grief, rather than temper.

"Hey. Some present." Grey looked in the bag. "A tail and ears."

"That was our pack's alpha. My dad. The new boss ran me off." Their messenger swallowed. "I was told to come to you. He said there was an opening for me here."

"I think Lowell made sure that pack won't be sniffing after us." Grey shook his head. "Damn. I didn't know the little bugger had it in him. His first try, too."

"His first try that he meant to win," Dek corrected and sniffed the bag. "All in all, it's a real nice token of his appreciation. Our little boy has grown up."

"You, pup. What's your name?" Grey turned to the gangly adolescent.

"Rossi."

"Well, Rossi, there's no time to clean you up, but mind your manners. You're going to be the ring-bearer."

"What?" The kid looked startled out of his misery, and Grey roared with laughter. "Welcome to your new pack, kid. We can do that ceremony after we get done with this silly-ass one."

"My God. You live in this huge place with no one but Lin and those two yummy men?" Sasha gave her the thumbs-up sign. "Some women have all the luck. Why didn't that big brute take one look at me and chase me down that night at the bar?"

"Hey, I invited you to the wedding. If you're nice to me, I'll throw the bouquet in your direction." Leila twitched the spaghetti strap of her gown into place and stared at the corsage pinned at her shoulder. "Is everything straight?"

"You're gorgeous." Thea hugged her.

"The other big one. Is he attached?" Sasha peeked out to where Dek and Grey stood, looking as *GQ* as Leila had ever seen them.

"No. Not exactly." Leila paused and grinned. "But don't get any ideas. You were right about Grey."

"I was right?"

"Yeah. He's gay. Just as gay as you said back in the bar. In fact, he'd probably love to jump Dek right now. He might even be willing to make it a threesome as long as he could get his hands on my husband-to-be."

"Leila, are you kidding us?" For the first time ever, Thea and Sasha both looked stunned almost speechless.

"Nope. But that's OK. We're all really, really close." Leila winked. "I might be willing to consider the idea someday. After the honeymoon glow fades."

Damn, she just might. Give her a little inspiration, a full moon, and Dek to make her feel wicked, and it could happen.

Her two buddies blinked at her, mouths open. Then they laughed.

"Damn it, girl, you got us." Thea shook her head. "You always used to be so nice, too."

Snickering, they all headed for the room that held the minister and Dek.

For a moment Leila thought she heard a wolf howl in the distance.

Vaya con Dios, Lowell.

"Go on, girl. Stop hovering at the door. I might make that man of yours change his mind if you wait too long." Thea poked her in the back.

Leila started and took a hesitant step into the living room.

No. There shouldn't be hesitation today. A bride should glide down the aisle, the center of attention. Like royalty. Like a princess.

"Mommy, you're beautiful!" Lin trilled out across the room, jumping up and down in her new sequined shoes. "You look just like a fairytale."

Dek smiled at her from across the room. Damn decorum. Leila picked up her skirt and ran to him. Straight to him. He caught her before she tripped over her ridiculously long skirt. Lifted her right off the ground to twirl her around. Her hair tumbled and her face flushed. And she didn't care.

Dek. Ah, Dek.

"Leila, I just want you to know something right now." Her groom cleared his throat and braced himself the way he hadn't needed to when he kept her from falling. "When we make the promises to love each other? I mean them."

"Ahhh." Thea audibly sighed behind her.

She wanted to sigh, too. Or weep. But Leila smiled instead. "If you make me cry and ruin my make-up, I'll -- I'll bite you after the ceremony, Deklin."

"More promises, baby? Then let's start this wedding thing now."

"I'm very glad I decided to run away with you all those years ago, Big Bad Wolf, seeing as it led us here."

Dek grinned, just the way he had back then, and whispered in her ear. "Just wait 'til tonight, Red. You know what big bad wolves do to little girls like you once we catch you in bed."

STAY

Chapter One

"Ahhhhhh. Ahhh, fuck, that's good!" The stranger gasped above him. The man's weight suddenly collapsed against his back as his temporary partner shuddered out the last of his climax.

Lowell shuddered, trying to catch his own breath, still gripping the wall for balance. He drawled out the words, forcing himself not to suck for air with each sentence. "Yeah. Yeah, not bad at all."

The world stopped spinning a split second afterward. The man pulled out and then off. Everything was back to normal. Lowell took another deep breath and stepped away from the wall.

"Ah…thanks, man." Lowell buttoned his fly and strolled away from the alley without another look. He'd learned no one appreciated good-byes, least of all himself, after a quickie.

When he got near the bar at the other end of the dirty little alley, he paused, trying to decide if he felt any better.

Not much. The immediate need had drained off, but not the underlying problem. Moonbeams hit his face through a break in the buildings surrounding him. Almost a full moon. Shit. That never helped his itch.

Lowell hesitated at the bar's battered door and listened to the music wailing inside about good times, bad women and cold beer. Why go back at all? He'd been there before -- maybe not this particular bar in this particular part of El Paso, but to enough bars just like it and enough men just like his already forgotten partner.

You'd think I'd be tired of this by now. Shit, I am tired of it. Thirty-one and still picking up the flotsam at two-bit bars to fuck.

Lowell grinned. Maybe the real problem was his cock still wasn't tired and it hadn't had any ass tonight.

He was an idiot. There was more than enough ass at home. Why did he hang out at these damn places and let himself get picked up like he was some kind of desperate whore?

Because I once was a whore. That's why. Sometimes going back to where he'd been as a scrawny kid, back when he was ready to bend over and be fucked on command -- literally and figuratively -- reminded him that his life now wasn't all bad. Hell, there were plenty who would envy everything he had right now. He was the one with the problem. He just hadn't quite found what he needed yet.

And odds were that he wouldn't find it tonight. He should give it up and leave. He had responsibilities now.

The volume of the music rose up in the bar, sending its false notes about the good times to be had. He wasn't restless enough to get suckered in by that, was he? Then again, he'd left his hat in the bar. No harm in getting it before he headed back.

Telling himself he was being stupid to linger, Lowell stepped back inside anyhow. The bar was smoky and noisy and like a million others. That was no surprise. There was nothing for him here and never would be.

Lowell walked to the back booth, where he could see his Stetson hanging on a hook against the wall. One minute, two minutes, and he'd be gone. The babble of drunken or excited voices hit his ears and he tuned it out. No more beers tonight. No more cock.

"I'm not interested." The cool voice that cut through his protective shield was female and husky and somehow familiar.

Pussy. That was something different.

His damn cock twitched. *Bad idea, cock. Pussy is way too dangerous for us.*

"If you're not, then what are you doing here?" The male voice answering her was slightly drunk and very unhappy.

"Maybe I should have said I'm not interested in *you*."

Lowell glanced over at the couple, deciding no one else cared whether he eavesdropped. The bar was getting more intriguing by the minute.

His eyes narrowed and his nostrils flared just a little once he saw her. She was a pretty girl. Tall. Reddish-brown hair, blue eyes. Flat stomach with a tiny ring attached to her belly, a fact she had no problem showing off since her skimpy little T-shirt cut off just under her boobs.

"Maybe you're too picky." The man started to get up from his chair.

Pretty and she smelled...He sniffed again. She smelled like someone he should remember. Lowell scowled, keeping himself from rubbing his forehead with an effort. Sex, no matter how meaningless, made you sluggish. Why couldn't he place her?

He didn't have time to think about it, though. The girl got out of her chair, facing the would-be pickup artist down. Her jaw jutted out as if she meant to confront him with more than words. The kid was tall and looked strong, but she was still facing a drunken man. Lowell knew what that meant.

Unless he intervened.

"The lady isn't interested because she's with me." Lowell stepped up to the guy's elbow and growled the words into his ear.

"With you? But you just stepped out with --" The guy stopped, measured how much taller and broader Lowell was, and sat back down. "Whatever. You probably deserve each other."

Lowell gazed at the almost-familiar girl and frowned. "Are you even old enough to be here?"

"I'm twenty-one. Had to show my I.D. at the bar to prove it, too."

She pouted at him and then the memories clicked into place. He knew that lower lip and how it stuck out. The rush of remembrance almost made him dizzy.

Lowell laughed and leaned over to flick the braid from her shoulder. "Bullshit, girl. I can do the math. You might be eighteen, Lin, but even that could be pushing it."

"Busted. This town is just too dang small. I don't know you, but you sound just like...*Lowell!* Of course it's you!" She flung herself at him and Lowell grabbed her, getting a nice armful of tits and hair and squealing laughter. "Damn, I forgot how pretty you looked. Your hair is shorter. And your goatee is just too cute."

Home. Damn it, she smelled like home and family. His arm closed around her just a little too tight and too long. He stepped back once he realized what he was doing, but her laughter had already faded.

"Now *you.*" She focused in on him as if he were tasty prey. "You, I was always interested in."

His cock twitched again. Damn it.

Lowell scowled at her. "Bullshit again, girl. The last time you saw me you were five years old and yelling at me to get you some cookies."

"Well, I was interested in the cookies and you. That's why I yelled." She grinned at him and then her smile disappeared. "Hey, I always liked you, Lowell. I missed you -- I cried for days after you left. You'd always been around to take care of me and then you were gone."

Lowell hunched up his shoulders, uncomfortable with the sadness just under the light tone. He'd missed her, too. He'd missed them all with an intensity he never wanted to feel again.

"Speaking of taking care of -- what are you doing out on your own, girl?" He took his hat with one hand and gripped her by the arm with the other. "Tell me on the way out. You shouldn't be here."

"Oh, c'mon, Lowell. The last --" Lin paused until they stepped out of the building and the door was safely shut. "The last were attack we almost had was from the pack you took over, you dog. That was over a decade ago."

"Right. Maybe that was the last attack for *your* pack. Now, where are your bodyguards, girl?" He knew just exactly how carefully her daddy would protect his daughter.

She sighed. "Rossi was supposed to be on watch. He's passed out in the last bar we went to."

"He didn't have any help passing out, did he?" Lowell looked at her. "And is he in a safe place?"

"He's fine. Everyone knows him at Jeeter's." Lin deliberately pressed her body a little closer to him, changing his grip to one that was more intimate than he'd planned.

"And did you do anything to him?"

Lin looked at him, those blue eyes completely blank and innocent. Lowell almost laughed. He remembered that look, too, and just how fake it was.

God, he had forgotten how much he loved her pack and all those little quirks that had kept them together.

"Don't do it again, girl. Otherwise, I'll have to tell your daddy. Were females aren't safe alone and you f -- frigging well know it."

"But you're the one who caught me, Lowell. Aren't I safe with you?"

Damn. There was that hunting look again. And damned if something inside wasn't telling him he wouldn't mind being caught.

"Of course you're not safe, baby. I'm not part of your family anymore. I've got my own pack, and I've been needing a fresh and tasty alpha bitch in it. Stop looking at me like that. You're too young for the job, little girl." He didn't need a teenaged tease to mess up his life. It'd be easier to lay the facts of were life right out and make sure she backed off. She was a virgin still. He knew that by knowing her pack. Besides, he could almost smell innocence on her. If he got closer, he would be able to smell it. He pushed that tempting thought aside. He wasn't trying to get himself interested. He was trying to keep her away.

But Lin just kept looking at him. For a brief moment, while she measured him for size, a thrill ran down his spine and centered in his damned stupid cock.

Down, boy.

"I'm no younger than you were when you took on that new pack and made it yours. And, pardon me for saying so, I'm smarter, quicker and female. I could whip your pack -- and you -- into shape before any of you could blink." She looked down at her hands. "Without even chipping a nail."

Shit. Why did she have to go and tempt a perverted fuck like him? He'd been good and done the right thing, but then she had to keep pushing. When Lin raised her gaze back up to stare at him without blinking -- giving him a direct challenge -- it tripped every were alpha instinct he'd gained over the years.

Promises he'd made long ago to protect -- the fears of what a mate could discover about him -- for the first time they were nothing compared to the sudden roar in his brain. She was calling to him. Daring him to mate. He'd never known how strong that lure could be until now.

Lowell bared his canines and closed in. Her neck, soft against his teeth, felt good. Right. And, damn, the sweet virgin taste and her quiver of submission kicked excitement into his bloodstream. *Mine.* Heat bubbled through his veins at the possessive thought. For that buzzing moment he stopped thinking and let his little head rule. Let himself do the thing he'd craved and feared for more than a decade.

"All right, then. We can do this the good old-fashioned way, if you want." His voice was muffled as he shook her, just a little, the way you did unruly puppies. "You're mine now, Lin. I'm claiming you. Welcome to my pack."

* * *

He was bigger than she remembered. That wasn't normal. People were supposed to shrink when you saw them again after years of absence. She'd always remembered Lowell as looming over her.

Damn. She'd grown -- some might say even overgrown, if you didn't like females to be six feet tall -- and he still towered over her.

Her neck throbbed from where he'd bit into it. He hadn't been gentle, the way the old Lowell always had been. She touched the mark, lightly. The bite had been dominating, old-fashioned, kind of patronizing. And exciting.

She'd spent thirteen years being an alpha's oldest child. Even if she hadn't been just the least little bit bossy all on her own, her position in the pack had assured her deference.

Lowell used to be deferential. Lin smiled. He used to be the lowest in the ranks, the omega of the pack. If he got too pushy, she could remind him of that. He'd been her babysitter, for heaven's sake.

Until he left and fought his way to alpha. Not many weres could say they'd managed that.

Alpha and omega. Lin stifled a giggle. That was funny, but not that funny. She must be getting a little nervous. Lowell never used to make her nervous. Hell, no one ever made her nervous.

But something still prickled at her skin, heightening her senses, making her jumpy. If it wasn't Lowell and nerves, she couldn't imagine what it might be.

"I owe your daddy a lot." Lowell's voice, sort of rumbly and faintly accented, broke her from her thoughts. She used to love the difference between his voice and the others in the pack.

"I owe Daddy a lot, too. Your point?"

"I'm letting you think things over again. Kid, you really think you're ready to take on me and my pack? No one will fault you for saying no. Hell, no one but me would even know."

That focused her the way nothing had since he claimed her. Lin leaned over and licked his ear. There had been an earring in it once. She remembered it, vaguely, as she traced the healed over indent on his skin. She wondered when he gave it up. There were lots of things to learn about him.

"Why would I say no? I say what I mean. I led you on back at the bar, but I wasn't teasing." She decided to be honest. At least a little bit. "I was made to be alpha, but I can't be anything but Daddy and Mommy's little girl in my own pack. You've got the only other were pack around here that I know of. I've been waiting forever for you to come back."

"I'm flattered. But, you know, there is that age thing. I was an adult before you lost your first tooth. And yeah, I really can remember you losing your first tooth."

He'd promised the tooth fairy would give her money. Lin scowled. That was not the vibe she wanted between them right now.

"Then you might finally be mature enough for me. I'm kind of hoping you've learned a few things since we last saw each other." Lin shrugged.

"What if I can't get it up?"

"What?" Lin gaped at him and saw the half-smile he couldn't quite hide.

"Maybe I think of you as part of the family. Or maybe I think you're too young and inexperienced to interest me in sex."

"Oh, my G --" Lin glanced down at those worn jeans and let out a laugh. "You -- you -- asshole. You almost scared me off. I think what you're packing is a whole lot different from what you're telling me, bucko."

She took a step closer, deliberately too close for comfort. His body warmth tugged at her. She tried to hide the catch in her breath, but his eyes narrowed again.

She better take the initiative before she was lost.

"Kiss me, Lowell." She paused a half-second. "If you don't, I'm going to kiss you."

"Shit. Oh, shit. I suppose I'm kinky enough to want someone from my family." He fastened his mouth over hers and kissed her, hard, showing the rough edge of his need with the scrape of his teeth against the tender underside of her mouth. The little bite of pain was perfect. Oh yeah, perfect. She arched against his erection and savored the feel of his cock rubbing against her mons. God, she hoped he was as big as he felt right now. Too bad they had clothes on. Too bad they were in public.

"First, we are so not family, you idiot. Second, I want to rip your shirt off and bite you right back, Lowell." She felt a little tremor under her nails, right where she was digging into his chest hair. "Third, I want to fuck until we fall down from exhaustion. I want --"

"I want you to mind your manners until we get home, girl. No need to spend our first night in jail for indecency, especially when we'd be given separate cells." He whirled her around, so his clothed cock was between her ass cheeks. She rubbed against that tempting heat and heard his breath catch. Mmmmmm. Even covered, his erection felt way too good. But his hands stayed firm on her shoulders, not letting her turn back to what they had been doing. His voice stayed firm, too. "My truck is right there. Climb in."

Chapter Two

Lin slid across the truck's seat to open the door. Lowell stepped inside, trying not to feel too deprived. "I wanted --"

She didn't finish the sentence before he had her pinned to the unyielding fabric. She found herself sighing into his mouth before she could think clearly. The memories of the high school boys she'd toyed with and the almost sexual possibility in her packmate, Rossi, faded as if they'd never existed. Nothing before had ever been quite as hot or urgent as this taste of Lowell in her mouth.

She wanted him. Not just that hard cock that was prodding her bare stomach and moving lower, but all of him. She hadn't even realized how much she'd wanted him to arrive, how deeply she needed him.

Maybe she shouldn't tell him so right now. As her mama would say, it was better to leave a man wondering. But she wanted to. Oh, yes, she wanted to.

It felt right. That was the most frightening, most sexy thing of all. He didn't know her -- he'd known a little girl a long time ago, not this woman who urged him on with a murmur and then a growl. But it felt as if he did. As if his body was meant to take hers.

When had he last known anything like that?

Never.

Submission. Domination. Grapples in dark places. Paid-for sex. He knew about that. Not this urgency that promised fulfillment whenever he wanted, however he wanted. Not little flickers of want that lashed at him whenever her fingers slid over his body.

Dangerous. Very dangerous.

He fought the craving to bite her again, hard. To hold her down like he would any wolf and dive into her for a few hours without thinking. He'd like to do that. He had the feeling she would, too.

But he also wanted to go slow. This first time was something that needed to be done properly. She was new to all of this and their kind mated for life. He had to get them started right.

She sighed, just a little, her chest rising and falling, and his hand was under that tiny shirt before he took a second thought about starting out right. Dear, lovely Jesus, the tight nub under his hand was already drawn up to an excited peak. He brushed his thumb over that piece of sensitive flesh and she whimpered.

"You aren't helping," he said.

Lin laughed. "I'll help whenever you do what I want." Then she sobered. "Fine. I can't believe you're so conservative. If you're going to be that old-fashioned, take me to your pack, then, so we can get on with things. But -- could you…play with me a little more first?"

He wanted to. He wanted to swallow her moans when he pinched those responsive nipples. He imagined how sweet they would taste when he licked and sucked them. Then he'd bury his face in the sweaty, musky liquid spilling from inside her supple young body right before he buried his --

"No. I don't play with something this serious." He lied with his most convincing tone as he fought what they both wanted. He had to go through with what he'd just told her. Things weren't going to go all her way, whether she helped him or not. What they really wanted didn't matter. He had to show her that of the two alphas in the pack, he was stronger.

The alternative was -- He pushed the seductive idea away quickly. Instead he thought about what was going to happen next, not what he wished would happen, and his heart rate slowed. Reality had a way of sobering him up.

"Brace yourself. My family isn't like yours. They're -- it's -- they're --" He tried to come up with the right word for the pack. There was none. "It's not safe."

"You haven't been home for a while, Lowell. I have one evil hellion baby sibling. I think I can handle almost anything your pack has."

Kids. Complete with a mom and dad. OK, there might be a few stray betas to keep it from being a picture-perfect human household, but she came from a real family, not just a pack bound together for survival. Lowell knew where and who she came from. In her world, a baby brother was dangerous. But Lin had no idea what she was walking into.

He started the truck, grinding the gears as he took out his frustrations on the clutch. Lin was just too young. She wasn't ready for ugliness. She wasn't ready to see what an alpha had to do to keep control of his pack.

She'd run.

She'd be gone before he had a chance to do half the things he was imagining. He should stop the truck now and let her go. That would be best.

Best for her. What about you? He fought the sudden thick longing that rose up in his throat, springing up from both his cock and his heart. The need almost choked him. God. He'd just met her again after years of no communication with his old pack, and here he was damn near dying at the idea of her leaving.

Danger. Danger.

She'd find out. Hell, they'd all find out. His pack. They'd sense his weakness and need. Once that happened, they'd be at his throat. He only stayed alpha because they thought he had no emotions in him except hot anger or cool control. That was all he ever let them see.

"Lin --"

"Now what? You better not try warning me off again."

He wasn't going to be sensible. Not the way need was gripping his throat...and his cock.

"No. Just...you may not like what happens next. You may not like me or what I do. I'll make it up to you later. I promise." He'd worry about how later.

She looked at him as if she could actually see all the sudden tension and lust roiling up inside him. See it and handle it. But how could she? How could anyone? Still, Lin nodded, as if understanding and wanting to reassure his inner thoughts. "I believe in your promises, Lowell. So let's get on with it so we can get naked and fuck."

* * *

He'd changed in the short time between getting in the truck and heading to his pack. Not *the change*. Lin couldn't remember when she'd last seen someone in her pack turn. Contrary to all the stupid movies, it didn't happen that often. Grey had, the time Rome had run off as a toddler and they found the kid playing near a rattlesnake. The rattler hadn't had time to know what bit him. Rossi had, a few times when he was younger and Dad or Grey had disciplined him. Lin had her suspicions about what happened sometimes at night, when she'd been firmly sent to her room by Mom and Dad. Dad looked a little too dangerous and Mom looked a little too bright-eyed. Not that either of them could keep secret the fact they had all kinds of sex. Things got too noisy. Finding out they were having weresex wouldn't be a surprise.

She was looking forward to seeing Lowell -- *her* Lowell -- turn into a beast for her. She was looking forward to finally being able to change herself. Surely after being with Lowell that would happen at last. It was embarrassing that she hadn't done so yet, to tell the truth.

But Lowell's change right now wasn't the one weres knew and craved, especially during the full moon. This was even scarier. The guy she knew was turning cold. She could almost feel the ice forming and the distance growing. When he stopped the truck, measuring her with flat, emotionless eyes, she had a sudden realization. *Do I know this man at all?* Wonderful. Lin swallowed. This was not the time for second thoughts. That chance left with the good Lowell several miles back.

This one looked a bit like Lowell's evil double. Lin firmed her jaw. She could handle a little evil. She'd signed up for this and she wasn't backing down now. Not just because Lowell looked different all of a sudden.

"Welcome home," he told her at the outside of the door to the house. But it sounded like a threat, not a promise.

When he threw open the door, she held her breath, feeling Lowell's tension under the ice and wondering what horrors awaited her inside. She looked inside. It wasn't what she expected.

There was nothing there. Nothing but the house.

She followed Lowell inside.

The house was enormous. Very modern, very empty. The walls were white and should look bright. Right now, in the dark, they looked flat and drab. Lin wondered if the walls would be overpowering during the day, when the sun beat through the windows and reflected on all that blank whiteness.

Nothing. There was nothing on the walls. No one inside the walls except Lowell and her. She blinked at the expanse of curtainless windows in the living room and had opened her mouth to comment on her soon-to-be mate's decorating skills, when she heard a rumble that might be a growl behind her. Danger! She whirled to face the noise, the hair on the back of her neck rising at the sound of a threat.

Four of them. Different ages, different sizes, different genders. But all of them were staring at her with the same hostile look. Damn. So this was Lowell's family?

"Who the fuck is this?"

The questioner was a woman who looked as unpleasant as her question. Lin bared her teeth, realizing as she did that she couldn't make as good a threat display as the were pack in front of her. A few were already wavering into the beginnings of their change. Those were some damn sharp, long teeth in front of her.

"Mine. She's mine." Lowell spoke behind her, his growl as frightening as the group in front of her.

There was only one of him, but by God, he was alpha and he was reminding them all of it. She got wet all over again at his display.

She saw each one's nostrils flare. Shit. They could smell her arousal. She refused to imagine she might be wafting off a little fear, but no matter what they could smell, the whole experience was like being paraded around naked.

"This is Lin Kinkaid. My mate. Your alpha. Lin, this is my pack. Our pack." Lowell didn't say it with pride, the way her father would.

"Hello." They continued to stand, silent and watchful. Lin narrowed her eyes. Even if they weren't sure of her, weren't they going to defer to the alpha's mate? Hmph. If they were waiting for her to prove herself, they weren't going to have to wait any longer. "Well? Didn't you hear Lowell? Do I have to tell you what happens next?"

"She's one of us?" The deep rumble came from the biggest man she'd ever seen. The amount of skepticism rolling off him was as big as the rest of his body.

"She's your alpha. She damn well is one of us, slick." Lowell reached out to grab Slick's shoulder.

"She's a Kinkaid. She'll never be one of my pack." The woman turned away, growling.

Shit! What have I walked into?

Lowell shrugged. "Dru, I've put up with you and your hatred for thirteen damn years. It wouldn't make me cry to see you turned out."

Lin tried to swallow and realized her throat was too dry. Expulsion was worse than death. Even the threat of it was almost unimaginable, but Lowell sounded like he meant every syllable.

"You owe me! You killed my mate to gain control of this pack!" Dru shrieked. "You threw my son out just because he might be a problem to you someday. Rossi was a child!"

Rossi's mother. This bitter woman was the mother of Rossi, who had arrived at her daddy's pack as a surly adolescent. No one had told Lin why Lowell was gone and Rossi was in his place. Everyone in her pack shielded her. Just like everyone in this pack seemed determined to yell the ugliest things they could think of in her face.

"With you around to egg him on, Rossi was going to get himself killed if he stayed. There was nothing left for him here except trouble. I would have thrown you out, too, except you were pregnant. Too bad I felt sorry for you. But I can rethink that earlier decision."

The kid behind Dru gave a whimper of distress. Lin saw the resemblance between the woman and the girl now that Lowell had given Lin the hint. Thirteen years. The girl was maybe thirteen and facing banishment with her mother or life on her own in a hostile pack.

Dear heaven. Lin wasn't about to celebrate her arrival by having all the other female members of the pack banished. Instead Lin smacked her hand hard against the wall. The thump made everyone turn to her.

"Dru. Take your daughter out of here. She's too young for the initiation rite. You can come back and join us or not, as you wish." Lin stared down the other woman. She didn't let herself feel any triumph as the older were's gaze lowered. Lin didn't point out what it meant if Dru didn't choose to rejoin the group. She didn't need to.

"Mia, you get!"

Without any more words, Dru grabbed her daughter and quick marched her from the room. There, that much was done.

Lowell glanced over at her and she almost saw a smile from him. Maybe. At least he didn't seem to have any problems with his mate speaking up. That was good, because Lin knew she wasn't going to stop now.

"Well?" She challenged the rest of the weres in the room. Shit, she didn't even know their names -- there was a huge guy standing with his arms crossed and the other one who was...well, smaller only in comparison to the mountain the first one was. The two of them had coffee-colored skin with a liberal dollop of cream mixed in. Strong features. They looked enough alike to be brothers. They might be brothers, for all she knew. Why the hell hadn't Lowell told her something about their pack on the way to the house?

"Yes, mistress?" The smaller one spoke up.

She liked that title said aloud even more than she'd thought she would. Lin nodded at him before she said, "Strip. We might as well all do it at once."

She'd never actually participated in an initiation into a pack -- she'd been younger than Dru's daughter when Rossi, the last were, had been introduced to her old pack. But she knew perfectly well what was expected and she certainly wasn't going to back down or "get" the way little Mia had. She was a big girl. She was serious.

Not to mention that she was the star of this show. No one was going to say she was waffling in her new allegiances. No one was going to think of her as a tease, either. Not again. She'd damn near heard Lowell's thoughts about that back at the bar, he signaled it so loudly.

"Wait." Lowell put his hand on her shoulder. His hand was warm, much warmer than the glacial tone he'd been using ever since they'd met his pack.

Not that she was going to let a little warmth confuse the issue. He was challenging her orders in front of everyone. She firmed her chin. "Why?"

"Because we're going to do this initiation my way. I'm going to get you ready. Gentlemen, your mistress and I are going to the bedroom. Wait here until you're called." And then, without a second's warning, he swept her up over his shoulder and hauled her away.

She didn't even have time to let out as much as a yelp in protest.

"You don't have to try to be protective of me, you know." Lin decided to take the battle to her mate, even though he was focused more on taking his clothes off. And, of course, it was only good manners to follow his example by taking off her own .

"Yes I do." Lowell looked up. She sucked in her breath when she saw the gleam in his eyes. All the ice was definitely gone. This was a warm -- hell, a *hot* -- man. Scorching hot. "You're my mate, Lin, and those rabid mongrels out there are my responsibility, and -- I want to protect you. I need to."

The sudden softness in the last few words made Lin pause before she pulled off her shirt. "Well, all right. Just so long as you understand I'm going to protect you, too."

God, his cock was so hard. He was just a bit furred all over. She could almost see the beast rising inside him as he got naked. And he was hers. All hers. Impatiently, Lin took off her shirt. She heard a rip as she tugged at it.

"You should let me do that." Lowell took a step closer.

"I shouldn't have let either of us do that. I don't have any other clothes with me." Lin glanced over at him. "But you make me forget about everything but getting naked with you."

The slow, hungry smile he gave made her stomach clench with need and nerves. What if she messed this up? Great. Now was so not the time for inadequacy issues to appear.

But --

"I've never done this before."

"I know. Your pack raised you right." The kiss he gave her bare shoulder made her shiver. "I'll be gentle. Mostly. At least, nothing will happen unless you want it to happen, baby."

"Don't call me baby. And -- and Lowell --"

"Yes?"

"If I don't -- you know, don't --"

"I absolutely promise you're going to have an orgasm, Lin."

Damn, that was a good thing about having an alpha to mate with. They were always so sure. Lin laughed and felt a lot more comfortable saying what needed to be said. "I figured that would happen. I'm about ready to come just looking at you right now. No, I meant -- you know -- the Other Thing."

Lowell raised his head, looking faintly baffled. Seeing as his cock was already nudging her thigh, Lin gave him extra points when he suddenly narrowed his eyes in comprehension. The man could fuck *and* think.

"You've never changed? You're a virgin and you've never changed?"

"Well, it happens, you know." Lin tried to ignore the warmth rising in her face. Great, now she was both a blushing virgin and untried were.

"And you hate that." Lowell smiled with such understanding that she forgot to be angry about him seeing her embarrassed. "I have an idea that might help."

"I'm willing to try anything." Lin kissed him, slow and deep, and told herself everything would be fine. "Anything at all, darling."

They heard a short yip and low howl outside. Great. The crowd was getting restless. All she needed was performance anxiety on top of everything else.

But Lowell touched her cheek and rested his face against her hair as if they had forever. As if it was just the two of them.

"Then let's get to bed and see if this works."

Nerves suddenly left as lust and love and need flooded her. Lin smiled back at her mate.

Because, you know, it was just the two of them. The only two that mattered.

Weird. The need and sweetness mixed when he saw Lin's vulnerability had been good. Damn good. But being helpless before her was even better. Lust gripped him hard and twisted. This was dangerous. Maybe she needed him like this for now. But she'd know, if she didn't before, how much he wanted this kind of sex for always. Then what would she think of him?

But what happened next couldn't matter. This was for her.

"I have my hands behind my head. They stay there, babe. This first time is your show." Lowell managed to say the words clearly. The palms of his hands cupped his head, his hands weighed down and helpless. His cock throbbed at the illusion of his being bound.

"I get to do whatever I want?" Lin looked him up and down before she gave him that direct predatory look that had turned him on so much back at the bar. It still did.

"Whatever." He wasn't sure how much longer he could talk.

She leaned over to lick a bead of sweat from his lip. When she raised her head, he could see her teeth as she smiled. He thought he saw her canines growing.

"That's just what I wanted. I'm in charge now." She growled. Both of them felt his cock bob up higher at the words. "I think maybe it's just what you wanted, too."

Shit. Their first time and already she knew --

She deliberately raked her fingernails from his stomach down to his thighs and he forgot caution. Forgot everything but what she was doing to him and how he felt when she did. He howled.

Her pubic hairs tickled his cock as she moved against him. So close. He panted, close to transforming and fighting it. She was wet. She was ready...

Not yet. Not yet. He had to let her take him this time. Had to stay human enough to let her.

And just the idea of her commanding him threw him closer to that dark, animal edge than he wanted to be. Stupid. If he wasn't so ready to explode at her next touch, he'd laugh. The more excited she got by being in charge, the more excited he got about submitting -- and the closer he got to shifting form. Once he changed, his beast would take over. That beast would demand to be dominant and he wouldn't let her take the lead.

Mustn't. Do. That.

He was hers this time. Submissive to her. His cock stretched hungrily, the pulse of his erection beating a harsh rhythm. Her hand circled the head of his cock, as if to test that pulse, and her grip tightened. She was almost too rough, but not quite. Instead, the slightest hint of pain was just right. Just too fucking right.

"This cock is mine." Her voice was fierce, ragged. She leaned over and he sucked in a breath just as she sucked him into her hot, wet mouth. Her teeth scraped against the sensitive head and his hips rose up from the bed, following her warmth.

Want it. Want her. Want. His nails lengthened as he clawed them into the back of his neck.

"You taste ready for me." She lifted her head, then rose and bit his shoulder roughly.

God, if this kept going on, he'd be a mass of scars from just one sexual bout with her. At the moment, the idea made him shiver with even more desire.

"I am."

"Taste me and see if I am, too." She pushed her cunt into his face and he almost cried over her perfection.

Instead he stretched his tongue deep inside her, sliding against her walls. Slick and welcoming, tasting of female. Yes. Perfect. He stroked her swollen nub and heard her gasp as if she had been hurt.

His cock was throbbing, going past that razor-like pleasure into pain. He had to come. But when she moved back, just long enough to slowly wriggle her sheath into place over his cock, he clenched his body, forcing himself not to spend. This was too good. He couldn't keep from grinding his hips against hers, though, moving his cock from side to side rather than thrusting up deeply, claiming her the way he wanted.

He could hurt her, but he didn't want to wound her. He'd rather be hurt himself. God, he *was* hurting. But this edgy torment was different. Even though the pain she inflicted was driving him insane, it was good pain. The best he'd ever had. Feeling each millimeter of her virgin channel stretch slowly open before his cock only increased the pressure of the pleasure-pain. Wet. She was wet and ready for his entrance.

He waited, forcing himself not to rush to the final conclusion. God, just the anticipation was almost enough to make him come. He licked his lips. When she reached out to flick the piercing in his nipple, he opened his mouth to soundlessly scream. He was beyond having enough air in his lungs to make noise.

"I wondered about your earring." She could still talk, though her voice sounded thick. He could almost listen through the blood pounding in his ears. "I see you didn't give up all your piercings."

She twisted the bar in his nipples sharply this time. The sensation zinged through his body and shot to his cock.

"Jesus God, have mercy!" He managed words at last. "If you don't, I swear I'll split you in half."

"Why do you think I'm doing this? Do it. Damn it, you wolf, *do* it. Hard."

He bared his teeth. "Wait. A minute."

He wasn't sure if he was ordering or pleading and it didn't matter. He paused, letting the sweat trickle down his spine while he savored. Virgin smell. Virgin feel. Sex. Lin. It was all Lin.

She half-whimpered, half-snarled.

That sound was too much for whatever self-control he had left. Lowell surged upward with all his strength, the last of Lin's virginity gone with his thrust. She was so wet -- with blood and sweat and excitement. And, finally, with his sperm. He wondered how drenched she was with his mark. His mating with her. His cum shot up from the base of his balls and spurted deep, deep inside her. Deeper than he'd ever been with anyone .

He didn't howl now. He roared, letting the world know as his whole body -- his whole world -- was rocked apart.

She opened her eyes, still panting. Dear Lord. If that was human sex with Lowell, what was the change going to be like?

"On your knees," Lowell snarled.

Oh, man. She was going to find out. She could feel the shift before she saw it and began to shake. Now. More of Lowell's words came out in a half-growl that she couldn't understand. She didn't need to hear the words when instinct told her what came next. She raised her rear up, obediently, crouched on all fours, completely vulnerable to whatever Lowell wanted next. Had she thought she wanted this?

God, yes. Despite the fear as she craned her neck to watch his face turn, his body transform. Hair. Teeth. Snarls.

She wanted it. He was an animal, but he was her animal. And she'd be his. Red heat rushed through her again, just when she'd thought there was nothing left after that last mind shattering orgasm. Her whole body burned.

The door opened.

The pack was there, answering Lowell's howl.

And her mind blurred even as her senses grew keener.

She knew, she knew. It had never happened for her before, but she was changing. The prickling through her body was different, but somehow right. The mingled scents of excitement and curiosity and mating...thank heaven, Lowell's warm scent was strongest...sharpened.

She was were at last. Fur covered what had been her arms. And she was covered not just by fur but by another strong were body. She was being penetrated by a firm, hard were cock. Her mate. Her alpha. The friction increased, first slowly, then faster. Faster yet. It burned, hot and fierce. It would burn her up.

Lin howled, too. And the door crashed completely open to let the pack pour inside.

Bodies crowded near them, but all she was aware of was the plunge of Lowell's cock inside her. The howls and yips shivered through her, adding to the bubbling lust and savage need slicing through her.

When she felt semen spatter over her fur, she raised her head up and rejoiced. Loudly. Something this powerful deserved recognition. The pack was here and they had responded to the strength of Lowell's and her mating. Her mind swirled again, just barely capable of recognizing motion and pleasure and the erotic pain of a jaw gripping her by the ruff.

"Mine." She heard the possessiveness in Lowell's howl, dominating the rest of the pack's noise.

And then the crimsoned sheen of her orgasm blinded her and the rise of her pounding blood deafened her as she shattered in front of them all.

Chapter Three

"You bastard! You couldn't wait, could you?"

"Wait? When does an alpha wait to claim what's his?" Despite mouthing an automatic response to the challenge, Lowell fought back the lash of guilt. He should have taken it slower. Should have...should have done something different.

Wolves took their mates without waiting for permission -- in fact, often they kidnapped a female from another pack. Hell, they killed for the chance at a female. But he knew this pack. Even more important, he'd been one of them and sworn to defend the members of Lin's family -- to defend *Lin* -- long ago. He should have respected her family more. He just didn't know how to honor her family if he kept Lin. And damn it, he intended to keep her.

"She just turned eighteen today. Her mother has been sick with worry."

Leila. Worried.

Jesus, no wonder he had let Lin twist him around her finger and make him ignore calling earlier. Now that he'd gone and done the right thing, everything in him was getting turned inside out. Old feelings somehow twisted and bled into the new. The smug joy of finally possessing his mate was being overbalanced by old guilt. Lowell felt his smile stiffen. He was much more familiar with the lash of guilt than the strokes of happiness.

But then Lin sat up in bed, lush curves spilling out of cool cotton sheets, her red hair trailing over his skin as she leaned over him to take the phone.

Lowell's dark emotions paused, trembling. My God, she was so beautiful. So alive. No one could be ashamed of wanting Lin. The shame would be in ignoring her.

"It's Daddy, isn't it?" She smiled at him and everything settled down again. Lowell wanted to rest his face against that smile and absorb it. He wanted to crawl over her and lick the hair tousled around her face. Dear Lord, the spicy, sexed smell of her made him itchy. "Give up the phone, Lowell. I'll talk to him. I can make it right."

He licked the sweet spot behind her ear as he obeyed her and watched his woman quiver. If anyone could make it right, it was Lin. His world already felt steadied. Centered. Focused. He had a pack and a mate. This was what he'd wanted all his life, even before he could put a name to his longings.

"Daddy? I love you. I'm so happy, Daddy." Lin curled her body up against Lowell and he let her warmth melt the last vestiges of cold fear inside. She was happy with him. "I want to come and show my mate off…No, don't growl at me. I do. I will."

Was Dek making threats to his mate? Lowell bared his teeth.

"And don't you growl, either, Lowell." She pursed her lips at him in what could be a kiss or a pout. "Of course we'll come by. It's my birthday, right? We can all be sociable."

Have two packs meet? At a civilized family birthday party? What did she think they were -- humans? Lowell almost laughed, but he knew Lin would take that as encouragement.

"No," he mouthed.

She made a face at him.

"At eight. Just in time for cake. Can I talk to Mom, too? Oh. Tonight, then. Love you both."

She clicked the phone down and bared her teeth back at him. And, God help him, he wanted to fall back down onto the bed, throat and belly exposed, and let her take a bite.

"Lowell, I can't ignore my family. I'm not made that way. They'd probably come after us both if I did, because they'd know I had been kidnapped." She crawled on his lap and nuzzled. "This way will be better. Trust me."

It was an accident that she was on top of him. She was being affectionate and sweet, not demanding and sexy. But his cock stirred, just as if they hadn't been making love all night. His hips arched, bucked against her.

Just like that, her gentle nose to throat nuzzle changed. She placed her jaw over his jugular, her teeth against the pulse of his neck. When she nipped, the blood raced to his cock and balls so fast, he thought he might faint, as if he were some stupid Victorian maiden in a story.

"Hours. I had no idea wolves could screw for hours." Lin grumbled the words against his throat, the puffs of air tickling sensitive nerves. "And I had no idea you could get it up so many times as a human."

"Complaining?"

"Praising. Now lay back and let me show you what we both want. Don't move unless I say so. You owe me for that last hour session. I think I may be a little sore. I want you feeling the same twinges I have."

She knew. She had to know what he was like. His cock was already leaking at the promise of what she might do. She crouched over him, like he was captured prey, and he sucked in a breath.

Lin wasn't ashamed or turned off or scornful with his submission. Her eyes narrowed to slits as she turned to bite his shoulder.

"Mine."

"Yours." He said it like a vow.

He wanted her to use him, to dominate him, to enslave him even more. Seeing her snap at him as she mounted him enthralled him. But she wanted it just as much and that made the deep, hot, dark desire surge higher.

He might be twisted, but she didn't care. He might be wrong, but she'd encourage it.

Jesus fuck. He'd stumbled across the one female in the world who was weak enough, strong enough, bad enough, good enough to be his mate.

She ground down, hard, pushing tight against his hips, so closely fitted against his cock that he could feel the pulsing in her veins, the hardness of her swollen clit, the wetness inside her channel.

He raised himself onto his elbows and sucked her nipples, already tight and ready. He whimpered, like he was a pup again, while he was waiting for...

She squeezed, milking his cock, her thighs gripping him, and, just like that, he came. Climaxed with racking, hard shudders as the blinding hot shots of cum poured through him. He couldn't wait, couldn't hold off.

But when he heard her triumphant cry, he knew she hadn't, either.

She collapsed on top of him as he sank against the bed, panting. Her hot body, the weight of her, pressed snugly against him and he wanted to do it all over again.

Perfect. She was perfect. How had a nasty little fuck like him found someone so perfect?

"Would you like to come along?" Lin looked at the two behemoths in front of her.

A long, deadly silence followed.

"No." The one Lowell had called Slick spoke up at last.

She decided to overlook the silence and the curt answer. For now. "You're welcome. My daddy would never do anything ...inhospitable...to my pack mates. Lowell might enjoy the company."

"Lowell, he can go," the other one said. "Maybe he can handle another pack. But we'd be trouble."

"You'd make trouble for my old pack?" Lin raised her eyebrows and sharpened her tone. Whatever their problem was, she wasn't going to let that go.

Slick smiled, all teeth and glittering eyes. "We're always trouble."

"Well, sounds to me like someone needs to sit you down and teach you to do more than make trouble." She eyed them thoughtfully. "Tomorrow we'll start working on that. Maybe a few etiquette lessons. Maybe some face smacking. Whatever gets the job done."

"What the fuck?" The smaller one gaped at her.

Lin fought a giggle at how she'd stopped their threat posture. She wondered what they'd do if she asked them to do something outrageous. The temptation to try itched at her, but she knew that wasn't being fair. Alphas shouldn't take advantage.

"Are you terrorizing the pack again, Lin?" Lowell was at her elbow, arriving so softly she hadn't even realized he'd come up behind her. His breath tickled her ear, just the way it did when they made love. "Be nice."

"Well, I could try nice, just for a change." Lin tucked her arm into his elbow and snuggled closer to him. It was just like a married couple.

She fought showing another little burst of pleasure. Alphas didn't go around presenting their emotions to everyone. At least, not in this pack and not these alphas.

The others had already stiffened and lost their befuddled look with Lowell's arrival. She'd have to work on them when they were alone and more easily surprised. She would also have to figure out just why Lowell hadn't developed more rapport with his own pack.

Sheesh. There was a lot of work for her to do here. She could barely wait to get at it.

"Thank you, Leila." Lowell took the plate carefully and placed it just as carefully on the table. Lin almost smiled, even while she felt suspiciously like sniffling with tears. The earnest politeness in Lowell's tone was almost too much.

He was trying so hard. He was such a sweetheart. And he was so afraid things would go wrong with her family.

She knew it. She was starting to feel his emotions like they were her own. The only thing she didn't understand was why he felt like he was so -- so imperfect. He was good, smart, capable, and damn amazing in bed. Lowell was frighteningly right for her. He was troubled when she was sure, reliable when she felt weak. Ying and yang, just like mates should be.

But doubt nagged at him. She would bet her first-born that Daddy never felt that way and Daddy was the only other alpha she knew. Alphas were difficult enough when they thought they were always right. But they might be even worse when they weren't sure.

Damn it, whatever was happening inside him, she wasn't going to put up with it. She'd make him feel right. As right as she knew he was.

She reached out to cup the small of Lowell's back, letting her fingers dangle innocently down, almost to the crack of his ass. A millimeter more and it wouldn't be quite so innocent. He tensed for a moment, then relaxed and accepted her touch. She could do that to him. For him. Once again she wanted to laugh and cry at the same time. Power seemed to spill effortlessly out of her. She was born to be this way, be with Lowell, to be-finally -- her adult self.

"So tell us about your family, dear. How do you like them?" Her mother was smiling at her, but Lin could see the tightness at the edge of her smile. She knew her mother too well.

Her family. Her pack. This family circle wasn't her pack any longer. The closeness she had to them now had to be replaced. She was bound elsewhere, to weres who didn't know her the way this family did. She was a part of a pack who maybe didn't even want her around. Some of the bright, perfect bubble inside her deflated just a little bit.

"We're still getting used to each other." Lin figured that was safe to say.

"They're going to love her." Lowell chimed in. "She's exactly what we've needed."

"No doubt."

Lin winced at the brittleness in her mother's overly bright tone. All right, Mom was unhappy -- maybe angry that her baby was gone forever. But there was something more here.

She discounted Grey's silence. That was just how he always was. Rossi wasn't around to sneer or snigger since he'd been banned from the party for losing her yesterday. If it had been up to her, she'd have given him a reward.

Obviously the rest of the party-goers didn't feel the same way. But what was behind the grimness of Dad's mouth and her mother's tapping fingers? Lin turned to Lowell. The same wrongness was there, behind his quick politeness. Yes, he'd been eager to please all night. Just a little too eager. A little too omega. That wasn't Lowell anymore.

Something was off here.

The three most important people in her world all thought Lowell was wrong for her. Or maybe they thought she was wrong for Lowell. *Why?*

"So when are you coming back, Linnie?" Rome asked. "We miss you."

The room got even quieter, if that was possible.

Trust her little brother to ask the worst possible question at the worst possible time. Romulus had a talent for it, even when he wasn't trying to be a pain.

"I'm not."

"Not *ever?*" Rome's eyes got big. Lin braced herself. Her brother's innocent look meant trouble.

"Just to visit."

"I get her room!" her brother yelled to her parents. "Hers is a lot bigger."

The noise covered the awkwardness. Gave Lin a chance to think. The only problem was, she wasn't sure she really wanted to.

Small talk. Chatter. That's what was needed.

"I *am* home, little brother. My own home. And I think I'm going to like the new boys a lot." That might be pushing it, since she hardly knew them. And what did it say about her that she still hadn't asked what the real names of their betas were? They'd done some damn intimate things together and she had no idea what their names were. That was just wrong. She should know. As Mom might say, becoming were was one thing, but being just plain rude was another.

The unhappiness in the room didn't ease with her words. No one said anything, which was almost unprecedented. Lin studied the other adults while she ducked her head to eat cake. What problems could they have with her mate? All right, maybe Lowell was a little bit older than her. Actually he was closer to Dad and Mom's age --

A bad thought hit. A thought that almost made her gag up the sweet icing on her birthday cake.

Pack mates did all kinds of things together. Intimate things. And Lowell had been part of this pack. Her mind filled with images she didn't want. Lowell. Grey. And her parents.

Somewhere in her head she heard the sound of a loud pop as her happy bubble burst completely.

Maybe she was imagining things. Lowell looked at her, then away. Maybe she wasn't.

* * *

Fuck this. Old habits and emotions be damned. He wasn't low man in the pack anymore and he wasn't going to act that way. He didn't have to be ashamed of anything. Not of being at the bottom of this particular pack once. He wasn't any longer. He didn't have to go sniffing after whatever the others in the pack chose to leave him. He was allowed to take a mate for himself now.

And who wouldn't take Lin as a mate if given the chance? If the alpha was strong and smart enough to hold onto a prize like her, he'd be insane not to. If he wasn't alpha enough now -- and he'd had a long time to become used to that role -- he'd learn to be better. He'd make himself good enough for her.

He was keeping her, no matter who wanted him warned off.

He could feel the trouble roiling inside her, her emotions reflecting his. He didn't want their newly forming bond to create unhappiness in her. She wasn't meant for unhappiness. Lin shone. She had when he met her and she'd been almost dancing when they got here tonight. He wanted her to be happy, to stay just as bright as she deserved to be.

But what do you deserve?

Without warning, Dek stood up. Lowell stilled for a moment, the old wariness and respect stirring in him as Dek lunged toward his ex-omega.

But times had changed. Lowell might not fight, but he refused to flinch at the attack.

"Let's be done with it." Dek growled low in his throat. "I just have one thing to say in front of the family."

"Then say it." Lowell growled back.

"She's your mate. When I found Lin, after all those years apart, I vowed she'd always stay with me. I wasn't thinking about her as an adult. You did. You took her. But she was mine first. One of my pack before yours. Part of me. And I'll hunt you and yours down if you ever hurt her."

Lowell relaxed against the grip Dek had on his shoulder. If that was all his former pack leader was concerned about, things were simple.

"You won't need to hunt anyone down. If any one of my pack hurts her, that one will be dead. I swear it."

"We'll see. Now I have something to say to you in private." Dek's tone didn't allow for argument and Lowell deferred to his old leader.

They stood and headed for the door, matching each other stride for stride.

"I suppose they're going to go chew on rattlesnakes for dessert. Honestly, Mom, how have you put up with that display for years?" Lin's words rang clearly behind them, just the way they were meant to. Lowell fought a grin.

"She's an arrogant female." Dek leaned up against the porch railing. "I love her, but that's the truth."

"I don't mind." Lowell let the amusement show, just a little. "She has other attributes that make up for it."

"I won't ask." Dek's mouth twisted. "She's my baby still."

"You said that before. Or close enough."

"I didn't bring you out here to repeat myself. This is more important than my feelings."

Nothing more was said for a moment. Lowell stared out at the view he remembered from long ago. Not much had changed. There was peace here at Dek's ranch. But only because Dek saw to it. He'd crush any threat against his pack. Dek never hesitated, always knew what to do.

But they appeared to be waiting now.

Dek's words, when they came, made no sense. "Lin never changed around us."

"She has with me. She's a were, sure enough." Lowell shrugged. "By the time she had changed, though, I would have taken her even if she wasn't."

"She *changed?* Then tell me this. Is she like us?"

How had Dek known?

Lowell swallowed. "You mean, does she grow fur and shape shift?"

"What the hell else would I mean?"

"Yes."

Dek let out a long sigh. "Then maybe it's all right after all."

"But --" Now Lowell hesitated. Then he started off with a babble of words. "I never saw a female who is more were. Every instinct she has is right on the money."

Dek tensed again at the first word. Now he scowled. "*But?* You said but."

Lowell's heart began to race. He wasn't even sure why. What Lin wasn't was so trivial compared to what she was. "Well. Don't take this wrong, but she's not quite...right."

"Shit! What does that mean?"

"She changes but you can still see the not-were. I don't think she knows. I didn't want to tell her and make her feel wrong. But her transformation still isn't complete. She crouches and you can still see...her. The old Lin. Her fur grows, but not as thick as most. She speaks to me, but the sounds are more human than were."

Dek shook his head and covered his eyes. Lowell gripped his old mentor's arm. "It doesn't matter to me, damn it. It doesn't matter to anyone in the pack who saw her, or they would have said something. The two of us, we still...err, we're right together. Perfect. It's fine. Better than anything I've ever had. With time, I'm sure she'll become even more --"

Dek put his hand down but kept looking away. "Do you think I care about your feelings or your sex life?"

"Then I don't understand anything about why you're asking me this."

Dek's jaw was tight. "Leila never changed. We've been together almost all our lives and she never has."

"It never mattered to you. Two kids, decades later, and the two of you are still burning each other up. Anyone can see that. I want that for Lin and me. I *have* that with Lin and me. Dek, I know my past hasn't been perfect, not what you'd want for your girl, but it wasn't that much worse than yours before you met Leila. It just took me longer to find my mate and settle in. You know what weres are like without a mate. That will all change now. Jesus, Dek, don't try to take this from us."

"I don't want to take that from you, boy. And even if I did, I'd never begrudge Lin. If she loves you, she can handle anything you could do. You know that as well as I do. She's my daughter and we value her for what she is. But I'm afraid. Leila and I are both afraid of what we've done."

No. Dek was never afraid. What the hell did he mean? Lowell shifted his feet, bracing himself. "Spit it out."

"Weres and non-weres can't breed. I don't know what Leila is. I thought she was some kind of latent were when I found out about Lin. Maybe Leila is. But our children aren't. If they don't change to were, true were, I don't think they can mate. Not a one has become were, and they're long past the age I was when I first had the change."

"Lin fucking well can mate -- err, sorry." Lowell blushed at Dek's glacial stare. "That wasn't what you meant anyhow. You mean you think we won't have children?"

"I'm almost positive."

No children. The reason one struggled to become alpha was to mate and breed. The whole purpose of the pack was to protect each other and the future.

"I see." Lowell stared down at his hands, avoiding Dek's gaze as the older man had avoided his earlier.

"You know...we both know...what that means. We love her dearly but if you want to void your -- arrangement -- with Lin, we'd understand. I'd understand if you want to walk from all of us. There'd be no bad blood between our packs. I'd explain to her."

Black loss roiled up in Lowell. He was alpha. He owed the future to his pack.

Fuck owing. Fuck the future. He wasn't going to face it without Lin.

"No! You could never explain that to Lin because it's not an arrangement. It was a mating. She's mine." *And I'm hers.* "We can work out something. Packs have lost litters before and managed. Hell, packs have killed pack heirs before and thrived. When other alphas took over, your parents' pack gave killing you a damn good try. You survived. You created another, stronger, better pack."

"Rogue weres, blood coups, and badly managed packs exist. But what would your pack want from you? What would Lin want?" Dek tapped his fingers on the porch railing.

His pack had always been ready to eat him for breakfast. He'd never been fully accepted since he first took over. Maybe he'd made a few wrong choices at first, but that had come from inexperience. This -- this -- was different. Keeping Lin was a deliberate choice to flout what the pack needed.

Of course, Dek's pack would have to decide, too. If they put the choice off for the next generation, it would only be more desperate for Dek's children.

Old habits died hard. Somewhere deep down, Lowell still believed Dek was the smartest were. The worthy alpha. Dek's ex-omega fought asking the question and lost. If he admitted he needed advice, so be it.

"What do you want to do about your own pack, Dek?"

"After Rome, there will be no one." Dek swallowed. "We haven't taken in anyone else since I realized what the future meant."

Oblivion. That's what no children meant for a pack.

"The hell with that. We still don't know if what you think is true. But if it is, my pack will make a different future if we have to." Lowell gripped his old mentor's shoulder, wondering if he'd have it bitten off. He'd questioned Dek. Defied him. "Damn it, Dek. I intend to find that new future with Lin next to me."

When he first saw Lin, he hadn't chosen her because she'd be a mother to his children. He'd needed her more than anything for himself. And it was Lin who had call to him above all.

Something eased in Dek's stance. "The future will come when it does and how it wants. Not even an alpha can change that."

"I'll take care of my pack. And I'll do whatever I have to for Lin."

Chapter Four

"Why don't you lighten up with your pack?" Lin arched herself up to allow him more access between her thighs. "Oh, that's niiice."

If she didn't care that they were up against the doorframe in the hall, not quite behind the concealing bedroom door, he didn't either. Remembering where he was was getting more and more difficult anyhow.

He was hard. Hard and wanting. She'd been all over him the second he stopped the truck, like she wanted him standing up against the metal door outside. He'd almost taken her then and there. He forgot now why he'd waited.

Once inside though, he tried for a little finesse. Instead of entering her as soon as he ripped her clothes off, he's just lifted that cute little skirt and stroked her soft wet pussy as if he had all night. The only objections she made were soft little sounds that weren't really protests at all.

Hell, if that's what she wanted him to do, they did have all night.

"All for you, babe. Everything."

His brain hadn't quite turned off yet, though. He's been an observer way too long to stop now. There was something else churning inside her. That's right. He had enough sense left to remember now. That's why he hadn't just gone for the sex she'd offered right from the start.

There was something else locked inside her. Something anxious. Something hidden. She couldn't tell what had happened between her father and him, could she? He was damned good at not showing his emotions, but she was his bondmate. Already she could tell things about him no one else could. And she'd say things he'd never take from anyone else.

Like, apparently, right now.

She was finally talking instead of whimpering. And he was finally calm enough to listen to her words instead of her body language.

"You were always so giving, Lowell. Back when you were an omega, you thought about what we wanted. And you wanted us happy. You're sweet, Lowell. I saw how sweet back then and just now at -- with the old pack. But you just snarl at your own family."

"I'm still giving. I'm gonna give you a mindblower of an orgasm in about ten minutes. Maybe less if you push my control." He mumbled the words, already sinking back into the scent and the warmth of her.

"Yeah, you give to me. Of course, I deserve all that worship." Lin giggled and then sinuously moved her clit against his teeth. They both grunted. "But why not shine a little warmth on the others?"

Lowell took the pads of both his thumbs and moved them up, pressed hard against her thighs. She squirmed. He knew she liked that. Besides, if he didn't use his hands on her, he'd have to start working on that aching cock of his. She'd told him to keep his hands off that.

And he had to obey her.

"I'm not an omega anymore." *Except with her. She had a leash on him.*

"You think being nice makes you weak? Ahh, Lowell!"

"Don't want to talk."

"You want to fight, then?" Lin laughed and suddenly leaned over to dig her nails into his ribs.

He squirmed this time. She threw herself on top of him, like a frisky puppy eager to play. He fell back on the floor with a thud, twisting his body to save hers. Damn. Her skirt slid back into place -- just barely. That little slip of material was just begging to be torn off.

"I remember how ticklish you were when I was a kid. Even I could make you giggle. The adults made you insane before they were done."

He remembered those long sessions of teasing in the living room. His cock bobbed.

"Jesus, not now, Lin." If she kept that touch going, he'd come all over her before he'd have the chance to service her. Even as he spoke, her fingers unerringly went to some of his most vulnerable points, stroking over his clothing. The material rubbed his sensitized skin. She knew all his pleasure points already. His piercing. The vein near the head of his cock. The skin between his balls.

"I bet if I tied you down and used some feathers, you'd scream." She brushed against his thighs, and he drew up in agony/pleasure. God, the ideas she could put into his head!

"What --" A male voice intruded on the growing haze of sex and laughter Lin was covering him with.

Three of them. The two huge male betas and tiny Mia stared at them.

"We heard these weird strangling noises."

Christ. He tried to pull himself together, but Lin was too good at provoking the helpless laughter, even in front of witnesses.

"You're tickling him."

"He's laughing." The voice sounded awed.

"Stop! Oh, damn it, Lin. That was evil!" He squirmed under her hands.

"He needs a little more laughing. Pile on!" Lin offered, her voice a devilish invitation.

Noooo. Lowell remembered the heat and the laughter from the old pack, the crazed almost-foreplay they would create together. The tickles that turned to nips and then panting, breathless collapse. But his pack wouldn't. They'd stand off, they'd watch while their alpha turned into a whimpering, laughing mush under their careful gaze. And he couldn't stop it. Couldn't stop Lin.

Oh my God.

Hesitatingly, Oscar bent over, his huge hands closing over Lin. Fuck, no. No beta was going to paw -- Lin twisted and somehow Oscar was sprawled over Lowell, with an *oomph* of surprised laughter.

And then the rest of them were entwined together, no one sure where arms and legs went or who was tormenting who, but in one sweaty, laughing mass that demanded more touch, more laughter.

The pack that laughs together and gets hot together, stays together.

Lin's thought slid into his mind right before her hand cunningly slid against his stiffened cock, under cover of some other humping body.

He was a millimeter from losing control and coming all over everyone.

No. He couldn't allow that.

"This is not a fantasy of mine," Lowell growled. "Everyone get up. And out. You weren't invited."

The laughter stopped. Slowly they all stood. Lowell glared and the others dropped their heads obediently.

But he could still feel a bubble of merriment in the room. Lin winked at the rest of them, deliberately shifting her shirt down from where it gaped. Then she smacked Lowell's butt.

"He's very, very ticklish. It's a terrible weakness of Lowell's."

"Mmmm." Oscar didn't quite agree, but his eyes twinkled.

Twinkled. Lowell scowled. Things were going to be hellishly difficult to put back in the old order. "Out!"

"Sure, boss."

"Whatever you say, boss." But he heard a trace of laughter still.

Lin got on her knees as they filed out and smiled sweetly at Lowell. "Now all we need to do is be nice to them some more, pay them a bit of attention and socialize them some more, and this pack will be fine. They'll be eating out of our hands."

"Lin, I wanted to be eating *you* out by now. Instead we had a little slap and tickle with a bunch of other weres and I'm horny as hell. And frustrated to boot."

"Horny even though it wasn't a fantasy of yours?"

"Damn it, Lin!"

"But that bit of fun was good for all of us. Don't pout. Shall we go into the bedroom, then? I promise to make it up to you." She kissed him slowly before she let her canines sink deep into his lower lip.

He gave a low hum of pleasure.

I promise to make you want me more and more, Lowell. Nobody else.

"So." Lin drew the ribbon in her hair off and shook the tendrils free.

She was back. Back in his room -- their room. Lowell looked at the small glittering trail of female ornaments she left through the bedroom. He didn't mind the ridiculously girlish clutter. She was claiming her territory in a human way, just as he'd marked her, were-fashion, much more primitively. He rejoiced because somewhere deep down, he hadn't believed she would return after being with her family's pack. That he would be enough to make her want to stay.

"So?" He still didn't believe it. He could sense danger in her overly casual pose and narrowed eyes. That little interlude outside with the rest of the pack had been just that. But whatever she'd wanted from it hadn't satisfied her.

Her next question almost echoed his own thoughts.

"What do you want from me really?"

"Want?" What the hell kind of question was that? He wanted his mate. He wanted to fuck her and laugh with her and be with her. What was complicated about that?

Lowell moved toward her. Whatever was going on, he wasn't going to let her run. "Just you. I thought I'd made that clear enough."

"No. We're playing games and not going anywhere. D'you think I'm just going to maybe…oh, smack you a few times, make you lie down and we screw?" Lin looked over at the neatly made up bed. Lowell felt the familiar first prickles of excitement run down his spine as he looked over to the bed, too. They'd gone insane in that spot a few hours ago but there was no evidence left of what they'd done. The pack had tidied up after them.

The faintest lingering odor of sex tickled Lowell's nose, just enough to tug at him but not enough to overwhelm.

"I don't know what you mean." He didn't have to admit that hearing Lin's suggestion made him swallow hard. "I haven't been playing."

"You haven't been truthful with me, either. We're mates now. I *know* things. I'm going to know more before we're done. Mated for life, Lowell. That's a long time to try to hide from me."

What truths did she want? He wasn't about to try to tell her about children now. Not when he was suddenly unsure of her. What if she wanted to believe it? That would be a damned good excuse to run from him.

Instead Lowell spoke aloud what used to be his most closely-held secret. "You already know that I like to sub when I'm non-were."

Lin snorted. "And you know I like you to obey. I also know that when you're were, you're totally dominant and you'd just as soon your pack not know there's any other side to you. Maybe that's why you're so freaking nasty with them. But that's not the issue."

Jesus. The thing that had kept him away from women for years wasn't an issue? But she was right. Lin was in charge of what happened now. He didn't have to think about hiding his preferences anymore. He could do whatever he craved -- which was whatever she demanded of him.

God, what freedom!

But then what was the issue? Her issue? He was sure no one had told Lin what her father believed. Lin wouldn't make him guess about a thing like that.

Hell, was this a female thing?

It might be useless, but he had to ask. "So what do you mean?"

"Lowell!" Lin shoved his shoulder. He almost staggered from sheer surprise. But, damn it, his cock stiffened at the rough contact. "I'm starting to figure you out. Can't you understand anything about me? Don't you know what's up?"

My cock is damn well up. I want your pussy rubbing me. I want you on top of me, that hot wet channel covering my hard-on...

Lowell let out a slow breath of air and backed off. He knew that wasn't what Lin meant. It was a damn shame, but he had to think instead of screw right now. If he got any closer he'd forget that. "You're upset. You have been ever since we had dinner at your parents'."

She sniffed, figuring something that obvious didn't deserve a reply. If she wasn't going to say what was wrong, he could think of only one other way to find out what the hell she meant.

Lowell shut his eyes, let himself open to Lin. First he received twinges of emotion that were hard to discern. But as he focused, the sensations grew stronger until emotion almost hissed out of his mate, even though she stood without speaking, without moving. He began to sort the feelings out. There was anger, plenty of that, but under that -- was fear?

Fear and hurt and jealousy.

"What the hell do you have to be jealous of? You already have me by the balls!" Lowell opened his eyes. "Jesus, woman, I'm yours. Totally."

"Are you?" Lin didn't look any happier.

Unhappiness with him, he could understand. He would have been surprised if there hadn't been any. Maybe even hurt. He was a moody bastard and hard to handle. But fear? Lin wasn't afraid. Not of drunks in bars, not of her new, less than welcoming, packmates and most especially not of him.

Was she?

He stared at her now. Unlike other weres, alphas were permitted, even encouraged, to stare. Then again, his mate was alpha, too. Lin held his gaze, giving back challenge for challenge.

That was when another emotion of hers swept in, one that knocked all the rest out of his head. Desire. Grasping, greedy need. She wanted to fuck. Hard and hot and nasty.

Hell, he knew what to do about that. And if fucking was all they ever had -- no children, no "true" mating by were standards -- well, he was already a pervert. He almost liked the idea. They'd have to make the fucking worth everything, wouldn't they? Damn. He already had.

He began to circle her, slowly. She cocked her head to one side, refusing to flinch as he closed in on her. But she didn't reach out for him, although now he could do more than feel her lust -- he could smell it. That musky scent made him want to grab her, but he sensed more lurking underneath.

She was torn. She wanted to fuck but she was resisting the urge. Resisting *him*.

Were instincts swamped his human ones. He was her fucking mate. Her alpha. What right did she have to resist?

"What makes you question me?" Lowell scowled.

Damn it. She was finding it ever more difficult to follow his questions. The humming buzz of lust jangled her nerves and made it hard to think at all. She was so damn confused. She was supposed to be angry and having it out with him. But now she couldn't.

He was just so male.

Ever since she'd changed, she had new, huge sexual hungers to contend with. Thank God her change hadn't happened until she'd found Lowell again. She wanted sex all the time. To be on top when she was not were and to be possessed when she *was* were. She hadn't been immune from lust before. Far from it. But this -- this itch was different and overwhelming. Now she craved it. Craved *him*. Her mate knew everything she wanted and just how she wanted it. Lowell got closer but she wasn't afraid of him moving in, as if for the kill. She wanted him to pounce on her, to make her fall back into the burn of the raw and physical. To be an animal.

There wasn't any shame in lust, and most especially not werelust. You simply wanted to satisfy your hunger. But she hadn't counted on that hunger always being there, crying to be fed.

Sometimes the human part of you could hold it in, could let other things like fear or anger stop you from the want. Sometimes nothing could. Right now she couldn't help herself.

Forget her stupid human quibbles. She wanted to burn all her concerns away, to take Lowell into her body, into her mind…losing her doubts and anger and confusion to the basic were desires.

Weres lusted and then they fucked. That was what they needed above all. Maybe, maybe she could understand and forgive what had to have happened before if Lowell had been as hungry for sex then as she was now. He hadn't had her and he'd have to have someone or go mad.

"Was this how it was with the old pack when you had no one?" Lin got the words out. "You thought you'd die if you didn't fuck?"

He was close enough now to brush against the thin cotton gauze of her skirt. The heat of him was stoking the fire inside her.

"I'd fucked a lot of times by your age, Lin. Or at least I'd been fucked. If I was good enough, I got paid for it. That's how I survived, until I met your father. I had no one and nothing, so I sold myself. I suppose you didn't know that."

That was something she'd think about later. The hurt and loneliness he must have gone through. Right now it was just confusing her. She wanted to focus on her own hurt right now. And her own desires.

"But did you want to fuck?" She stared at him, trying to see his face in the dark, trying to find answers without him finding out what she meant. "More like need to. Have to."

"Yeah. Of course. Hell, Lin, I was young and I'm were. I wanted it all the time. When I didn't run and get something real, I'd dream about it at night. Sweat for it. Any kind of fucking would do. But mostly I fantasized about fucking a warm pussy. I spent hours imagining what it would be like…I damn near rubbed my cock raw at the images in my head. I'd done a lot of things by the time I was your age, but never that."

"Not until you met a pack with a woman in it."

He stilled. Lin tried to feel his emotions, but her own were too tangled, too ferocious to let his in.

Lowell stared at her. "What? That's what this is about? You want to slip a cock ring on me because of…"

"Because of my mother."

"*Leila?* Because you're jealous of your *mother?*"

Nausea rose up in Lin's throat. And why the hell did he sound relieved?

"Yes. No. Tell me, Lowell. I have to know."

"You think your father would let anyone, especially an omega, get inside his mate? You think Leila would let me?" His voice lowered. "You think I'd sneak around and shame my alphas by screwing one? Would you do that, Lin?"

"This isn't about me, damn it. Don't even try to make it about me. There was something! I know there was something. I could sense it tonight!" Lin clenched her fists, sickness replaced by frustrated anger, because she still wasn't getting to what he was hiding from her.

Lowell shook his head, as if to clear it.

"We're all weres, Lin. Whatever there was, it never went further than pack rules allowed. Yes, your mother is female. She was sexy. She still is, damn it. She's alpha and she can do what she wants with the rest of her pack. And I was a horny little beast who lusted after her. I'd have done the same after any woman who would look at me cross-eyed."

"But you left. There was a reason you left the pack. We loved you and you loved us. Was it because of her?"

He sighed. "Yes. But even more, it was because of Dek."

"*Daddy?*" She really didn't want those images in her head. But if Lowell fucked someone and not a woman…

"No, I don't mean I wanted to fuck Dek. Not that -- err, never mind. I mean I was a starving mongrel and I knew I'd only get to sniff at Leila as long as he was around. Neither he nor your mother would ever allow more. More importantly for you, I wanted to stick to pack code. Strange as it may sound, I honored my alphas even more than I wanted sex with Leila. But it was best for all of the pack if I left. We all knew that could change, especially if I could constantly see them -- smell them...Shit, there'd have been nothing but grief for us all if I stayed."

His hands bruised her shoulders as he gripped her, but she didn't care. She moved even closer against the vee of his legs, rubbing against him. She was almost beyond making sense of what he said, but his sincerity and lust got through. He wanted her. He was totally focused on her.

"Thank you. For telling me." Whatever he'd done or not done, he was hers now. It wasn't important enough to ask.

She did anyway. "But you did have women? Later?"

He hesitated. "Not many. Not nearly enough for you to be jealous. There was one non-were who was almost important to me. Since you're going to keep asking, yes, I liked screwing her. A lot. Almost too much to give her up when the pack needed me to move on. After that, I kept away from non-weres. It was too complicated and I like pussy way too much. It was ironic, really. I made myself alpha because I wanted to mate. And once I became one, I had to be alpha first, horn dog second." He bit her shoulder. "I can be both with you. Thank God."

"Yes." There was still something more. She sensed it. But she couldn't think or say more as she arched her neck back, submitting to him.

"Lin, I need you. And I'm going to keep you, no matter what."

All the tension leaked away, leaving just warmth. She knew a new tension was going to fill her soon, but right now she savored the rough bearded stubble that abraded her neck as Lowell nipped and licked her skin. She wanted the quick, hot darts of pain as his teeth closed in on her.

She wanted to surrender to him this time.

She wanted him to rip the thin skirt with one impatient tear, just the way he did a heartbeat later. Her nipples hardened as the night air and then his mouth touched them. He suckled hard, forcing them to even tighter peaks.

And then she wanted to fall back just the way they did a moment later, half-on, half-off the bed, bowled over by his impatience and hers. When he pushed her legs apart and entered her, hard and hungry and unwilling to wait, she shivered with excitement.

Lin moaned when she realized his weight held her down. Her heart was beating so rapidly, she wondered if it would stop from overuse. She tried to move her hips, to deepen the thrust of his cock inside her, but not being able to move made her even wetter and hotter. Hungrier for not being allowed to satisfy herself. Her nails scored into the light furring of his chest, leaving a trail of red welts.

She struggled and panted. He ignored her and that only increased her sharp need. His own hoarse groans echoed in her ear as he thrust deep and then deeper yet. Everything stoked the burning that tingled from her clitoris and radiated out through her body.

She wailed as Lowell's breath whistled out of his lungs. Finally he drew back slightly, allowing her to move. The bed shook underneath her and her legs, clinging to his hips, drew her body up and smacked against him with each thrust.

She wanted to do more. She wanted to snarl and snap at him. To offer her human belly and then her ass and be forced to submit, just like the lesser ranked were. The only thing that stopped her from the change was her total pleasure in what was happening as he used his non-were body to subdue her, to claim her, and to pleasure her completely. He was heavy and sweating and no longer focused on her wants. This was what *he* wanted. Her. He wanted her. Were form or not, this time he would be an animal who wanted to come inside his mate.

And that pushed her even closer to her own satisfaction.

She tensed, biting her lip, clutching for the sheets that bunched under her back. She was so close to the ultimate pleasure that the tremors of her release had begun to shake her body. She was so close to the edge, so delightfully, fearfully near to toppling...

But he stilled above her. Refused to move. She'd kill him. She'd -- Lin shook her sweaty hair out of her eyes and blinked at the man above her. Her breath caught.

For someone who was doing his level best to drill her through the bed, he looked...tender. He studied her for a long moment, as if he'd memorize every frustrated, quivering inch of her. Then he smiled, a little crookedly, and she saw the suddenly elongated length of his teeth, changing the tenderness to something more feral. Good. He wanted to change as badly as she did. Wanted to and was resisting that want because what they had already was so good.

His chest pumped in and out, the flash of metal that pierced his nipple sparkling in the dim reflection of the moon. He gripped her wrists and pulled them up above her head.

"Wolf. Human. Both ways. Any way. I claim you, Lin. D'you understand? Always. No matter what."

"Yes."

She couldn't say anything more. She didn't need to. With a long growl, he lowered his head against her and began to pump again, even harder. Hot liquid spilled into her already heated body, even as he kept thrusting.

Lin released a long, thin howl of joy as she came, fiercely, her body racked with her orgasm. Lowell collapsed on top of her a moment later. He hastily rolled off.

"My God." Lowell covered his eyes with his hand.

"Yeah."

"Topping is hard work."

Lin snorted, too weak to laugh.

They both heard the faint scratching at the door. Lowell sat up, his body shielding hers. "What?"

Slick opened the door hesitantly. Once again Lin wondered if he'd shuffle his feet while he spoke. "Boss -- you had a phone call."

She'd thought the ringing in her ears had been from her climax.

"And?" Lowell sounded as impatient as she felt.

"You were busy. But -- but --"

Damn. Was the entire pack waiting outside, listening to them, waiting for them to finish? Part of her wanted to shrivel up in embarrassment, but another part exulted. Let them listen and long for what she and Lowell had.

"It's her father." Slick glanced over toward Lin and hastily looked back at the floor. He held out the cell phone. "Trouble."

"What kind?" Lowell reached for the phone.

Oh, dear Lord. Had her parents been listening in by phone as well?

The beta moved his hand back, not letting Lowell take the phone. "I dunno. The kind that makes an alpha call and say he needs help. He said you had to keep it private."

Lowell growled. Slick swallowed and backed out of the room. Lin didn't think the other were had to worry, but then she'd never seen Lowell quite so unhappy.

"What is that beta's name, anyway?" Lin asked. She knew it was a stupid question but, insanely, she thought conversation could postpone what he'd hear next.

"Oscar." Lowell answered absently.

Odd name for a trouble-making behemoth. She should ask what his partner's name was. Big Bird? Ernie? She should --

She didn't want to hear what the trouble was. She was tough, sure, but she didn't want to hear it. Eventually she would. Maybe she should insist on ignoring her father's command for privacy right now, but she let Lowell stride out and shut the door. She needed a minute or so to collect herself.

It must be bad. Very bad.

Adrenaline surged and she crouched in a fighting stance, without knowing what she needed to fight.

"God *damn* it!" Still naked, Lowell began to pace as he held the phone. "What the fuck kind of game is this?"

He almost fell over his pack when he turned. Orders of privacy long since forgotten, the two male betas kept creeping closer, straining to hear the rest of the phone conversation. Lowell might have laughed except for his rising annoyance and puzzlement.

"All right. I understand that you didn't call. There's no real emergency. Who gives a damn about Rossi being gone? He's nothing. Probably just passed out somewhere. Unless --"

Lowell raised his head and the rest shrank back when they saw his eyes.

"Where's Dru?" Lowell demanded.

Oscar cleared his throat. "She's been hiding in her room ever since you smacked her down, boss. It's been kind of nice to have the peace."

"Make sure she's still there." Lowell spaced his words out, his voice almost gentle.

Oscar goggled before he spun around and ran as fast as a huge man could, even faster than last time.

"I'll kill Rossi. No, I'll cut off his little head since that's the only one that ever did any thinking. I know they're planning something. And if Dru has even the slightest idea about making trouble, I'll --" Lowell knew he was snarling, babbling, the words turning into one huge snarl as the change began. But the hair was standing on the back of his neck and he could feel the wrongness.

Dek hadn't called him at all. Hadn't thought it worth mentioning that Rossi had been gone since their supper together. Certainly hadn't said anything about it being an emergency. But someone had called to say he had. Someone had demanded Lowell's attention on the phone.

Wrong. Something was wrong.

"Jesus fuck, Lowell, she's gone!" Oscar was back and panting from the exertion. "Everything is cleared out. The kid -- Mia -- she's hiding in a corner, crying. But Dru's run from the pack."

They all gasped.

Oscar kept talking through the shocked silence of the others. "You never should have kept her on. She was never any good for this pack. And I know she couldn't have been that hot a piece of ass since you stopped fucking her years ago. But this is your fault. How did you think she'd react now that you've taken someone else for your bit --"

Oscar stopped in mid-word when Lowell dropped the phone and put his hand around the beta's throat. The silence changed from shocked to deadly.

"What would Lin think if you killed me, boss?" Oscar almost screamed, his voice shrill with fear.

Lin.

"Shut the fuck up."

Wrong. Very wrong.

Lowell ran back to the closed bedroom door. Lin knew the rules and even though she'd flouted them when they met, she'd obeyed them ever since. She was always with him or a member of his pack in case of danger.

His pack. His pack was supposed to protect their alpha bitch. *He* was supposed to protect her from everyone.

Lowell tore open the door and stared inside.

The window was open, letting heat into the air conditioned chill. Cold. Despite that window, it was too cold in the damned room.

"She's gone." Oscar was at his heels. "You let them take her."

With those words, in one blink, Lowell did the impossible. He turned were without any time to change at all.

Oscar saw the danger too late. He had only started to transform, already too late to defend himself, before Lowell was on him.

"Shit, I didn't mean anything! You can't kill me for telling the truth, you bastard!" Oscar yelled.

The words meant nothing to the red blood lust in his head. He was going to kill.

"Oscar isn't the enemy, Lowell! Are you listening?" It was a female voice and that reached him when nothing else might. The words were something Lin might say, almost the way she'd say them.

But it wasn't his mate. Lin. *God, Lin, where are you?*

Slowly Lowell focused. Mia stood sandwiched between the two angry weres, looking sick with fear. She ignored the beta and spoke directly to her boss. "Don't be angry with your pack brother."

Not that she'd seen a lot of pack spirit here. But it gave them all a moment to breathe. To think again.

Jesus, he didn't want to human think.

I let Rossi go. I let Dru stay. It's my fault. Weak.

Mia cocked her head as if she could hear him. "Why are you still here? Aren't you going to find her?"

The sizzling anger whooshed back but with it came control. Ice. That's what he was. That's what he needed.

Damn straight he'd find her. He wasn't that weak.

Mia's face crumpled as she realized there was no immediate threat to her or the pack. She took in a deep breath and let it out in a wail. "Oh my God. You have to find her. Now what?"

A long howl rang out behind the sobbing girl. The death howl. Lowell heard the cry echoing in his own throat and then the return wail from his betas.

Mia might cry and pretend not to know the answer, but they all knew exactly what would happen next. But it was too early to be were. Like it or not, they needed to think.

Lowell shuddered, gritted his teeth and let the surge of transformation seep into his body.

"You might want to go find your jeans, boss. If you're back to feeling human again." Oscar rubbed his non-were throat as if Lowell had actually gone for it. "Sounds like there's work to do."

Chapter Five

"It's all right. Really. Really. I'm here. I'm here." Lowell laughed down at her, just out of reach, almost the way it had been when she was a child. Annoyed, Lin stretched out to touch him.

Lin woke up with a jerk, tears on her face.

It had been a dream. She could almost hear Lowell, though their matebond wasn't letting her hear his thoughts, now when she most needed to.

Maybe because her head still hurt from where she'd been knocked out. Taken and captured without a sound because she'd known these wolves.

"Not yet, baby. But soon." For a moment Lowell's voice rumbled in her head clearly. And then she went under again.

He and Dek met formally, their packs standing at the alert behind them. Lowell had never seen anything like the meeting -- never heard of anything like it. It was an alliance in a world where packs never formed partnerships. But now they had a mutual enemy and the same goals.

"I've started searching Rossi's haunts around town. Talking to people he's talked to." Dek's fists clenched, ready for battle. He relaxed them with an effort but they balled up again before he was done with the sentence.

Lowell almost pitied the poor non-weres who had to answer the questions. If he'd had any pity to waste.

"Dru hadn't settled in here yet. But I've been checking out the last few places we've lived. Calling in a few favors to find out if she went back." The two packs whined uneasily, close to were, even in human shape. Lowell knew why. He might have shifted back to human form, but everyone could smell the were on him, not far below the surface. It made all of them restless.

Too damn bad. He was on the hunt. It wouldn't take much to turn it into a blood hunt. It was hard enough to stay focused and thinking when he wanted to rend and tear. Where the hell had they hidden themselves?

"Mia." Leila snapped out the name.

Lowell's eyes narrowed. Mia. He'd changed to human so he could think, but he hadn't been thinking smart at all. Thank God someone was. Lowell beckoned to the group behind him.

"Come here."

Mia walked reluctantly forward. Everyone had ignored her and her hysterics after she'd delivered the bad news. After all, Mia was no threat. She still wasn't. If she'd been in were form she'd have crawled forward, belly to the ground, to meet her alpha.

Lowell knew that his temper made it unwise for him to question the miserable little thing before this. But it had been stupid to let temper get in the way for so long. Mia might be reluctant, but she was still a potential source of information. No matter. Leila or Dek would do the interrogation, which was just as well since he was close to losing control.

"Sir?" Mia whispered the word.

"What do you know about what's happened here?"

Mia shook her head violently.

"I didn't -- I wouldn't --" The teenager was incoherent, seeing up close the cold rage in Lowell's face.

Time for some feminine sympathy. Lowell glanced at Leila, took a deep breath and gathered patience.

"Why didn't Dru take you along?" Leila grasped Mia's hand. It was shaking so hard that the woman almost had to use force to hold onto Mia's wrist. "It's all right, Mia. We aren't blaming you, aren't out to punish you. You're still one of the pack."

"Yes. Oh, please, believe me! I wouldn't go." Mia began to sob, tears trickling down her chin. "She said we were going to be a new pack, but I said I didn't need a new one. She smacked me, but I wouldn't go."

"Did she say anything about Lin? About where they would go?"

Mia shook her head.

"Moth -- Dru said she had a bargaining chip to keep them safe. To make sure we'd be a pack. She said I was a fool and ungrateful --"

Lowell broke in. "Did she do anything? If she didn't say anything, did she do anything to let you know what would happen?"

Leila shook her head at him. "Don't cry so, my dear. You'll make yourself sick. Wipe your eyes and think for a moment. We'll wait."

Lowell didn't know how Leila could stand it but somehow she was holding onto the shaking Mia, the way she would have Lin, letting her cry it out.

Where are you, Lin? Damn it, speak to me.

The embrace worked. Mia's sobs calmed at last. She swiped at her eyes and spoke steadily. "I've been thinking. I know a lot about my moth -- about Dru. I watch her. You have to, because if she gets angry, she gets ugly. But she wasn't angry. Not until I said I wouldn't leave." Mia's face was tight with concentration. "Then she said she didn't have the money to do everything her new pack wanted, but she would soon and then I'd be sorry. I'd see what I'd given up too late."

"Money? D'you think that's all she wants?" Dek broke in.

Lowell had money. His security service was world-class and world-famous. They'd been bodyguards to some of the most important people in the world. And Dek had money from his business ventures. Probably even more than Lowell did. Fuck. Money was easy.

"I think that's too easy." Lowell rubbed a spot between his eyebrows, hating to say aloud what he knew they were all thinking. "She's too angry to be satisfied with money."

"But if that's even a part of it, then she's nearby, to get it from us." Leila couldn't keep the hope from her voice. "And to watch and gloat."

"If they're still here, Rossi has to have found the spot for them to stay. Someplace where they can find out what we're doing." Dek began to pace.

Some place that Rossi would find. Lin knew where Rossi liked to go. She knew how Rossi thought -- better than anyone else in his pack or hers did. They'd been companions, even if forced ones, for many years. If she'd been trapped or disoriented, she could still figure him out.

Lin. Think, damn it. Then tell me.

He hadn't picked up anything since she was kidnapped. What if she couldn't tell him? What if she was too badly injured or -- He wasn't going to let himself think what she might be.

He saw Leila sway just a little. Damn, the woman was strong, but the uncertainty was killing them all.

"Leila needs rest. She's running on adrenaline right now."

"Decided to take on the care of both packs, boy?" Dek's words made Lowell stiffen. But the other male alpha in the room didn't sound angry at him. "Lin is enough work on her own."

"That she is."

Jeeters.

The word made no sense, but it sounded like Lin's voice. Had she called to him or did a random thought finally hit his brain? No matter. Lowell took a deep breath and focused. He searched his memory.

"The night Lin left Rossi behind. He was at Jeeters."

Grey scowled. "It's where he always goes. He's dragged me there a few times. There are people there who'll do a lot of ugly things for a nice price. I don't hang with them, but everyone knows who they are."

"Bingo." Lowell knew he was smiling wide enough to show all his canines. An ugly smile. "You can tell me about them in detail. Give me names and descriptions. I don't want to make any mistake about who they are."

"*We* don't want to make any mistakes." Dek cut in, eyes glittering. "Jail's not a good place for weres."

"No one will know. We'll keep everything within the pack. Two packs. Hell, we'll keep it even tighter. It's just between our families." Leila looked at them, all trace of weakness gone. "Guess we owe you a chance to get your own back as well, Lowell."

Pack rules were tight, but using kin-family? When invoked, that was closer, more secret, and more sacred than pack law. That was why it was used maybe once in anyone's lifetime. But Leila was right. This was too messy to get all the pack involved. And the situation was a once in a lifetime emergency.

"Understood." Lowell nodded, ignoring the yip of protest from the rest of the pack, just like he pushed aside the brief delight at being counted kin. "Just family. The only one who won't go is Rome. He's too young yet."

"We deserve a chance at those two rogues," Grey snarled.

His own pack snarled behind Lowell.

"Thank you for standing with us." Lowell swallowed. He hadn't been sure before this that his pack would. "But this time -- this one time -- it would be better without the pack."

Lin shook her head. She was groggy. Disoriented.

The water. The food. Lin tried to think if anything had tasted off, but her brain was too fuzzy. No matter. She couldn't risk tasting any of the things her enemies had prepared for her. She could be a little hungry and thirsty until Lowell came for her.

For a moment, she thought she heard him howling.

Chapter Six

"Keep away from the door." Leila spoke with quiet deadliness.

Someone would die. Tonight. In front of the rest. Lin absorbed the knowledge as she heard the almost soundless growls of the weres around her. She wasn't as steady as she could be, since she'd carefully hidden the food and water given to her for the past day, but her brain was clear enough to know trouble when she saw it come in the door.

The family's entrance had been almost soundless, but terrible nonetheless.

"Fine. You found us. We still win. It's not what we planned at first, but if you touch us, Lin's throat is ripped out. You took me once, Lowell. You tricked me into putting aside revenge because I thought I would be your alpha bitch. I don't believe in putting aside revenge any longer." Dru's voice was as cold, as certain, as Leila's. "You have the girl tight, Rossi?"

"Yes." He was the only one who looked terrified. Hadn't Rossi known what would happen? Or had he just wanted to please his bitch mother when she ordered the unthinkable?

Rossi really had never been too bright.

But he clutched Lin just as tightly as a smart man would. His hand was steady on the knife and his head was slightly bent toward Lin's throat. Weapon or his own teeth -- either could tear away her life.

Lowell had already begun to circle. He said nothing, just hummed the lowest of rumbling growls. Dek followed him, his growl matching Lowell's. Lin licked her lips. This was what Lin had heard of but never wanted to see -- the death circle. The move to find the weak spot. Dear Lord, her family was moving in for the kill.

"You better not mess with us." Rossi backed up a little.

She saw Lowell noting every move Rossi made. Every mark on Lin's face. They'd bruised her when she finally came to and tried to struggle.

She knew Lowell. For that alone, they were going to die. For all the rest, they'd die horribly.

"Quietly," Leila said. "We don't want any interference from outside."

"If you don't do what we say, we'll --" Dru began.

"You'll do nothing! Enough!" Lin let the beginnings of her change begin to rip through her, releasing it faster and more painfully than ever before. Rossi took a half-step back, and that was enough for her to spring.

Dru's face went slack with astonishment and Lin almost laughed. Hadn't Dru ever seen a were change before?

Perhaps not one who changed while in motion. Lin lashed out with a still-human foot pointed toward Dru's throat. Dru, the source of all their pain and anger. She'd like to smash her.

Instead, in mid-leap, Lin twisted and launched herself at the person who held the knife.

Rossi's mouth gaped. "What --?" he began before she landed, knocking over Rossi and herself.

Wait! Lowell barked a warning, much too late.

"What is that half-were bitch doing?" Dru screamed and the glint of a gun flashed in her hands.

Were against loaded weapon. Not a good match. Maybe she should have thought instead of felt. Too late now.

Crack! The bullet hit flesh.

Lin braced herself for pain, even as she swiped at Rossi's neck and his knife clattered to the floor. They could die together.

Someone screamed. Rossi?

"Hush, child." Leila's Southern belle tone rang incongruously through the room. "Lin, girl, next time use your head."

Her mother pointed her revolver down toward the floor. Dru lay on the floor. She twitched more and more slowly a few feet away, gradually, in her death throes, making her final change back to were.

"Lin! Let the boy go!" Leila shook her shoulder. "He won't cause any more trouble for us."

The buzzing in her ears gradually subsided. Lin swallowed.

"Yes, Mama."

"What --" Rossi tried again after he cleared his throat. "What are you?"

Lin scowled. "What the hell do you mean?"

He seemed to be taking the failure of his plans and the death of his mother in stride. But why the stunned reaction to her transformation?

Lin paused and thought. She had just *spoken*. Out loud. In English. That couldn't be. Weres didn't speak.

"You're not human. But you're sure as hell aren't were." Rossi backed up, eyes shifting between her and Leila. "Shit, you're some kind of freak!"

Lin blinked. She forced herself not to look for a mirror. She couldn't be sidetracked now.

"Get out." Lin said in a clear, human voice. "Shut up and get out, Rossi."

Rossi began to walk away faster, but when he did, he took his eyes off the wrong were. With a slow, almost casual swipe, Lowell reached forward and clawed the rogue from cheek to chest. The wound would run deep before it scarred over.

Another scream rang through the room. Rossi clapped a hand to the blood streaming from his face and ran.

Dek crouched, snarled and sprang. For a moment he worried the neck of the now sobbing Rossi and then his arm. A snap of bone rang clearly through the room, before Dek deliberately stood and turned his back, showing how little he cared about a counterattack from Rossi.

Rossi crawled this time, clutching his arm, and managed to stumble to his feet at the door before plunging out. His new life, one where he'd run from the buzz surrounding his reputation, had begun.

Lowell gave a long, lazy yawn of contempt, with all his teeth and tongue showing, and shook the blood from his paw.

No need to make it too easy on him. This will help the fool remember not to fuck up again.

"Will you weres kindly change so we can leave and take care of our girl before anyone arrives? I'd rather all they found was a dead wolf. That'll look odd, but better than what they'd find right now if they investigate all those screams." Leila's voice stayed steady and calm.

"Can you manage, love?" Lowell, half-human and half-were, turned to her.

"I'm all right." Lin steadied herself.

And Lin's world slowly transformed back into the more ordinary human one she knew.

When they silently filed out, no one looked behind at the bloodied canine carcass on the floor.

"I'm sorry, Lin." Mia stood as if she was before an executioner.

Tired. She was so tired and confused. But Lin pushed away the weariness long enough to smile and touch Mia's worried face.

"There's nothing to be sorry for, Mia. Between either of us. You stayed with the pack while we dealt with those who tried to tear the pack apart. You're one of ours. What happened before is done."

Mia relaxed a little.

"You're all right, then?" Oscar took a step forward, one eye on the watchful Lowell.

"I will be." *Once I can get all these crazy emotions under control.* There was something very wrong that she needed to deal with. "Now that I'm home."

"Welcome back, boss lady."

"Back off and let her go sleep. Lin, that's what you need right now." Lowell scooped her up as if she was a baby again.

"I -- I'm afraid to sleep." She whispered it in his ear.

"I'll watch. You don't have to be afraid."

"What did Rossi mean, Lowell? What did I do wrong?"

They were home. Back in their bedroom. He'd watched and waited while she slept, memorizing each breath she took. But now she was awake and alert and he needed to do more than just be thankful she was alive. Lowell tried to figure out how to stop the inevitable.

He shouldn't have let her take charge. Should have stopped things before she changed.

Almost changed.

"It means nothing, babe. You're my mate and you're were enough for me. More than enough." He ventured a long nuzzle from ear to neck.

She didn't even twitch. Lin just sat there, eyebrows knit.

"Is that why I get thi --this weird vibe from everyone? I thought my family was unhappy about you. But was it about me? Because I'm a freak? Not were, not human. And I was too stupid to even know before this."

"You're not a freak. You're not stupid -- at least, not unless you keep on talking like this. I told you it doesn't matter."

"Don't try to hide this from me. It obviously does matter. But why are the others so bothered? We're happy. We're mated. Some weres change once in a decade and no one wonders about them. So why am I wrong? I look a little different. I might grow into being more were someday. Right? Don't you think so?" She turned to him.

"Why not? I never heard we were on a schedule." Lowell wanted to put his arm around her but she'd snap at him. The wave of misery emanating from her wasn't even needed. He could see from her narrowed glance and restless movements how she felt. He couldn't tell her what her own parents believed. He wouldn't let her know barrenness was a good possibility.

"Right. So why --?" She gasped. "Lowell, no!"

Too late. He tried to shut his mind down, but too late. Idiot. Moron. He'd forgotten how close their bond was. She'd heard him.

She crouched on the bed, as if she was going to spring for his throat. Shit, maybe she was. He braced himself.

"What do you mean, barren? We've barely started to even try for kids."

"It doesn't matter. It's just a crazy theory and it doesn't matter. We're mated. Bonded, sealed together. Children or no children, that's what is. If you left, there still would be no children, because I'd never mate with anyone else. But we'd be separate. Alone." Christ, he hated to argue with an angry woman. *His* angry woman. There was no way to win this one.

If only the sadness wasn't seeping out from her and leaching into him. It was taking away all the annoyance and leaving nothing but grief.

He was going to have to do something.

"I love you, Lin. Human or were or something in between. I want to marry you. We can promise to be together in sickness and health…"

"Yes!" Lin stopped. "But I shouldn't. Not if I'm not meant to be here."

So much for understanding. Lowell snarled, the sound reverberating through the room.

"Shut up. Just. Shut up." He gripped her hair, pulled her head back. "Mine. That's all you need to know. Believe. You're *mine.*"

Eyes wide, she looked like she might argue. He tightened the grip and stared her down.

When her gaze fell, he pulled her tight against him. His cock was already hardening against her.

"Stupid. Rossi and Dru were so stupid. If they'd known I was so useless, they'd never have kidnapped me as if I were some sort of prize --"

"Take your clothes off, before I rip them off." He showed his teeth, already lengthened and sharp. "Looks like I have to show you who you belong to and who's prize you are."

"Dominating sub."

"Oh, no. We don't play if you're going to be an idiot. This isn't a game now. You're going to have to find out who is really boss in this relationship."

Indecision. Deep unhappiness. And desire. Were lust, running hot inside her. He could feel all of it warring in her body and he hung on. She'd been through so much that she deserved some peace. Instead she had to make a tough choice right now. And she had to decide the right way. She had to stay with him.

Her lips pursed and then quirked into a smile. Her body relaxed against his. She scraped her teeth against his chin before she whispered, "I already know who is."

He smiled, too. He wanted to do more than smile. He wanted to laugh or weep with relief. She was back. His Lin was back again. "I guess we'll just have to see about that."

"And we'll have to talk to the pack. Let them decide what to do about me."

No. Lowell swallowed the instant reaction and skimmed his hand down her arms instead. Lin was right. She was always right about what was needed for the pack. He was the one who didn't always care what was best for the others.

"All right. We'll talk. But what they say will make no difference between us, Lin. Believe it."

"Just -- let's fuck first. I need that. I need you. I needed you for so long and you weren't there." Lin looked near tears.

"We'll fuck any way you want, babe, just so long as we do."

"Shut up and lie down. I need to let some energy out and you need to stop giving the orders and just feel." Lin wondered why she even bothered with the second sentence. Lowell was already unbuttoning his jeans with her first words.

"I want you to do something special for me. Please."

Was this what was called topping from below? Lin scowled down at him. She was at a disadvantage because while she might have a hell of an imagination, her mate knew about many different ways to pleasure, all very intimate.

And both of them wanted to forget about everything but pleasure for just a moment. The rest was too overwhelming. Too hopeless. She wanted the oblivion that sex would bring to them.

When in doubt, weres fucked. Wasn't that the rule? During her ordeal, whenever she was conscious and able to think, she'd craved Lowell's body. Trapped, hopeless, wanting him.

"I give the orders this time," Lin growled.

Now she was with him and the situation still seemed hopeless. It didn't matter. She didn't want it to matter. She wanted him. She wanted to be in charge of him and his body, making them both shudder and climax.

"But we'll both like this. Look in my drawer." Lowell was stripped down completely and her breath caught once she took the time to see him properly.

Lean and hard and just lightly furred. No male were should be so hairless even though she loved the feel of his skin under her palm. She tickled his skin with her tongue. Tasty.

Then she leaned over to see what he had wanted in the nightstand. Dear Lord. She couldn't even imagine what half of these things were meant for. Lin fumbled with the contents, drawing something out almost at random.

"Ohhh." Lin held up the metal and leather ornament. "Will you wear my ring, darling?"

"Cuffs first." His face was tight with longing, well beyond jokes. Lin ached at the sight.

She ached more by the time she finished with the cuffs, making sure his wrists were tight against the headboard, his legs stretched out underneath her body, restrained and helpless and all hers.

"You do as *I* say. In bed, you're mine." Lin kept her inflection precise and cold. He was going to trust her and then follow her, no matter how inexperienced she was, or the game wasn't worth starting.

It hadn't ever been a game, really.

She fastened the ring around his cock, testing the snugness and inwardly rejoicing that she'd done it with a minimum of fumbling.

"I don't do this much. It's dangerous." His eyes gleamed up at her. "If I change…"

Wolf, cock ring, tethered. Not a good image. And what about Lowell, whose swollen cock showed how much he was enjoying his restraints? What was it like to never be able to do what you want because you had no one to back you up, no one to tell? It made her want to kiss it better for him, but she knew this wasn't the time to baby him.

Lin bent over and, instead of kissing him, she scraped her teeth just lightly over his cock. He writhed underneath her.

The hum of excitement inside her upped a notch.

"What do you want now, fella?" She whispered it. "What haven't you told me yet?"

They shouldn't know each other so well so soon. But they did. She was going to know him better yet. Every dirty thing he had kept secret from everyone else. She was going to get it out of him. And it was there, waiting. Lin could almost hear the secret he was crushing back on his tongue.

What could he still be keeping inside?

She looked back into the drawer. His personal little stash of treasures. Then she smiled.

"This. You want this."

The vibrator buzzed as she held it up in her hand.

"It's big and powerful." She set the speed up a notch. "How often have you pleasured yourself with it, Lowell? How often did you want the real thing up inside you while you did yourself?"

"Maybe that toy was for…others." Lowell licked his lips as he watched.

"Maybe that's what you told them." She smiled. "I suppose I should give you at least a little lube before I use this."

Despite the tight bond against his cock, a small drop of precum glittered on his cock's head. So pretty. So were the sounds he made when she slicked lube between his ass cheeks, probing for the hole.

He sucked in his breath when she slipped a finger inside. Was this how she felt to him? He was hot and tight. Mysterious. Something she wanted to explore. She inserted her finger up just a bit higher, working her way up carefully past the initial resistance.

"My balls are turning blue, babe." He gritted the words out.

"They'll be deep, dark navy blue before we're done." They were both gulping for air. Lin had never seen anything quite so arousing as a man with his body quivering and his face set in a grimace of combined pain and pleasure. Hers. Her man. Her pain and pleasure to mete out, a gift to him.

"What do you want, Lowell?" She ran a finger over those blue balls. "I need to know. Even more, you need to tell me."

Lin gestured and he arched his back up, as high as the restraints allowed. She laid the vibrator between the cheeks of his ass, and he shuddered along with the toy.

"You don't need to know all my sick fantasies, babe. You seem to do fine on your own." Lowell's voice still held a thread of amusement through the lust.

In fact, he still sounded much too much in control.

She inserted the toy suddenly and he jumped. Then, with it buzzing inside, his ass now flat down on the bed, she pushed her full weight up against him.

Her face was a quarter inch from his when she hissed, "I said to tell me."

His muscles were so tightly locked that they shook. She wasn't sure if he was tensed to keep the toy caught inside his body or the words bound inside his head.

"Why?" he gasped.

"I could sense it, but this time you have to give me the words. You have to give me everything." Lin stroked the sides of his throat. "Because I want it, Lowell. Because I'm ordering it. And because you are meant to obey me."

"I want…you. Doing whatever you want to me."

"But that's not all." Glimpses of impossible, erotic images began to dance at the edge of her mind. She licked his chin. "You want more."

"There is no more. Nothing more than you."

"I like that response, Lowell." She eased away, up onto her elbows so just the tips of her breasts rested against his chest. His lungs were pumping as fiercely as if they were having sex. She edged her sex to fit against his rigid cock.

"Mistress." He mouthed it, almost beyond speech.

The images tumbled into her mind, stronger and wilder. Heat. Sweat and groans, tangled arms and legs. So many arms and legs. So many…

Her fingernails bit into the flesh near his flat nipples and he shut his eyes.

"But you're lying. What. Do. You. Want?"

"You. Others. You standing, me kneeling and sucking you, someone else taking me. Taking me hard." Sweat beaded down Lowell's face. "Me fucking you while someone fucks me. Letting go. More. Being overpowered. Overcome. Jesus God, Lin!"

She could see it. Feel it.

His control was gone. He was tearing at his cuffs, rocking the bed as if they were having sex right then.

"You want a cock inside you while you're inside me. You want --" She slipped on top of him, so slick that she didn't need to force that big erection inside her. His cock fit inside her like a key in a well-oiled lock. " -- to feel like *this*."

She rocked, keeping pace with the vibrator.

"Ohgodohgodohgod." The sound of Lowell's choked, gasping words gripped her by the pussy. "Let me loose, Lin. Let me fucking loose before I go out of my mind."

"You can trust me, Lowell. I'm going to take care of you when you go out of your mind. I'm always going to take care of you." Suddenly she couldn't say more. It was like electric currents running through her body. The blinding heat of insanity clawed at her too as she arched herself back, trying to absorb everything, every shock of his thrusts.

The mirrored images of ferocity, of lust, of pure sex slammed into them both. Lin pinched her nipples, imagining the biting kisses of her mate as he fucked her. It was so close to reality -- she felt the sharpness of the punishment. She wanted it as much as Lowell did. She wanted to see his ass as some huge cock plowed into it. She wanted, she had to...

She came, the twisting force of lust almost blinding her. She was amazed her heart didn't stop from the strength of her release. Her legs trembled as she tried to stay upright.

She opened her eyes, blinking, as if she and her surroundings were transformed.

Then she looked down and gasped. Lowell had felt her relief but couldn't follow. Not yet. She slid off the strong body below, her shaking fingers just barely able to finally unfasten Lowell's bound cock. He ignored her intervention, eyes shut, teeth locked on his bottom lip, caught up in his own desire. Lowell rode the vibrator a moment longer, a few viciously brutal thrusts more, his muscles straining. Then he screamed as his body snapped like a sprung bow, and his come spurted up, falling against his chest, spattering against his sweat-matted hair.

There was blood on his wrists. Lin swallowed past the dryness of her throat and crawled over to completely free him. She licked his skin, kissing Lowell's blood, the salty wetness reminding her of his spilled come. Delicious. No wonder weres sometimes had to fight bloodlust, the desire to maim and devour. No wonder they sometimes failed the battle.

She wasn't going to think about the battle she had been in. Because it wasn't bloodlust she felt now. She laid her head against his shoulder, fighting tears.

"Lin." Lips brushed her hair.

She hadn't known what it would be like. Her hand grasped his. She curled it tight around his palm, careful not to brush against his wounds.

"Are you angry? Jealous?"

She shook her head at his anxious words, unable to speak.

"You were about Leila. And that was -- well, I won't say it was nothing. But it went nowhere. Then you heard about Dru. She couldn't resist rubbing that in your face. I did fuck her when I first became alpha. I was confused and she was there. Afterward, I felt guilty and she worked that guilt to stay. But now this..."

"Stupid. I didn't give a damn about what Dru said or what you did in the past. I don't care about some passing stranger you might have a fantasy about. I'm only jealous when there might be some real competition. My mother might have been competition if things had been different." She smiled up at him, letting them both know she was being truthful. "But I'm your mate now."

And your perspective changes when you think you're never going to see your mate again.

Her heart still hammered. Her body was still mush. And her soul...she was very afraid that Lowell had taken her soul away from her.

How could she be jealous of his desire when it made her so hot? This was different. This wasn't about pack and family. It wasn't even completely about sex. It was something he craved, deep down, and now he had passed the craving on to her.

Her body and soul was his body and soul now. She had no more control over it.

"Lowell --"

"Hmmm?"

"Nothing." There were no words to explain.

He stood up and squinted, obviously searching for his clothes. Lin hugged her knees against her body as she sat, staring at him.

His eyes focused on her and he shook his head, as if to change the direction of his thoughts. Then he loped over to her and rested his mouth against her nose, almost as if they were muzzle to muzzle.

"Nothing? I think not." His mouth slipped against her cheek. "You're everything, Lin. You frighten me. Almost. I want to show you how important you are."

"I like being able to frighten you. Almost." Lin felt the warmth soaking into her.

Chapter Seven

Believe it. Believe it.

The three remaining pack members didn't visibly react to their alphas after the announcement. Mia stared out the window. The two beta males looked at each other.

Believe. Believe.

"And? So?" Oscar's shoulders were set, his growl a clear threat.

"I intend to remain alpha." Lin spoke over the jittering echoes of her stomach. "But I can't promise you any future. Any children."

"We're not stupid. We got that." Oscar's partner -- Enrique -- snapped.

"Hell, if it were just about him --" Oscar jerked his chin toward Lowell. " -- I'd vote to toss him. Stupid asshole."

"Now wait a minute --" Lin stopped. "You mean, you don't mind?"

"Of course we mind. We're a pack. We want children around. But you're all right. You make the asshole laugh. We'd probably never find another female able to do that."

"You stood up for me despite what my mother and brother did to you." Mia's voice was soft, but it carried far enough.

"You're one of us. We'll wait it out and see what happens." Enrique shrugged. "And we'll stick together. Stick with you."

Believe.

"Thank you." What else could she say without getting teary and stupid? Oh. One other thing. "Lowell isn't an asshole. I just need to get him to mellow out with you folks. That is, if you mellow a little back."

"Don't try, Lin. What do I care what they think of me, as long as they keep their tails between their legs and their heads down when they see me?" Lowell's harsh voice suddenly softened. "Besides, they're smart. They know I'm a mean asshole and they know what they've got in you. That's all they need to know."

"Yeah. Don't push it too far, boss lady. Some things are just impossible to accept." Oscar almost smiled.

He's wrong. They're both wrong. But she'd fix it. Nothing was impossible right now.

"I have time to work on it. It'll be a piece of cake." Lin kissed Lowell and then reached out and squeezed Oscar's hand.

Oscar looked almost as shocked as if she'd set fire to his fur. But he gave the slightest of squeezes in return.

* * *

"If he wants to do this shit, why isn't he saying anything?"

"He wants it, all right. Bad. Look at his fly." Lin gestured to where it tented. "But he knows he's supposed to say just two things during all this. *Please* when he wants it harder and *thank you* when you're done."

Lowell's pants weren't the only one sporting a hard on. Even in the darkness of the alley they all could see it. The guy laughed, a little uncertainly, but there was definitely eagerness in his tone when he said, "And stop isn't one of his words?"

"Not tonight. I'll be the one who says that, if it needs saying." Lin dug her nails into her mate's shoulder. "But I'm betting there won't be any need."

The man's eyes shifted from Lowell's cock to her. Eagerness was definitely overtaking the hesitation he'd had just moments before. "You're staying?"

"I'm the reason for the show, buddy. You just bet I'm staying." Lin cupped Lowell's balls, and he shifted his weight under the pressure.

"Hell, why not?" The stranger was already pulling at the fastenings of his pants.

Lowell pushed down his own, baring his ass to view.

"Nice. You have any lube?" The man paused a minute.

"Yeah. But don't use too much. He wants to feel it." Lin licked her lips.

Their temporary partner left all hesitation behind with those words. There was a small spurt as the man snatched the lube and spread it on his rising shaft and reddening head.

He was big. Trust Lowell to pick out someone big. He would feel it. So would she.

Lowell lifted her and braced them both against the wall.

Things blurred for a moment as she absorbed the gasps and groans before her and then the jolt of a cock entering Lowell. She could feel the push and pull of the third person's frantic jolts inside Lowell when Lowell entered her.

It was too much. It was perfect. She gripped him hard, his hands under her ass, her legs over his shoulders. Every harsh beat, every stroke he absorbed, she could feel ripple through her.

When Lowell shuddered, she did too -- and felt reciprocal movement in the other man. Lowell panted like a dog over her, holding her tight.

"Please."

Harder.

"Please!"

Harder.

"Oh my God," Lin whimpered.

She shattered, pinned against the wall, pressed by the weight of two male bodies. Ignoring her release, their frantic coupling continued. Dear Lord, it was stoking her again. She shifted, trying not to cry out.

Lowell's head dropped into the space between her shoulder and neck. He bit, hard, as he rocked and ground his hips against her -- against the other.

"T-thank you." She wasn't even sure if Lowell said the words or she did.

"Oh, yeah. Oh fuck, yeah." The man screamed in turn.

And then the hot roller coaster ride was over. The stranger didn't meet her eyes as he backed away. Lowell still gasped for air.

There was nothing more. No sounds except for the steps their former partner made as he walked away from them, the noise growing fainter and then disappearing, leaving just the two of them together again. Just the two of them in the darkness of a warm night. The moon had just started to rise.

The faintest of breezes cooled her skin.

"Lowell?" Had it been wrong? Was he angry with her for making his fantasy real?

Maybe that was all she was good for now. Being part of a fantasy. If it was, and that was what he wanted, she was going to give it to him. They'd enjoy what they could have together and not regret -- not ever regret -- what they didn't have.

Lowell's eyes were wide, unfocused for a moment as he caught his breath. Then he squinted at her. Really saw her there, standing under the moon's rays. The sweat beaded his face as he smiled.

Her beautiful Lowell. There was nothing wrong with being his fantasy.

"Damn, baby. That was good. You're good." He bent, kissed her hand. "All good. Perfect. I don't deserve you."

"Lowell --" Her breath caught. She couldn't bear him to start that now. Not when she was trying so hard to feel worthy herself. His insecurity was so ridiculous when he was everything a were was meant to be. It was her. For her, perfection was too far away.

But maybe it wasn't so hard to keep believing. Especially when Lowell kept coming up with new ways to show how much she meant to him.

His voice roughened as he continued, just as if she hadn't interrupted. "I don't deserve you, but I'm damned well making sure you stay. Forever."

When she had dreamed of being top dog, she'd never thought of how complicated it might become.

Her head drooped and then she raised it up. Stared straight at her mate. Complicated was one thing. Weak was another. She had to be strong when she told him the truth he needed to hear. "I'll stay. I have to. I'm yours."

HOME

Prologue

Bright-eyed, Rome crouched lower, waiting for the next yahoo who might crawl out his hole and try something new. He could use the exercise. He wasn't afraid of a bar brawl, even with the odds against him. Except for The Change. A little too much excitement and he might give the cretins in this place a real surprise with his transformation. Then he'd be both bright-eyed and bushy-tailed -- and have good sharp teeth and claws to top things off. So be it. They'd started the fight, after all.

He didn't listen to the catcalls and noise. Instead he kept his eyes and ears open for whoever moved next. Someone threw a beer bottle and the light on the ceiling swayed, the electric glow giving a weirdly strobe-like effect.

A split second later the outer door opened and everyone's attention turned to the newcomer. For just a moment the waves of light played over his face, as if it was a theater marquee.

"What the hell -- ?" The gravelly voice at the doorway was cool, despite the words.

Rome tried to stay alert, tried not to stare at anything but the crowd in front of him. But prickles rippled over his skin and the hair on the back of his neck rose.

The face had been revealed clearly in the eerie light. He knew that voice very well. He'd lived with that face and voice, night and day, in his dreams and wide awake.

He'd vowed when he left that he was never going to listen or dream about that voice again.

He'd lied to himself.

"Stay out of this, Grey." Rome jammed his elbow, hard, into the fool who thought he had a chance to take him off guard. The man crumpled to the floor, whimpering. "Stay out or take me on."

"Shit, boy." The new man took a step forward.

Rome whirled, adrenaline surging, and grabbed Grey by the collar.

"Didn't you hear me?"

They were almost mouth to mouth. Shit. Yeah, it was Grey all right. The same scars criss-crossing his face. The same scowl. Grey said people were put off by his scars. He'd even seriously thought Rome should be put off because Grey was older. But there was a hell of a lot more to him than some old wounds or grizzled hair. Ah, hell. Grey's scent was just as sexy as ever. His body was just as muscular, tough and potent. Rome swallowed, his throat suddenly going dry.

Grey barked out a short laugh. "You're getting mighty close for a fighting man. Do you want to fight me or fuck me?"

Both. Holy God, he wanted both.

"Why're you here?" Pushing Grey away, Rome kicked out, landing a blow right under the chin of the bartender, who had been inching toward his nightstick.

"To fetch you back, boy. We need you."

"Why?"

We need you, wasn't *I* need you. But then Grey wasn't much for telling folks what he wanted. Hadn't that been the problem? Grey's dumb ass, "I don't feel anything" act was why Rome had vowed he wasn't ever going back. And he wasn't.

Grey slammed the next would-be brawler onto the bar and then slid the unconscious man onto a bar stool, where he slumped, completely out for the count. "Well, like they said in another family, we've got a little proposition we don't think you can refuse."

He wasn't doing what Grey or the rest told him to do any more. But somehow Rome found himself inching out of the bar, when a few minutes ago all he'd wanted was to stay and fight. Grey was at his back -- protecting him? Herding him? -- both were possible. But neither of them bothered to say anything until they stepped out into the night air.

Then it seemed Grey had plenty to say.

"Shit, boy, haven't I told you to keep out of stupid damn brawls? I don't care if your wolf is up and you want to go howl. Fighting like that just isn't smart. Non-weres can get the best of us if there are enough of them. I'm proof of that. If it hadn't been for your Daddy -- "

"I know the lecture. How Dad saved you from death when you got into a fight where you were outnumbered. How I'm just a stupid pup with no sense. How you should never try to mess with anyone when the odds are bad. I've got it memorized." Rome threw his hand up in the air. "Now you need to ask me if I care."

"You're an idiot, Rome."

"I'm on my own now. All grown up and not listening to what my elders tell me. I'm not going back."

"You fucking well are. I promised."

"Ohh, because you promised. That's why. Be honest. You wouldn't give a damn if I did die in some damn fight. Good riddance, I'd finally stop bothering you. Right?"

Before he got his answer, lightning struck -- lights danced in front of his eyes before darkness slid, peacefully but inevitably, around him.

Grey spat once, flexed the fist that had knocked Rome out and looked down at the huddled heap in front of him. Damn, the boy had turned out handsome. Handsome as his daddy, but with his mama's pretty eyes.

Pretty boy. He'd never gone for pretty boys before. Non-weres would call Rome a twinkie. Weres didn't like things that sweet. They went for meat. Preferably raw. But damned if this twinkie wasn't tempting. Rome had been tempting him for years, in fact. When he wasn't getting Grey mad enough to do something like hit him.

Ah, hell. There was no way around it, no way to make little of Rome or ignore him. Rome wasn't just a pretty boy, even though he had the face of an angel. If he had been, Grey would never have looked twice. What he was remained to be seen.

The kid had a tongue on him, though. He could hone right in and make a man's head buzz.

You don't give a damn. Right?

Ask me if I care. Do I?

"Yup. I guess I forgot to ask if you cared." Grey hoisted Rome's dead weight over his shoulder and headed for his truck. "But then again, boy, you forgot the part about even when it looks safe, you still gotta keep your eyes open."

Chapter One

"I'm getting tired of stalling. If we have to play nice much longer, I'm going to forget myself and bite them."

Lin grinned at Leila. "Sorry, Mom. You wouldn't be all that effective seeing as you can't change. Maybe you should ask one of the pack."

"Oh, shush, smart mouth." Leila began to pace. "I can't help it if the rest of you get hairy and toothy during the full moon."

"Weres rule, humans drool."

Lin's mother swatted her after that response. The rest of the group didn't crack a smile.

"This strange pack isn't going to wait forever. I've been doing some investigating. They're not known for playing nice but apparently they're willing to try because they badly want a breeding female." Lowell tapped his finger on the chair's arm rest. "If we cross them, however, I wonder how long they'll stay pleasant?"

"Maybe they know your rep as well and don't want to challenge you." Lin hopped onto the arm of Lowell's chair to hug her mate.

Lowell shrugged. "Whatever. I appreciate your support, Dek and Leila, but this is about an offer for someone within my pack. You may boss your own pack but neither of you are Alpha here. It's my problem. My pack and my problem."

Mia froze.

And it's about me. Not that anyone has checked for my opinion lately. Then again, I'm just the omega. The omega who happens to be a breeding female. And we have a pack desperate enough to consider having a non-alpha for breeding. A pack desperate enough to make a formal offer for me.

She glanced over at the alphas in the room and reminded herself to keep her mouth shut. Over the years Mia had come to like and respect not only her alphas, but also the alphas of the neighboring pack, who happened to be her mistress' parents. That didn't mean she felt comfortable speaking up when they were meeting.

"It's not necessarily all your problem." Leila looked at Dek, who nodded agreement. "We have a proposition to make. One that might solve both our problems."

"What problem?"

"Our own breeding issues. What if you tell the outsider weres that you've already accepted an offer from our pack for Mia?"

Mia let out a small, surprised yelp.

"Who do you have to mate -- ?" Lowell glanced at Dek and hastily turned his eyes back to Leila. Definitely not Dek.

Everyone knew that Dek and Leila were thoroughly bound to each other.

"Rome left you months ago. No one knows where he is. Besides, I thought he had the same -- uh, fertility problems -- that I have. He is my brother, after all." Lin spoke calmly, but her jaw was clenched.

Mia had figured out that Lin wasn't going to be having any children for their pack. Everyone knew it wasn't for lack of trying on Lowell and Lin's part -- good Lord, trying wasn't the term for what the two of them had been up to for the past six years. But six years was a long time.

"No, not Rome." Leila shook her head.

Lin continued, "We would have accepted a formal offer from you years ago but you have the same problem that we do. There's no one. Our pack has Lowell -- "

" -- who would rather not have his balls removed for trying anything with anyone but his mate, thank you -- " Lowell smiled, briefly.

" -- and Oscar and his mate, who are just as bound as Lowell and I are."

And just as infertile. Two beta males who bonded with each other didn't upset pack dynamics, but they'd never produce children.

Mia swallowed. Both their packs were so small. Too small. Lowell and Lin had Oscar, his bondmate, Enrique, and her. Leila and Dek once had Rome in their pack but he left after the fight with Grey --

Mia, probably because she had the most at stake, saw it first. The idea was so stunning that she actually spoke up without permission before all four of them. "Grey? You're offering *Grey*?"

* * *

"Grey, you fucking asshole." The words might have sounded more forceful if they hadn't ended in a hiss. "What the hell was that sucker punch for?"

Grey handed him some aspirin and a glass of water. "Just a love tap, boy, to remind you I still care."

There was a brief pang of relief when the younger man swung his body up from the bed and grabbed for what Gray held out. Rome had been lying so still on the motel bed, breathing so heavily...

"Bull." Rome gulped the medicine and the liquid with his eyes shut. "You never gave a damn about me. Do you think I'm going to forget about the last night we were together?"

Gray sure as hell hadn't.

"We were never together, Rome."

"We might not have had sex -- well, technically -- but we damn well were together."

"You were too fucking young. And you're still too fucking young for me. You're not even twenty, for God's sake!" Grey heard himself yelling. Damn it! He was known for keeping calm. When did all that half-concerned, cool amusement vanish? How the hell did this pup get under his skin? No one had done that for years.

No one but Rome. Shit, the boy had inherited some gene that let him zero right in and gnaw at a man. Got it from both his parents, most likely. Damn Rome's whole family. I'm an idiot for putting up with the pack of them all these years.

Decades.

Decades of wanting. First Rome's daddy and then him. Knowing he couldn't have either of them for real. Knowing it was wrong and stupid and futile to feel that way.

"You're wrong. Wrong about us," Rome whispered.

Wanting.

Just like the want he saw in Rome's eyes, now that they were open and looking straight at him. Still. Rome wanted him that bad still. No one had ever had that look for him. Just him. A burn rose up in Grey's throat, almost stopping his speech. He got the words out anyhow.

"I hurt you once. I figured you'd get over it."

"Oh, I did. Licked my wounds -- and someone else -- after I crawled away from your bed that night. I didn't die from you saying no, Grey. In fact, I've done just fine on my own and with other people, both in and out of bed." Rome's lips twisted. "But I knew then and I know now that we could have built up something even better together. We should have. It was your stubbornness, your blindness that spoiled it."

"Maybe it just delayed things a mite."

Rome didn't answer. Grey couldn't blame him. He didn't know what to say himself to that last sentence.

"What does that mean?" Rome sounded shakier now than he had when he first came to.

"Why don't you take your pants off and find out?" Hell. He really hadn't meant to say that out loud.

"Don't try to shit me, Grey."

Then again, maybe he had meant it. His body hummed with excitement. What the hell did he have to lose? The kid was already angry with him for not having sex. What difference would sex make?

"Hey, where's all that sweet talk, boy? I'm giving in, letting you have your way with me. It was all 'I love you' when I wouldn't put out." Grey unbuttoned his shirt. "Are you telling me you won't respect me in the morning?"

He heard a shaky sigh.

"Unbutton your pants, too, Grey, and I'll bet I respect you a hell of a lot. I remember the monster inside there."

"It remembers you, too, boy." His cock stiffened, as if in agreement.

"Rome. Call me Rome, damn it, not boy."

"Then let me see what kind of man you are."

It was a wonder Rome didn't rip his pants, he got them off so fast. Grey would have smiled, but when all the blood in your body was rushing to your cock, it was kind of difficult to remember how. The kid didn't bother to pace himself, just tore his clothes off and let Grey see.

God. Damn. It.

The body was as perfect as his damn face. This was no kid. Rome was a man. Hard muscles, furred chest, tight ass. Rome's cock was already jutting out in excitement. Oh, yeah. He was just as tasty as Grey had imagined in his fantasies.

Grey stopped, pants halfway down his legs and said, "Suck me off."

"We've been there before." But Rome's eyes were shining. "You better plan to go a little further than that tonight. Or are you going to back off again, old man?"

"Your ass is going to know where I've been soon enough. But I want your mouth right now." Those full lips and those teeth with just the slightest overbite. That freaking agile tongue, longer than any non-were's. God, yes. They both wanted it, no matter what might be said out loud.

Rome was on his knees and drawing Grey's leaking cock inside almost before Grey had told him what to do, the kid's cheeks already hollowing out as he began the suction. Oh yeah, this boy knew how to suck cock.

Grey clenched his hands into fists, fighting the urge to spew right then, right into that clever mouth. It had been too long since Rome had done that and it had ended too abruptly.

"Jesus, don't tell me to stop this time, Grey. Don't." Rome murmured the words against Grey's aching shaft. Grey shuddered, holding onto Rome's shoulders before he slid to the floor.

"You can bet I won't. We're not stopping until we're both dripping wet, cross-eyed and face down on the floor." Grey loosened his grip long enough to transfer it into Rome's too long hair. He thrust hard into Rome's mouth and that mouth let him in. Harder, longer, faster. He thrust deeper than he had in years with any of his partners.

Grey was too damn big for most people and he'd learned to be considerate. Fuck consideration this time. He finally had a partner who knew how to match him. Rome was already making him forget everything but the animal that wanted more.

And Rome was giving him more.

Jesus, he was buried to his balls, with Rome's lips still wrapped around his cock. And the kid was murmuring approval and making things feel too damn good...

"Shit. Not. Yet." Grey forced himself to stop.

"You'd better be planning to finish this or -- "

"Or what?" Grey didn't wait for the answer. "Get on your hands and knees. I want your ass bad."

He was damn tempted to jerk himself off as he watched Rome obey him. What could be sexier than seeing a man get ready for his cock? Especially this particular male. But he wanted to finish off inside Rome this time.

God, what a pretty ass. And it was presented to him without an argument, just the way he'd asked. That was prettier yet. The kid had positioned himself on the bed in front of the yellowed motel mirror. So Rome wanted to watch? Grey realized his fingers were shaking as he spread lube into that tight hole. God, he better not fuck up in front of an audience. He didn't think it was possible, though. If this turned out half as good for Rome as it was for Grey right now --

Grey didn't finish the thought. He couldn't. He knew he couldn't enter Rome immediately. Not if he wanted Rome begging for him. It would be over too fast. So he thrust one finger in and smiled, a tight grin, when Rome twitched against his hand. He used two fingers then, scissoring against Rome's passageway and then three, grinding his palm against Rome's ass.

Rome whimpered, a heart-felt wail, and abruptly stopped.

"What the fuck?" Grey'd meant to drag things out as long as he could, make Rome want it, remember it, crave it.

Crave him.

"I'm not -- " Rome cut the words off as if they were strangling in his throat.

"You're not what?"

Not interested? Shit. Grey almost whimpered himself.

"I'm not -- begging. I won't. Not this time. Oh Jesus, Grey." Rome backed against his hand. "Maybe I am. Just fucking do me."

That was it. Screw foreplay. Grey had just enough control to enter slowly. Carefully. He needed care. How much experience could the kid have? He'd been a virgin when he came to Grey first, begging for what he hadn't known.

Yeah, the kid remembered last time as well as Grey did. Rome had pleaded and wailed and, oh God, he'd been so sexy doing it...

It had almost been as sexy then as now and the feel of him as Grey entered that narrow little hole. Jesus, it clasped him already, ready to clamp down.

I want you. I want you to be the first. The only, for as long as you want me. Grey, you won't be sorry.

He hit the tight muscle ringing the passage inside and paused.

"Grey!" Rome sounded lost, panicky.

If he stopped now, he'd die. Combust and die. But Grey couldn't hurt this fallen angel lover of his. He'd go slower even if it killed him. *Madre de Dios.*

Hell. He hadn't thought in Spanish for years. Not unless he was close to losing *it. Slower. He had to go slower. Count to himself.*

Uno.

"Yeah?"

Dos.

"It's so good. I never knew it could be this...good." Rome thrust back, the mirrored image showing his face contorted with lust. And when he impaled himself on Grey's cock, his mouth went slack with satisfaction.

That was when Grey lost it. Lust hazed his sight. He knew friction against his cock, tight and perfect. Heat roared through his body. Howls. Pleasure. More than pleasure.

Grey's teeth sunk hard into Rome's neck, claiming him the way weres did. He could think about why he was making a claim later. Much later. Right now all he could think of was yielding flesh. He shook Rome's neck and growled possessively, low in his throat.

"Oh God, Grey, I'm coming!"

Warm spunk flooded over Grey's hands from where he was gripping his partner's cock and stomach. Damn it, that was perfect -- his lover's come flowing over his hands and then onto Rome's body, seemingly forever. He heard Rome's guttural sounds of pleasure as he shook underneath him and Grey got set to milk every last drop.

Rome bent and managed to lick Grey's arm, the way a mate did to show submission. Trust. Love.

"Oh, *fuck.*"

Grey's last remaining control snapped and his climax roared through him like a fireball, exploding through his body and into Rome's.

* * * *

"Why not just artificial insemination?" Mia hoped she didn't sound desperate.

"We thought of that ourselves." Lin looked briefly at her mate. "We don't know if it would work. But even if it did, weres mate and bond for a reason. Even if this isn't quite -- usual -- you still need a strong male to protect you and the baby. Who feels some bond toward you. It's dangerous out there for a pregnant were. Or one with a small child to care for."

"It's dangerous for any female alone with a baby, were or not. I've been there." Leila put her hand on Mia's shoulder. "I know this seems like we're pushing you into something that isn't at all usual, but we do care about you. We want you safe, Mia."

"But you care about the pack more." Mia couldn't keep the bitterness from her words. Damn, that was why she should never say anything. Words were too dangerous.

"We care about you and both our packs. This way the two packs would be united with another bloodkin tie between us."

Bloodkin. She had none left. At least none she would ever acknowledge. It was her bloodkin that had tried to destroy the two packs when she was a kid. Some packs would have turned her out or even killed her. But her pack had defended her, said she was one of their own and Dek's pack had agreed.

How could she forget what she owed them?

"I -- I can't handle Grey. He won't want me anyhow. He doesn't care about females."

"He cares about his duty to the pack."

"That's not going to -- to make him get it up!" Mia saw the men hastily hide grins. "I'm female. He's not interested."

"I have a plan -- " Leila began.

"So do I." Mia swallowed and fought against years of obedience. She fought against breaking her promise to Rome to say nothing. Nothing about the night he ran to her for comfort. Nothing about their feelings. But this was too important. She rushed the words out. "Get me Rome. Grey and he have always had something between them. And…and…"

"What?"

"And I've always wanted Rome. For a while, he wanted me too. Get me Rome and he'll get me Grey. This is one time when weres won't have a problem with sharing."

The rest of the room stared at her and she felt her cheeks heat.

Weres had no problems with sex. Almost any kind of sex. But asking for permission for a threesome from four alphas… Mia hid her face in her hands.

"Actually, my dear, that was my plan. You're sharp, even though you're so quiet." Leila patted her on the head. "Grey's orders are to fetch our lone wolf home. I expect Grey to be back here with Rome before we have time to blink."

Chapter Two

Mia crawled into bed, exhausted. This bedroom was her refuge and had been so for years. It was the same room she'd had ever since the pack had made El Paso their home base five years ago. But she was different now -- or she was supposed to be. She was an adult and soon her whole life was going to be different. Grey would bring Rome back. Grey always did what he said. And then...and then...

Things would be different. So different. In a way she was grateful something was staying the same in the middle of such promised upheaval. Nothing in her room had changed. Here were the same high school posters, the same paint. And the frightened thoughts skittering inside made her feel like the same terrified teenager who used to cower from the rest of the pack and hide here alone.

The window was open, letting in a slight breeze and almost dispelling the heat that had built up during the day. Mia stripped and lay on top of the covers. The forecasters had said there might be a storm brewing, but that was probably wishful thinking on their part. It probably got dull saying nothing but heat and sun all day, every day. El Paso weather rarely changed.

It was almost the way it had been when Rome showed up that night. She'd been itchy and nervous then, with no real reason for it. Maybe she'd smelled trouble ahead.

"Let me in, Mia."

"You know, when big bad wolves say that, you're supposed to lock the door. Then they blow you -- or at least your house."

"Not funny."

He hadn't been in were form then. Not exactly. But she could sense the feral quality in his stance. Even if there hadn't been The Change, something was different. He was different.

He smelled like sex.

He leaned against her window as if he might just come in whether she said yes or not. Because he knew it didn't matter what she said. He knew what she wanted.

Mia swallowed and realized she was going to let him inside the bedroom window, even though it was a stupid idea. The wrong idea. A bad idea -- he wriggled through the open screen the second she unlatched it.

Something about Rome always made her act a little adolescent. Maybe it was because they had been adolescents together. But tonight she was acting wilder than she'd ever let herself. First the blowing remark and then letting him see her like this...

Maybe it was the full moon.

He leaned against the wall, saying nothing.

"What?" She fought the urge to cross her arms over her chest as he looked her over. He was the one who had trespassed into her private room, not caring if she was dressed or not.

After that first long, assessing look, he smiled. A knowing smile. That gaze and that grin were so charged that it made the hair on the back of her neck stand up. If she'd thought she smelled sex when he was outside, the scent was doubly strong now.

Damn it, that just wasn't right. This was Rome. He might act superior to her, but among weres, they were equal. Equally low. He was an omega, just like she was -- at the bottom in the pack ranks. An omega didn't demand sex. An omega probably shouldn't even think about sex unless someone in the pack said to.

Even so, Rome smelled like sex and -- beer. Mia's nose wrinkled.

"Are you drunk, Rome?"

"Not enough, baby."

She would have left then, although it was her room and she was naked, but she realized there was something else Rome smelled like. Sex and alcohol and tears.

Oh no. It couldn't be. Rome was tough and macho. She might be tempted -- had always been a little tempted -- by the virile Rome. She'd always been able to resist that Rome. But this Rome? She'd always been a sucker for the injured.

Mia put her hand on Rome's shoulder, and he flinched, just slightly.

Definitely there had been tears.

"Who hurt you, Rome? What's wrong?"

"No one. Nothing."

"Stop being so manly for a minute. You came here for a reason. If you aren't going to talk, why bother?"

"What makes you think I came here to talk? And fuck it if I'm too manly for you." He looked down at the floor. "Maybe that was Grey's problem. I'm too manly. Or not enough."

His laugh sounded like a sob and, as if he realized it, Rome cut it off in the middle and took a deep breath instead.

"Grey?"

"I don't want to talk about Grey. I don't give a damn about Grey right now."

"I don't think that's true, Rome. I've always known how much you worshipped him." Mia could never figure out what anyone saw in that silent, rather menacing beta, but then he probably saw even less in her. He never even talked to her. Everyone knew he didn't give a damn about women.

Rome went back to staring at her, as intensely as before. "That's bull. I never worshipped anyone. Except -- well -- look at you, all stripped down and built like a goddess. I could worship you."

He might be avoiding the issue but it worked. Mia knew she was blushing. She liked to ignore her looks since they meant nothing. Omegas didn't mate. Omegas only had sex if the higher ups in the pack demanded it of them, but that wasn't an issue in this pack. Her looks didn't matter to anyone. In fact, lately she'd almost forgotten what she looked like -- which might be why she was here, defenseless in front of a hungry were who was definitely noticing her appearance.

"I look like a woman. What of it?"

Sex. The smell of sex strengthened. Mia licked her lips and tried to ease the dryness in her throat.

"What of it? Jesus, Mia, you've got breasts like a porno star's, except they're real." Rome came closer and Mia stiffened. He didn't touch. But the way he looked made her as itchy as if he had. "And your ass. That is one fine ass." He stopped and whispered, "I even like those big, big eyes of yours, staring at me like I'm going to gobble you up."

The big, bad wolf had definitely arrived tonight. Mia took a step backward and tried to rally. "You have the hots for Grey. I'm sorry if you two had a fight, but why run to me?"

She'd known. Rome might have fooled non-were girls -- and fooled around with them, too. But any were knew what Rome wanted as soon as he got in the room with Grey. The awareness of the older man's presence, the scent of arousal. It was very clear.

Rome didn't flinch this time. Instead he ran his tongue over his teeth, as if he were preparing for a meal. "What of it? I'm not some one-team fan. I definitely like women. And, Mia, you're right. You look like a real woman."

She'd always been a bit ashamed of how she'd developed. Her human change as an adult was almost as dramatic as her were change and sometimes even more bewildering. After all, a buxom blonde wasn't what she was like inside. She'd been scrawny as a kid, almost as thin as a boy. That suited her better.

But Rome's gaze was hot and carnal and admired the shape she was now. At that moment Mia wasn't ashamed of what she'd become. She deliberately straightened her shoulders and lifted her breasts. For the first time in forever she looked right back at a man, giving him a direct challenge back.

He was an omega, just like she was. But Romulous Kinkaid didn't let that stop him from being bold. Why should it stop her?

She turned off the nagging little voice that was ready to remind her why. The pulsing of her body kicked up a notch with every second that Rome kept looking at her and drowned out the old, scared Mia.

"How much do you like women, Rome?"

She'd wondered about him before. When the most gorgeous weres west of the Mississippi lived as close as Rome did, you wondered. He hadn't ever acknowledged her in particular. Not at high school, even when they were the only weres there. He might have looked her over then sometimes, she thought. Mia couldn't imagine why.

It wasn't just that they'd come from different were packs, even though the packs were friendlier than most. But they also had little in common except being were. Rome had been a grade behind her but she'd envied his assurance. Mia had always been afraid she might betray who she really was among the non-were. Not so Rome. There was no cowering for him. She'd faded into the hallways while Rome swaggered down them, oozing attitude and daring anyone to stop him.

No one did. No one dared. She didn't want to now.

"You want me to show you how much I like you, Mia?" His smile was as lethally assured as it had been when he was on the football team.

"You know, no one would ever take you for an Omega."

"That's because I'm not. I'm a lone wolf."

"My God!" Mia raised her hand to her lips to hide the gasp. "When did this happen?"

That was a life every pack member knew to avoid at all costs. The life of a lone wolf was dangerous, often violent, and usually all too short. It's what her brother had to become when he'd been punished and exiled. No one had heard of him again.

"Tonight. As of tonight I don't belong to anyone." Rome didn't look afraid, but she saw the pulse hammer in his throat. She could sense the emotions roiling inside him.

Fear? Regret? Desire? All of that and more. Rome had feelings all right, just waiting to leap out if someone wanted to let them free.

What about belonging to me?

Mia bit her tongue, the need to ask that very wrong question was so great. Then she yelped at the pain of the bite. Her teeth were lengthening, sharpening -- she was close to The Change. Dear Lord, Rome was exciting her enough to make her turn were.

"What about being with me?" That was Rome's voice, almost echoing her thoughts. "For tonight?"

That was almost, but not quite what she'd been thinking.

Rome kissed her and she forgot everything else. She put her arms around him. "Close enough. Staying with you tonight sounds...fine."

When he bit into the sinews at her neck and shoulder, she growled.

She was the one who ripped his shirt off. After that she wasn't quite sure how the rest of his clothes were shucked, but he was naked and hot and urgent against her skin and she didn't care about anything more except having him inside her.

A sudden, unexpected breeze blew through the room, letting the wind brush against their bodies. She shivered and spread her thighs.

"You're beautiful, Mia."

"You're saying that because you want to have sex," Mia said the words accusingly, but she knew it didn't matter. Even though she hadn't changed form in front of him, she was achingly aware of being were right now. She didn't care why he'd said those words. He didn't have to say anything. She wanted sex, too. More than anything else in the world. He'd managed that when he first showed up at her window.

"I want to have sex and you're beautiful. Jesus God, who wouldn't want to have sex with a goddess?" His voice softened. "Who wouldn't want to have sex with you?"

She almost cried. How had he known the right words? Those were the ones that made her reach over, take his thick cock and guide him home.

They were both trembling. Hot and sweet. Not as fast as she'd thought would happen. Not as fierce. Slow and tender and gentle. As if they both cared. As if they both had forever and ever.

His hands skimmed over her skin. She nuzzled against the softness of his throat. And he edged in slowly, slowly, filling her. Gentling her as he took possession of her body.

"Ah, Mia."

Rome claimed her and she surrendered. He kissed her tears away -- the ones of joy and the ones of hurt, because even though he was gentle, she was a virgin.

"I don't want to hurt you ever, love." He whispered it against her ear and she believed him.

There wasn't hurt then, only slick wetness and delight that built inside her. At first her body was hesitant, awkward. Rome moved against her, the bump of their bodies changing from a slow dance to a hot beat. The friction that hurt at first edged slowly into deep, dark pleasure.

And the pleasure built higher yet as he licked her flesh and his fingers glided across her skin. She was wet and panting by then. And the pleasure built, built until it burst. She screamed and cried out in the darkness of the night. The pain and the fear had long since left, and soon even the frenzy of want disappeared in a warm wave of sated pleasure.

There were no tears when she came.

There were no tears during that night while the full moon bathed them and Rome woke her up to send her up into the glittering stars with his fingers and tongue.

The morning was different.

Her tears came when she woke up, the hot sun in her eyes dazzling her, but not so much that she couldn't see he had left the way he arrived, through the open window, without a sound.

Chapter Three

"God damn it!" Grey roared the words but knew the woman in front of him wasn't going to even blink. "You know me. Why're you asking me to do this?"

Except it wasn't asking. It was an order. Women didn't give in when they wanted something. Even something as insane as this.

He'd known this woman for years. She was his alpha, his mistress, his boss. They both knew he'd have to give in.

But this was lunacy.

"Leila. It's not going to work. You have to know that." He tried. He tried to sound reasonable and submissive at the same time.

There was no flicker of give in Leila's expression or her voice. "It has to."

He wanted to howl. He wanted to snarl.

When he'd brought Rome back, it had been like bringing him home to the family. He'd thought he was only bringing him home to the family. Rome had sulked, but Grey hadn't cared. With the kid by his side in the truck, everything had felt so damn right again. Back to the way things used to be, but better. Much better. He hadn't quite gotten there yet, but Grey figured somehow he'd find the words to explain to them all how things were between Rome and him. When they reached the ranch, Grey had almost swept the younger were up in his arms and carried him over the threshold.

But Rome wasn't going to be the bride. Mia was.

There were no words to explain that at all.

"You can still have Rome." His designated bride said, very softly.

That was supposed to make things all right again? She was insane, too.

"Jesus. You're all willing to use the kid as...bait? A sweetener for the deal?"

Mia shrank back as if he'd planned to hit her.

Grey looked at his balled up fists and realized she might have reason to worry. He forced himself to relax his hands. Relax his shoulders. He'd try reason again.

Grey used his calmest tones. "This whole set up isn't right. It's not fair to Rome -- "

"It's fine, Grey. I don't -- mind."

Grey swung around and stared at the idiot behind him. Rome couldn't have said what Grey thought he just did.

"Are you crazy, too?" Grey forgot about the calm tone. "You're the one who kept telling me you didn't want to go back, you'd never return to pack life and now that you're being ordered to be some kind of -- some sex toy for me to get it up…"

And he wasn't going to get hard at just the concept.

"Well, yeah. There is that. But I don't mind." There was almost a smile on Rome's face. "Really. And you're only partway right. I wouldn't be just your toy. I'd be Mia's sex toy, too."

He didn't want to think about the images that reeled around in his mind after Rome spoke. Or the looks on his alphas' faces.

"And we'd be his toys, too." Mia spoke up again, warily waiting for Grey's reaction to her words. "Don't you get it? Rome wants us both. He doesn't want any ties to the pack any more. This way he can do and get everything he wants. Everything."

Everything encompassed a lot with someone like Rome. The younger were had either spent a long time studying the Kama Sutra or he'd been on a sexual odyssey that boggled the mind in the few months since he'd left the pack. Oh, shit. Grey was getting hard now thinking about just what might have happened.

He ignored his damn cock and said, "This is never going to work."

Rome shook his head at Grey right before he walked over to Mia, put his hands on her shoulders and smiled into her eyes.

The damn flirt. What did he have in mind? Then again maybe Grey didn't want to know. He had lived with

Romulous long enough to know the kid's mind worked fast and twisted.

"Shut up, Grey. *I'm* going to make it work. It's going to be damn good for you, babe." He turned and looked at Grey and winked. Freaking winked. "It's going to be good for you, too, Grey. Real good. I promise."

Grey was tempted to smack Rome upside the head again. Or wrestle him to the floor and show him and everyone else how they made things good.

And it wouldn't take a damned woman to make it that way.

This is never going to work.

Mia wanted to scream the words but she couldn't even make a squeak. This had been her idea. Hers and the other females of both packs. But now she was sure it had been another bad idea. She'd been coming up with some stinkers lately.

And how was she supposed to act? How were they supposed to act? There were rules. Rules about bonded pairs. Rules for humans. But this wasn't a bonding or a wedding.

She wasn't even in her own room, where she might have been more comfortable. Everyone had decided they should "meet" -- nice word -- at Dek's and Leila's ranch. So here she was, standing in the kitchen, all alone in an empty, rambling house wondering what she should do. Stand in the living room and wait until the terrible two decided to make an appearance? Find a bedroom and strip?

She poured water in the kettle to make tea instead. Something calming. She wiped her hands on her jeans and tried to settle in.

Grey was ready to jump. Rome laid his hand, palm out, on the muscles of Grey's back. Grey tensed under his touch.

Rome fought his grin. One of the toughest men he knew was completely unnerved. And he'd probably take Rome apart with his bare hands rather than admit it.

"She's more worried than you are. Trust me. Mia is a good person. Sweet. It'll be fine."

Grey grunted. "Sweet and good? She belonged to that evil brood that tried to kidnap your sister and take over her pack."

"She couldn't pick what litter she came from. But back when they did that shit, she chose to help us, even though she was just a kid."

Grey didn't say anything more, but his scowl was ferocious.

"You'd think we were about to have another bar fight." Rome pushed open the front door.

"I'd rather."

Rome shrugged. He'd tried. He really had. There was nothing else for it.

He kicked the door shut behind him with his boot and whirled Grey up against the wall. As he unbuckled the belt of Grey's jeans, he could feel Grey's cock starting to straighten up and take an interest.

Rome ground himself against that cock as if he had paid for a quick ten minutes. Hard and nasty and hot. Grey gasped.

Rome swooped in and nipped at his lover's bottom lip. He took Grey's low growl as encouragement.

"I'm not always gonna be the bottom, Grey. You'll have to live with it." Rome growled when Grey bucked against him.

Gray looked like he could definitely live with it. He'd figured Grey was an equal opportunity partner. Betas knew how to take orders and Grey had been the beta in his pack for a long time.

Rome pulled the shirt out of Grey's pants and dove inside, fondling that killer cock a little roughly. Rough was the name of the game this time. Rome wasn't going to give Grey time to think.

Blind need roared up in him, the way it always did when he got his hands on this man. Feel. That was all they needed to do now. Just feel and go by instinct.

Rome pulled Grey's pants down and began to jerk him off. It didn't take long before that big cock was full and hard, dripping with liquid precum.

"This is just the start, old man," Rome said between his teeth.

The door slammed and she jumped. The tea slopped over the edge of the mug and onto her hand. She hissed and sucked on the red spot, waiting.

There was the rumbling murmur of male voices and then nothing.

What was wrong with those men? They weren't even going to acknowledge she was there? Mia stalked toward the front door, scowling, and stopped short.

Right there in the front hall. My God.

Rome had Grey pinned against the wall and Grey had his eyes shut, his neck bent backward. She could hear him gulp as he thudded against the picture frame that already hung at a crazy angle above his head.

They grappled and if you didn't notice their clothes were half-off, you might think they were wrestling. The muscles on Rome's back flexed with effort and then he surged forward again in a quick, harsh rhythm. Grey's hand gripped his shoulder as he grunted.

Mia swallowed. She could feel a slow burn rising up from her pussy, spreading through her body.

So primal. So strong. So…beautiful.

And she'd never be part of what those two felt. She was outside, looking in yet again. The heat that had warmed her chilled in a moment.

Rome turned. His eyes glinted. "Well, look at the little were with the big eyes."

She tried not to stare at his erection but -- dear Lord, there were two of them, huge and hard to miss. The heads were flushed dark and they stood erect, full of life and power. How could you help but stare?

Rome slipped something glittering and small onto Grey's cock.

"What the hell do you think you're doing, you little pervert?" Mia jumped at Grey's gravelly voice but Rome just snorted.

"You'll be down on your knees praising God that I am one in a bit. Or at least down on your knees. That little contraption is going to make sure you keep it up, Grey."

"And he sure is up." Mia clapped both hands over her mouth as Rome roared with laughter and stalked toward her.

"Damn it, I do love you, Mia. I missed you."

Not enough to come back unless Grey dragged you here by the scruff of the neck. But Mia didn't say that. What was the point? That would spoil...that would spoil whatever happened next. She was beginning to want what happened next quite desperately.

As if she got a reward for her discretion, Rome lifted her as tenderly as someone might lift a small child -- more tenderly than she'd ever been carried, even when young -- and placed her between the two of them.

"I think it's time, Grey." Rome kissed her, just a whisper of a kiss.

"Oh, Jesus. Maybe I should have had a couple of beers first."

The near-terror in Grey's voice softened the fear in Mia. She wasn't ever going to think of that tough wolf as wounded but...but he wasn't quite himself right now. She could tell that.

She found herself patting him on the shoulder. Then she froze when he glared at her. Oops. This wasn't a stray needing comfort. It was stupid of her to forget that.

"Sorry."

"Oh no, baby. Don't be sorry about petting. Grey likes it." Rome told her. Grey snarled.

"Oh, yeah. Right. Of course. I can see that." Mia tried to smile.

"He'll learn to like it. Trust me." Rome flicked her cheek. "We're all going to learn to like a lot of things. But why don't you try something he likes even more?"

She frowned in puzzlement and then clued in. There was definitely a nasty were side to her because once she realized what Rome meant, every muscle inside her clenched. She'd already been hot. Now she was combustible. Her nipples were tight. Her breathing quickened. Oh, yes. She wanted to. She wanted what would happen. She wanted everything.

Shaky, she dropped to her knees and licked.

Grey's cock was different from Rome's. But not a bad different. They were both exciting. She ran her tongue along the length of his shaft, experimentally.

He tasted different. He smelled different. But still good. Still male. Not Rome this time, but Grey.

Grey, who was going to put this cock inside her, whether he liked it or not.

His cock jumped against her cheek and she chuckled, softly.

He'd like it. She was taking this as a challenge. A very direct, up front challenge. She sucked the tip of his cock and he thrust forward, hard, into her mouth.

"Are you ready?"

Rome had moved behind Grey. His voice wavered for a moment -- with anticipation? Mia didn't know.

She also didn't know if Rome meant her or Grey. It didn't matter. Grey's body moved, accepted Rome's entrance inside. She could feel Grey's muscles tighten and relax as Rome penetrated him. In turn, her mouth tightened around Grey's cock, exploring the alien metal encircling him. Cool metal and hot, hard muscle.

Grey's body jerked as if electrified.

"Rome, stop it, you fucker...fuck, oh fuck, oh *fuck*...that feels sooo..." Grey's voice caught.

"He can't talk." Rome was panting, but coherent. "That's good. That's really good. Now, Mia. Now."

They weren't bonded so she couldn't read Rome's mind, but she didn't need to. They all knew what was needed. What they all wanted. She stood and positioned herself. Grey's eyes opened. His jaw was clenched hard and his eyes looked wild. This was how he must look right before The Change. Before the wolf took over and the animal burst free.

Mia smiled into those eyes and for a moment he focused on her. Oh, yeah. He was tough, but no one was that tough. He was hungry. Too hungry to resist her. She gripped his hips and Rome's hands slid over hers. The three of them were locked together for one frozen moment, unmoving.

Here we go.

Grey shut his eyes again and plunged into her, hard. The frozen moment exploded into motion. Rome rocked against Grey's back and Grey pushed into her.

"Oh my God," Mia gasped. She hadn't expected anything like this -- anything so --

Amazing. Hot. Rough. Overwhelming. She grabbed for Grey's sweat slicked shoulders with one hand and then nudged against Rome's hard abdomen with the other. She was slipping, falling into a need that radiated out from the core of her.

Ohhh.

"I can't hold on -- " Rome gasped. "Oh, Jesus."

His hand fumbled, pulling Grey half out of Mia. She gasped a wordless protest even while Rome grasped Grey's cock.

There was a clink of metal on the floor, then Rome plunged hard into Grey and Grey slammed into her. They moved together, gasping, cursing, body falling against body.

Pleasure heated into explosion.

Mia squeezed her vaginal walls tight, tore into Grey's shoulders with her nails. Rome's lungs whistled for air against Grey's back. Grey groaned and swayed between the two of them as if they were fighting for his body in a wordless, unacknowledged tug of war.

They all howled together.

Rome recovered first, of course. He slowly disengaged himself from where the tangled pile of exhausted bodies had ended on the floor and got to his knees. Grey opened one eye to watch Rome give a long, slow stretch of his body before the kid put his face close to Grey's.

"So what was it like for you -- doing both of us? Doing Mia?"

"I don't want to talk about it." Grey didn't know what to say.

Even worse, he didn't know what he thought about it. Sex with Rome had been great. The kid always rang his bell, no matter what they did. Sex with Mia was...different. He was afraid to think beyond that.

"I think he's embarrassed." Rome's eyes sparkled with mischief. "Trust me, Grey. A few more times with Mia and when you think about it at all, you'll wonder why you passed on women all these years."

"Hmm. Do you really think he's embarrassed? He looks too pleased with himself for that." Mia looked demure but Grey didn't believe the prim façade for a minute.

"Yeah. See that blush? We need to relax him. Make him loosen up." Rome stood up, staggered just a little, and leaned against the kitchen counter. "Whew. You two know how to take it out of a guy."

For a minute Grey couldn't remember how the hell they had made it into the kitchen. He stared up at Rome. No. No matter how he tried, all Grey could remember was heat and motion and mind-numbing pleasurable sensation. They could have moved through the entire house and he wouldn't have noticed.

Rome fished out a banana from the kitchen fruit bowl and gently slid three fourths of it down his throat. Mia raised an eyebrow and then lifted up one hand. Rome pulled her up with one easy motion.

Grey decided staying on the floor until his head and body stopped spinning left him at too big a disadvantage so he got up, shaking his head like he'd just gotten out of deep water.

"Deep throating a fruit? How…obvious." Mia went to the refrigerator to take out a box of ice cream. She scooped a generous portion into a cone.

She'd want to talk about it, of course. Women were even worse than Rome for talking and Rome was bad enough.

Mia cleared her throat and both men turned toward her. Grey braced himself.

Mia smiled, before daintily taking one lick of the ice cream cone in her hand. "Now this is delicious. A nice, subtle flavor to it."

There was a smothered snicker from Rome.

"Guys are crude, babe. And visual." Rome swallowed again, taking another few inches of fruit down his throat.

Grey looked at one grinning were and then the other. "You two are beyond crude. You're freakin' perverted."

Mia slurped her dessert this time. Rome began to peel another banana.

"Want some, Grey?" Rome offered. "There's plenty more where that came from. You probably need to keep your energy levels up."

"Sick and not ashamed of it," Grey growled.

"Maybe Grey would prefer to see…a cucumber." Mia leaned against the counter and tilted her head back to catch a stray spill of her confection. Rome snorted.

There wasn't going to be any deep, meaningful conversation after all?

"You're sick and I'm getting hungry. I don't think I can wait until dinner." Grey gave in and laughed, taking Rome by the hips to grind against him.

Mia laughed, too, ignoring the slight twinge in her chest as Rome molded himself against Grey. Of course Grey would pick Rome. Of course --

Grey's hand snaked out so fast she didn't have time to evade him. He pulled her tightly against the two writhing bodies, turned and frenched her. Hard. Deep. Lingering.

The twinge in her chest changed into a pounding excitement. The feel of Grey's tongue and then Rome pulling her even tighter against their hips --

Mia said, "I guess we are crude. And freakin' perverted."

"When are you two going to learn I'm always right?" Grey muttered the question against her hair.

He was horny as hell and still laughing. When had that last happened to him? Grey couldn't remember when. Not even when he was as young as the pair surrounding him. Jesus, the feel of them pressing against him with their hot bodies made him want to snicker and fuck them both into oblivion.

Truth was he'd never been this way. When he was their age he'd been healing from the wounds he'd received in a damn fight, hiding himself from others' pity. And falling in unrequited love with an alpha.

"I think chocolate sauce would be really tasty," Mia said. "Mmmm. Right here." She licked the pulse of his throat and Grey bit back a moan.

She was soft against him. He hadn't ever wanted soft. Hadn't trusted soft. Women were tricky. All gentle on the outside and cruel on the inside. That's what he'd learned as a kid, hiding from those so-called foster mothers of his. He shouldn't think this one was any different. Mia's mother hadn't even bothered with the gentle on the outside. Her mother had been pure nasty until the day she was put down. God knows Mia's brother had learned what bad tricks he could from the evil bitch. Luckily he'd been too stupid to become more than a nasty lout.

He should keep on guard with someone who had that heritage to live up to.

But Mia…no, he'd never felt like this about any woman. He wasn't even sure what *this* was. Except somehow she was part of Rome and him and sex. And the laughter. And Rome, damn him, was probably right about how he'd feel toward this particular female.

How he felt about her already.

Rome was tickling the inside of his thigh.

"Sex on the kitchen table, anyone?" Rome gasped the words. "Jesus, everyone. Sex. Please. Hurry."

Damn it, just looking at Rome's face, all tight with need and lust, made Grey want to come like a teenager.

Jesus, that was what had happened. He was turning into a kid again. A different kid this time. One that trusted, laughed. Got sex when he wanted it. He didn't understand why either of them had agreed to this. He couldn't figure out why it had worked so far. He didn't care.

A kid didn't need to think ahead.

Grey bit Mia's shoulder and then grabbed Rome by the hair and dragged him to the table, straddling him. "Fine. Dessert first and dinner after, since you begged so nicely."

Mia's laugh mingled perfectly with Rome's curse.

Chapter Four

"They're trying to trick us. Lie to us." Dunne looked over at the slighter man who hunched over the table, smoking. "We played fair with them. Why would they do that?"

"They're bastards." The other man crushed out the cigarette but stayed hunched. "All of them."

"But you sent us to them."

"They killed my father and mother and messed me up." Absently, the man rubbed the rough patch on his face and then his arm. "They have my sister. She's all I have left. I don't want her with them."

Dunne snorted. "Right. All you have left is your sister and you'd sell her to us."

"I didn't say I cared about Mia." The visitor laughed, soundlessly. "She stayed, didn't she? With them. She picked them over me."

Dunne mentally crossed Rossi off his list of conversational partners for the next few minutes. Rossi wasn't important, even when he was on an irrational rant. Rossi's sister was. There weren't enough female weres around to be choosy and this one was prime. Good-looking, submissive and the right age for breeding. What more could his Alpha need?

Maybe cooperation from the girl's pack. They'd been courteous enough but somehow they never said yes or no. Eventually Dunne realized it didn't matter what they did say. The girl never materialized. But his weres had been put on the alert. They'd seen her taken to another pack's den. Apparently their legitimate offer had been rejected without the courtesy of a reply.

Dunne kept himself from fidgeting with his napkin. He wasn't nervous or impatient, and even if he was lying to himself, he wasn't going to show it in front of this low life. He'd get the female. Now they'd have to use other methods, less gentle ones. That could be arranged.

Maybe she wasn't as virginal now as his Alpha had first wanted, but she was still ready for breeding. Hunt was a reasonable guy. He wouldn't be happy but he'd accept that he'd get what he needed, if not everything he had wanted.

Dunne swallowed. It was his own damn stupid problem that he wanted so badly to please Hunt. To make things perfect for him.

He cut into Rossi's droning whine. "Yeah, fine. The two packs are both filled with curs. Now tell me something more useful about them. Every detail. If they aren't going to help, I need to know their weaknesses. I need to know their strengths. I need to figure out how I'm going to get your sister Mia away from them."

* * *

He slipped behind her in the near-darkness of dawn and hunkered down, not quite touching, not quite close. The porch stairs creaked as they accepted his shifting weight.

"Hello, Grey." Mia clutched the warm mug, letting the steam pour over her face. The morning air outside was still chilly.

She'd known he would be the first to check on her after the orgy last evening.

"Hello. How are you feeling this morning?"

She'd known, too, his voice would be hesitant, even though he had been quick to see she was all right.

Was she all right? What had they done yesterday? Something more than uninhibited sex. She didn't have a name for it. She was afraid to have a name for it.

"A little sore. A little…confused." That was as good a word as any for her feelings.

"Yeah." With a slow, easy motion he rose and walked away from her.

Alone. She hadn't felt alone until he joined her. She'd been the way she'd always been. He and Rome -- they were changing things.

Was that good? Bad?

She didn't know.

She wasn't even sure if she was glad or not when he returned with a mug of coffee for himself and settled next to her once again. They sat together, silently.

"Do you -- " She cleared her throat.

"I've heard -- " He began and stopped.

"Go ahead." She bit off the nervous laugh. "I didn't have anything important to say."

"I've heard some packs let betas have mates. Have children." His eyes were holding steady on her but she wouldn't look. "It's just that out here, there are so few of us. So few women. I've only heard it was possible, never actually seen such a pack."

"What are you getting at, Grey?" Mia traced the rim of the mug. "I never heard of you wanting a woman. Or children."

"I haven't. I don't. Exactly." When his hand touched her side, she jumped. "I'm sorry."

Ridiculous. After all the things they'd done to each other in some were lust-induced madness, it was stupid to be so nervous because his fingers skimmed her hip. Mia forced herself to smile. Relax her muscles.

"No, I am. I'm being stupid."

"Maybe." He almost smiled. She could see it in his eyes as they warmed. "I just started wondering, probably the same as you, about what happens now. If you are pregnant."

"I might be." Mia looked down at her stomach. "Rome and his family figure he can't get any were pregnant. So if I was -- "

He knew that. They all knew it. That was why he was here, wasn't he? Why she was letting him do all those incredible things to her. At least that had been the reason.

His hand, huge and brown and callused, slipped over her stomach. Rested there.

"I do want children. I never thought it was possible, so I never let myself imagine it. But -- " he stopped.

They stared at the hand against her jeans.

"You've got big hands." Mia laughed, no longer nervous. "I didn't mean that as a comment about your other…parts…though they're big too. But your hand is almost as long as a new baby."

"God." He breathed the word out, staring hard at his hand.

"I'm scared about having a baby, Grey. About everything that's happening." Mia let herself admit it. This Grey, the Grey she was discovering, would understand.

"Me, too." He moved his hand away, the faint warmth still lingering. "Guess we'll be scared together."

Will we? Mia wasn't so sure they had a together. There was more than the two of them. She'd wanted Rome first and been willing to put up with Grey. But more than she or Grey -- or Rome or a baby -- was involved. This had been meant to help two packs.

"Grey -- "

Rome's arrival was noisier than Grey's. The door banged open and he stumbled out, his hair still standing up and stubble on his face. Mia smiled. You couldn't help but smile at Rome.

"Coffee?" Rome's face was innocent as a baby's and as hopeful.

Grey handed him his untouched mug. Rome took a large swig and sighed with satisfaction. "Perfect."

Mia stood up. "No need for you to go fetch another, Grey. This time I'll fix one. Like someone else could have done for himself."

She moved back into the kitchen. Rome smiled sleepily at Grey. "You trying to spoil me?"

"Can't do what's already been done." Grey heard the soft sounds of a woman puttering in the kitchen. "The coffee was almost gone. She's making more."

Just for him. When was the last time anyone had done that?

"You spoiled me and she's spoiling you." Rome's smile broadened. "This is going to work out, isn't it."

There seemed no question in Rome's mind about the outcome but he was young. Grey wanted to believe, but he'd been around too long to have the same certainty that life would work, that the future was meant to be good.

Grey shrugged. "It's a risk. No way to know if we can pull it off."

"But now you want it to work. That's a hell of a lot more than we had going before yesterday."

Grey stared down at his boots. "I'm thinking someone is going to get hurt."

"Grey." Rome leaned forward, gripped his shoulders. "You know how bad I want you. You know how good it is with us. Right?"

"For God's sake." Grey shifted uncomfortably. "Yeah. I know. Why the hell do I have to say it?"

"How much better was it with Mia?"

"It was great. And none of us wants to hurt the other," Mia said, coming up behind him.

"No. We don't want to." But in Grey's experience sex and caring about someone always did hurt eventually. Some things shouldn't mix.

He looked over at the woman who had walked into his life. Mia looked so delicate there in the dawn. Fragile. Like whatever it was he felt for her -- for her and Rome together. Fragile things got broken too easily.

Mia looked at the two men who had dropped into her life. Rome, still focused on his coffee and Grey who was focused on…her? She ignored the flutter in her stomach at the thought and deliberately spoke briskly. "Then we'll just try to keep things that way. You don't scare me so much any more, tough stuff. Underneath all that growl is marshmallow." She leaned forward and kissed him on the nose. "Here's your coffee. Drink up and don't worry, big guy."

"Don't patronize me, little girl."

Rome laughed. "She wouldn't dream of it. But watch out. I've always suspected once she got over being a scared little girl, she'd turn into a tigress."

"I turn into a wolf, Rome. Much better." She could feel The Change trembling inside her. "Now. Let's try it that way."

She saw a brief hesitation on Rome's face before he smiled, slow and hot. "I don't think so."

"Why not?" Mia almost pouted. And why did he get to give the orders anyhow? Her wolf was calling to her.

Heat rippled through her. Not just sex heat, but The Change. It had been a long time since she'd done this. Omegas weren't encouraged to try their inner wolf out very often. As she settled down, let herself absorb the difference, she looked over. Grey crouched, his face changing from human to feral. The scars were still there, but covered with fur, they barely showed.

"No -- "

Rome backed away, half-laughing, half-serious.

Mia rested her nose in his crotch. She snorted. Things smelled different now. Sharper. He still smelled like Rome. Just more so.

"Shit! Mia, I mean it -- "

Stiff-legged, Grey danced in front of the only one of them still non-were. Grey crouched. They knew what that meant, but even as Rome braced himself, Grey knocked Rome to the ground. He worried Rome's hair.

Rome covered his face and throat. "You guys don't take no for an answer."

The male wolf mounted Mia, dry humping her, his back to Rome. They all knew the depth of the insult.

"Ah, to hell with it then -- " Rome's words ended with a howl.

Rome moved in a blur. Mia couldn't see him clearly. During The Change she couldn't always control her senses and he was fast. Lightning fast.

He barreled into her and they rolled on the ground. She offered her neck, submissively. Rome's teeth closed over her throat, gently, but not so gently that she couldn't feel the sharp prick of canines.

The growl above them deafened her sensitized ears. Grey stood over them both, demanding obedience. Rome snapped in the air, not trying to go close to the other male's jugular but not cowed, either.

Mia crouched, waiting.

She didn't have to wait long. Rome mounted her, keeping his muzzle close to her neck. She thought she could feel the extra weight of Grey as he mounted Rome, but she wasn't sure.

Flashes of heat and the dizzying smell of sex surrounded her. She groaned, deep, as Rome moved. Wolves could mate for hours. She wasn't sure if she could bear it, but she was more than ready to try.

Hardness inside her, friction, warmth, pleasure. Vaguely she knew the thrusting against her was different. That would be Grey's doing, as he entered Rome, changing the sensual beat.

Rough. Fire. Spots danced in front of Mia's eyes and she trembled, almost bucking her rider off.

He moved inside her, deeper yet, and she shuddered with the first roll of satisfaction. It moved through her like fire, scattering her. Making her whole. The hard knot of a canine penis swelled inside her.

More. There would be more and more yet.

Mia's mouth dropped open in a wolfish grin.

* * *

"I don't understand." Mia stared at her two alphas. "Why would you take on a job without me? I'm your electronics expert."

She was damn good at it, too. The men could provide muscle and intimidation when their security contract called for it. She provided the surveillance hardware to back up the threat.

"Oscar or Ric can make do for this one." Lin smiled at her. "We think you're too valuable here to send you out on some three week contract."

"I'm too valuable to do my job?" Mia fought the next words. Swallowed them down. Alphas didn't care for contradictions.

"Mia, what you're doing right now is more valuable than the rest of what the pack can do combined. We can provide overpriced security for some spoiled heiress with our eyes closed. That's just our work. But you? We're counting on you to make a baby."

If I'm not pregnant now, I'm never going to be. She didn't say those words aloud, either. Mia didn't really want to chat about why. But between Grey and Rome she'd been taken every way there was. Some of those ways had to include getting her pregnant.

"All right then. I'll stay." Mia sighed. "Of course."

Chapter Five

I'm not some mindless breeding machine, to be set aside whenever I'm inconvenient.

Mia thought about all the things she'd wanted to say to the pack as they got ready for travel. She'd been with them all these years. She'd thought she'd been valued for her contributions.

Now she was only valuable if she could produce a new crop of babies.

Of course she hadn't said anything. Omegas didn't rail or complain. Omegas did what they were told and then steamed away inside.

"Hey." Rome flicked a finger against her cheek.

Mia jumped. She'd been so absorbed in her thoughts that she hadn't even realized Grey and Rome had arrived. She scowled. Of course they would arrive. They were the stud service.

And she was being an idiot. What was wrong with her tonight?

"Maybe I *am* pregnant."

Grey's chair clattered to the floor as he leaped to his feet. "Are you sure?"

Why couldn't she keep her mouth shut now after being quiet all day? And was he happy or terrified over the possibility? She couldn't tell.

"No, I'm not sure at all. Sorry. It's just that I'm getting -- temperamental, I guess. I knew what was going to happen before we had sex, but now it bothers me."

"Sex bothers you?" Rome looked horrified.

Guys never understood anything.

"No, idiot. Being used for just one thing."

"You can use us for that one thing, too, babe. It works both ways." For once Rome's sexy smile didn't make her insides curl.

Grey was smart enough to be quiet. Or maybe he didn't care enough to talk. It didn't make any difference to them how she felt. Grey and Rome had each other. They didn't need her. Except for babies, of course.

Oh, God. Now she wanted to cry.

"I need some time away from testosterone," Mia said. "Far away."

She stalked out of the room to dead silence.

"Women." She wasn't sure which one of them said it, but it made slamming her bedroom door shut all the more necessary.

Mia glared at the bed, with only the prospect of punching her pillow to cheer her up. Maybe she was pregnant, not just saying something off the top of her head. Her emotions certainly seemed out of control right now. If she was, then what?

Grey had never wanted her in the first place. She had no idea why Rome wanted her, other than her being female and available. Probably that was enough to make him want to have her. For a little while, anyway.

She sat down on the bed and hid her face. Once she'd had a baby, Grey and Rome would be gone. And she'd be --

Nothing. She was tired of being nothing.

She took a deep breath and her eyes widened. She cocked her head, suddenly alert to something outside her own misery.

Something was wrong. She could smell it.

Smoke. The scent of it was faint at first, but her nose was keen enough. She straightened and sniffed. It was definitely getting stronger.

"Grey! Rome!" And closer. The smoke was getting closer. "Help! Where are you?"

They might be gone from her life someday but right now they were around and she wanted them to be even nearer. Now.

Silence. Mia ran to the door, ready to rip it open. They wouldn't ignore her when she called for help. Not unless they couldn't answer.

Shit. Oh, shit. She'd left them on ugly terms and now --

"Damn it all to hell and back." Grey's faintly accented voice called to her, the accent and voice thicker than usual. "Girl, stay where you are. We're coming for you."

Years of obedience fought with common sense. If there was a fire, she had to get out, not sit and wait until it reached her. Mia looked at the window. She could hear the hissing of flames now in the hall. It would be dangerous to come to her room through the house. They might not make it. They probably shouldn't even try.

"Get out. I can manage here!" she called.

No answer.

She put her fist to her mouth and bit hard to keep from screaming. A lifetime of obedience warred against a terrified need to survive. She waited, shaking. Everything in her screamed to run but she stood, fighting her gut instinct.

They were coming. She knew they'd be there for her. She wasn't going to screw things up for the men.

The bedroom door crashed open. Without a word, Rome scooped her up close. Grey stood apart, scanning the bedroom window, and scowled.

"No good. It's too exposed here and too many people know where she sleeps. We have to go back." Grey jerked his thumb to where she could hear crackling flames.

"Go back? We have to get out!" Mia did scream this time. Enough was enough.

Grey shook his head. "We're being burned out for a reason. I expect they're waiting for us to run outside."

"Fine. So we won't do that." Rome slung Mia over his shoulder.

"What do you mean we won't and who is they?" Mia said her face up against his ass. Maybe she'd be able to think clearer if she wasn't choking to death.

"Busy. We'll explain later." Rome patted her butt.

She'd waited for these idiots?

"If we live through this, I may kill you both," Mia warned before she began to cough.

They all ran down the hall, Mia hauled ignominiously over Rome's shoulder, her rear in the air and her legs dangling across his chest. She was torn between fury and fear. When Rome stumbled and began to cough, too, fear won.

"What the hell are we doing?" She gasped the words, holding a sleeve across her nose. "You can put me down."

"Crawl. There's fresher air closer to the ground," Grey snapped the order out. "I can take her if it's getting too hard."

"Fuck. Off. I'm keeping her." Rome sounded choked but sure. He stayed on his feet.

"Call 911." Mia tried again.

"No. This is were business. We don't need others to know. My guess is they're trying to get to you, Mia." Grey was the only one who sounded unaffected by the smoke. "They want to burn us out and then grab you."

She'd grown up on stories of what packs did to get female mates. She'd seen what her own family tried on Lin years ago.

Lord help them all.

No. They had to be wrong. This had to be some sort of accident. No one broke into the pack's house that easily. They were the security experts, for heaven's sake.

But then why weren't the smoke detectors beeping? All she could hear was the fire hungrily crashing through the house, looking for more to devour, and Rome's rasping breath.

"Maybe it's safe. I don't see or hear anything." Rome squinted out the window, peering through the blinds.

"You want to risk a life on it?" Grey snarled.

Mia spoke up fast. "Sure. Mine."

"No." The men chorused the word together.

"Listen, if this is were business, they won't try to kill me if I go out because they want me alive for breeding. I can keep them busy enough so that you can escape. And if no one tries for me, then we're all safe."

"I'm fast. Once I'm outside, I could take out the fuckers." Rome rode over Mia's words as if they were meaningless.

Grey touched Mia's shoulder, then Rome's. Mia could barely see his face through the smoke, but she could tell from Grey's iron grip that he wasn't holding them for reassurance. He was planning on physically keeping them from leaving. "If need be, I'll go. I know more about getting out of bad situations than you two kids ever will. But it's not that bad yet."

Not that bad?

Mia wasn't sure if she wanted to bite the two macho idiots or kiss them. Someone was going to have to give in and be saved. Otherwise they'd all sit together until they burned alive.

And those two males were stubborn enough to do it.

"Listen, I'm not worth dying over." She began to cough. "That is, if you're right."

"I'm thinking I'm right. But no one here is going to die. And you're not trading yourself for me." Grey rasped the words in a low and menacing growl.

His battle voice. She was sure of it.

"Besides, we have reinforcements, Mia. We're not gambling with you." Rome's voice was just as hard.

Reinforcements? They could have mentioned it.

"All clear!" Dek. Of course. She'd forgotten they had another Alpha around. Mia could have wept at hearing the familiar voice outside. "Get the hell out now!"

Grey surged to his feet and knocked his shoulder against the closest window. Blessed fresh air rushed in. Mia found herself pulled off Rome's shoulder and tossed through the air.

She landed on the ground outside, barely in time to roll away as Rome hurtled through the window. Grey followed more sedately, climbing out and swatting at his head with his Stetson.

"Did you -- have to throw us?" Mia gulped.

"Well, things were a tad close." Grey cleared his throat. "Damn ashes were falling off my hat and getting on my hair and shoulders."

Rome just hunched over, gasping.

"Are you all right?" Dek kept his eyes scanning, squinting into the horizon, his rifle still raised. "I'm calling the fire department now. Don't think they'll see anything they shouldn't at this point. I sure as hell can't."

He flipped open his cell phone.

"Did you see -- catch -- anyone?" Mia asked.

"No, damn it. I missed whoever was hiding out here."

Had there been a "they" out there, the way the men insisted? She wanted to believe this was some accident even though her gut screamed at her. Damn smoke. She couldn't think after it fogged up her brain. Instead Mia turned and threw up, almost on Rome's boots.

Appalled, she opened her mouth to apologize.

"We have to get her to Leila. Mia might be pregnant. All that shit she breathed in can't be good." Rome picked her up again, cradling her this time instead of hauling her.

"Leila is right here. You think she was going to let me come alone?" Dek almost laughed. "Well, you're still young yet, son."

"We'll deal with this later. Mia might need attention right now." Grey spoke up. "I had to toss her out kind of rough from the house. She might have gotten hurt when she landed."

She really ought to take down that chauvinistic attitude. Neither of them were alpha and both of them had been through the same thing she had. But Mia decided she would do that later. Right now it sort of felt good to be fussed over, even if it was to protect the baby as much as her.

"You all are going to get checked over. Now. Before the firemen start asking questions." In the distance they heard the distinctive whine of the sirens. "Leila! You can come out."

"You damn well better believe it." Leila looked grumpy as she joined them, still holding her revolver. "Don't think you can make me stay in the truck next time. And no, I didn't see anyone peel out by way of the road. Damn it. They were too slick for that."

She looked over at Mia and crooked her finger. "I might as well do something useful tonight. I need to check all of you out."

"I'm really fine." Mia held back.

"I'm sure you are, sweetie. But let's make sure. I didn't take all those veterinarian classes just to twiddle my thumbs when they might be needed." Leila ran her hands down Mia's shoulders and began to pat her stomach. "Anything hurt? Do you feel sore?"

She'd forgotten that Leila had an interest in trying to figure out what medicine would help weres. They didn't exactly have problems you could take to the local neighborhood doctor.

What would giving birth be like? She didn't even know how to start planning. Could she go to a hospital? What if the pain and excitement triggered The Change? Maybe Leila would be her midwife.

Except -- oh. She was a little slow as well as a little sore, but she knew the signs by now. They'd happened often enough.

"Um, Leila? Ma'am?" Mia lowered her voice. She didn't need a public announcement for this one. "I think I've figured out my problem and it's not pregnancy."

Leila paused in her exploration and looked at Mia's face.

"It's the exact opposite." Mia gestured, hopelessly. "Don't tell the guys right now, but I think it's that time of month."

Chapter Six

"Rome, why are you doing this? We're safe. Our packs can handle this. All we have to do is wait for them to finish up a plan. Trying to take this pack on alone -- that is *not* safe."

Rome tried to relax his jaw. There wasn't any need to yell now. This was Mia. She didn't yell much. Well, unless she was trapped in a burning building. His jaw tightened at that thought and he tried again to get control of his emotions.

But he was exhausted as well as tense, a lousy combination. He and Grey had gone toe-to-toe and shout-for-shout for almost an hour. That damned Grey could be one stubborn jerk. It didn't matter. Grey had met someone who could out stubborn him. Rome was still going to find the freakin curs who had tried to burn Mia's pack house down, with them inside it. Then he was going to make them wish they'd never been born. Why was that so hard to understand?

Mia was as determined in her way as Grey was, but she was less likely to slug him. So he shrugged and tried talking again. "I'm not one of the pack, Mia. Not yours. Not Grey's. The only one who can handle the insult to me is me. And I want to do it. I want to real bad."

It was more than an insult. It was an actual nagging ache to pay back the people who tried to hurt Mia and Grey. To make sure they'd be kept safe. He'd had to hunker down and watch his companions choking. Wait and wonder if they would all die while he did nothing. He wasn't going to stay feeling that helpless. He couldn't live with that.

And he was tired of talking about it. He was going to do something. Preferably, something very violent and very final.

"You really think you're alone?"

Rome almost laughed at the naiveté in the question. Sometimes Mia was so -- so innocent. Those earnest eyes of hers actually looked surprised and worried. "I really do."

"What about your parents?"

"They love me. But I can't be what they want me to be for the pack. And if I can't do that, they'll have to find someone else to do it. They have others to tend to."

He'd disappointed his parents first.

"All right, then. Are you telling me you still feel alone after everything the three of us have done together?"

Rome didn't answer. Why keep going on about the obvious? He'd already done enough of that with Grey.

He'd disappoint Grey and Mia next.

"If you don't want to answer that, Rome, you'll really hate my next question."

"Oh, goodie."

"Do you love me, Rome? Grey, yes. I know how much you're a part of Grey. But I don't understand why you pulled me into your couple."

He gave a half-laugh but said nothing. Couldn't say anything. There it was. The big question all women asked eventually. For some reason he hadn't seen it coming this time.

He could brush it off. Kiss it away. She'd let him. He could tell she was terrified about asking.

Or he could be honest.

That would hurt.

But this was Mia. She was valiant, even when she was afraid. Especially when she was afraid. And she had offered to give herself up for him and Grey back when she was sure they were going to die. He didn't know how Grey felt about that, but her offer had damn near made him cry.

He had to be honest with Mia. He'd danced around the problem just now and she didn't take the hint. Time to stop hinting.

"Couldn't you tell what was wrong when we all mated? Why I don't belong?"

"Wrong? What was wrong with that?" Mia stared at him. "I couldn't tell anything except that I was having enough climaxes to black out. You and Grey had me so keyed up all I could do was feel. That's usually what I do as a were anyhow. Sense. Feel. I don't analyze."

He could leave it at that. Not press into the old hurt and shame threatening to engulf him right now. She really wasn't getting it. Maybe he'd been a better con artist than he thought.

But this was Mia. He owed her. She was one of the two most important people in his world. All right then. He'd get on with it.

"You had to be able to tell after we changed. I'm not one of you. You and Grey -- you're weres. I'm nothing."

"Rome -- "

"My change doesn't make me -- I'm not were. I'm not human. I don't fit." He jumped up and began to pace, avoiding looking at her face. "I'm not asking for pity. That's just what it is. I'm not meant to be a pack were. And I'm not meant for you or for Grey or anyone, no matter how good the sex is. Not for keeps. You two -- I gave you two to each other because you're right together. You two. Not me."

She just stared, clearly not understanding. Rome prayed for patience and tried again.

"I remember when the packs used to leave us alone, back when we were kids. No. Not kids. Twelve, thirteen."

"We were the youngest and the Omegas. Of course we were left alone while the adults were busy."

"That wasn't the only reason why." Rome patted her butt. "They were testing us out. Seeing if there was any potential."

"Potential -- oh. Oh!"

"I was interested."

"You didn't act interested."

"I was too interested to be able to admit how much. Damn, between you and Grey, I was getting really worked up. Seemed like both of you were around all the time but just out of reach. I spent a lot of time fantasizing about one or the other of you. Or both. A lot of time. I bet telling you some of those fantasies would still make you blush."

"That long ago?" Mia was blushing without him having to say they'd lived out a few of them already.

Sweet. She was sweet enough to eat.

"And then the alone time during visits stopped."

"I sort of remember that. I was flattered to become part of the adult circle." She smiled. "I was annoyed you were younger and you were included too."

"I was fourteen. When I first Changed and they saw I was like my sister. Not quite were enough but not human either." Rome looked forward. "Dad didn't give me hints any more about how to lead a pack. My mother dropped those grandchildren hints. I wasn't the heir to the pack any more. I wasn't going to have any chance at being Alpha."

He couldn't explain any more. It was beyond humiliating to think of how it made him feel once he was old enough to realize what he lacked. How lost he was.

"Hollowness. A gnawing need that will never be filled. Couldn't be." Mia said the words in his head, not with pity, but as if she was feeling the same thing. As if she knew right then what he was feeling.

"Oh, Jesus." Rome stared into her face. She looked as shocked as he felt.

Was she sensing his thoughts and emotions? She wasn't bonded to him. She couldn't be. That would mean -- he didn't want to think what that would mean. He'd accepted he was meant to be alone, never to have...

A bondmate. One that knew what you thought, felt what you did.

"There was nothing wrong with you during The Change. You smelled right. You felt right. Very right." Mia moved closer, held him. "What else does a were need?"

How could you resist Mia? She warmed the coldness inside him with more than words. She used her own body. He could sense little prickles of warmth flowing from her to him as she pressed against him. Gradually Rome relaxed. His body fitted against hers. He brushed his lips over her hair. "How do you do that?"

"What?" Mia's fingers were already burrowing under the loose shirt he wore, ready to strip him out of his clothing.

"Make the impossible sound easy." He nipped her earlobe.

He wanted to bite her hard. To mark her. Claim her. He kept his grip gentle, though. He'd be gentle even though he shook with the need to possess her.

No. No. Now wasn't the time for something he wouldn't be around to finish.

"Oh. I suppose I learned from you and everyone else around me when they convinced me to join you. This whole situation should be impossible, but somehow we're here."

The gentle heat turned up to boiling. She brushed her tongue against one of his nipples and his lips curled back at the sensation. He bared his teeth, all of them, *wolf-style*. His cock was harder than he could ever remember.

Sex. He could definitely start and finish that with her. Uncomplicated, beautiful, hot sex. His balls drew up tight as he smelled her arousal. The ache was almost a pain.

"Damn straight. And I think we should take advantage of it." He picked her up, tilted her against the wall, and buried his face between her breasts.

Heaven. The smell of woman. Of Mia. The musky scent of arousal and what must be her monthly change. Weres -- at least this were -- reacted to that new difference as if she was in heat.

Damn. He'd wanted her back in high school bad enough to hurt. She'd been dangled in front of him and then taken away and he'd wanted her -- everything -- back.

Of course he'd wanted anything he could screw back then. But he wasn't a high school kid any more. He'd like to think he'd gotten a little more selective about who he laid nowadays -- then again it was easy to be picky about partners when you had the exact ones you wanted.

Still his little head had been smarter than usual when it first took notice of the only available were female in town. Now that he knew Mia, he realized she was even sexier, sweeter, better than he'd fantasized during class.

"But I'm -- you know. Not exactly up for sex." Mia looked completely embarrassed. "I suppose those were hormones of yours don't want to pay attention to *that.*"

OK. She wasn't a fantasy. He could live with it.

"No, they want you especially because of *that*. But if you're saying no to straight up fucking, we'll manage something, babe."

"All right." She curled against him willingly, even though her voice was uncertain. "I guess my hormones don't want to pay attention, either."

Weird. He wanted her. His body sang with want. It would be good, whatever they did, and he wanted it like he wanted to breathe. But sex felt...incomplete without Grey. Was she feeling the same thing?

"You're in my own room and you started without me? Haven't you ever heard about waiting for your host?" Grey's graveled voice was the answer to everything uncertain still swirling around inside Rome. Trust Grey to know when to make an appearance.

Steadied, Rome waved at their partner. He didn't want to think about how right it was to have Grey with them.

"Hurry up, old man, or we'll finish without you, too."

Grey's eyes narrowed and then he began to unbuckle his belt. "Wouldn't like to see you try it."

Rome wasn't sure if that was a statement of fact or a threat. It didn't matter. When Grey's jeans hit the ground, it was clear from his stiff cock that no one would have to wait for long.

Better yet, Grey didn't seem to still have a mad on.

Rome turned Mia over, flipped up her skirt and slapped one butt cheek, pausing to admire the rosy glow.

"This way will work for all of us. Damn, I like Mia's ass."

"I like yours. You want a spanking, too?" Grey was already circling the rim of Rome's hole, spreading it with cool lube and hard fingers. Grey shoved two digits down together with no more preliminaries. Rome swallowed and tried to keep his legs steady. He rubbed his back against the pelt on Grey's chest until his breathing slowed down some. Damn, he liked the feel of Grey -- fingers, hairy hide, everything.

"Rome knows you like his ass. Everyone knows." Mia sounded amused as she arched forward, giving Rome easier access to her own sweet butt. "I suppose I should be honored you sometimes notice mine instead."

"I'll get to your ass soon," Grey growled at her, but Rome heard the humor lurking there. Grey never yelled at Mia. Then again, that would be difficult to do. Especially when you were about to have sex like this.

Perfect. The words sang inside Rome. No one ever got perfect but this was…

Hot. Tight. So fucking right. It almost hurt, it was so good.

It was like hearing Grey's words in his head. Or maybe hearing his own thoughts in Grey's. Except that the inner voice sounded like Mia. Rome's hands stopped tracing the pretty blue veins in Mia's legs.

"What the hell -- "

"Don't. Ask," Mia said aloud, her voice thin. "I'm just…I feel like a telephone wire or something. What's going on in your brain is spilling out and over."

It wasn't just his brain, though. She'd heard Grey.

"Can we think about it later?" Grey asked aloud. "You all are distracting me from what's important here."

He couldn't be bonded to Grey and Mia. Weres couldn't bond more than once even at the best of times. But Mia was hearing them. Their thoughts. And he felt so...so...

Connected.

Then again, Grey could be right. If they thought too hard, they might stop screwing. Grey's cock was so close --

Jesus, Grey was huge but he hadn't grown a few inches overnight, had he? Grey's entrance made him feel full, damn full. The pressure almost hurt. But Rome didn't wait too long for things to ease up. He moved against Grey's cock fast, savoring the length and breadth of Grey in his ass, wanting the pleasure enough to endure the sting. Everything fit together soon enough and he didn't want to stop for thinking or foreplay any more than Grey did. Any more than Mia did, either, judging from the impatient little twitches and murmurs underneath him.

Grey hit the right spot, the one that made Rome moan every time.

Rome moved over Mia, resting his head against her shoulder. She had her arms draped over Grey's bed, bracing herself for the two men pumping against her. Which was going to start just about *now*. Rome thrust forward gently. Home.

Mia whimpered and pushed back, just like he had for Grey.

And they stayed, unmoving, for a long, impossibly long moment just like that first time.

Mia and Grey. They were slick against him. Soft and hard. Soft cries of delight and rough cursing. Surrounding him. Enveloping him in sweat and heat and strength and gentleness. Sensation layered over sensation. Differences that combined into one.

Then, like before, like always, they all moved in a sudden burst of energy and lust, matching each other stroke for stroke. More. He wanted more. Rome found himself holding Mia's breasts, her soft nipples hardening in his hands as she squirmed against him. Grey was holding Rome's hips, not letting him move while Grey pounded hard inside him, just the way Rome wanted to do to Mia. Instead Rome waited, half in warm female flesh, dying to get further in.

Mia moaned, clamped down on what was in there already. Rome shook with wanting more. Damn that Gray.

Gray hit the perfect spot again with one sure stroke and Rome shook with satisfaction. All right. He wouldn't damn Gray yet.

It seemed like forever, posed midway between satisfaction and torture before Grey let him free. Instantly Rome pumped himself inside Mia, hating to pull out but making up for it with the fast slide back in.

Damn it, they all wanted more. Nastier. Harder.

I want to be between you and Grey next time. It's like being between two explosions waiting to happen. So powerful. I love being with you both.

Mia moaned again, shuddering, fitting him like a tight fist.

Rome shook his head, but Mia's words echoed there, heightening the edgy need. Knowing what she wanted from her thoughts, hearing Grey's gasp against his back -- he felt the rush of his come surging up from his balls. This wasn't just sex. It was better than sex.

But the sex was fucking good. Oh, *yeah!*

Rome gave in as the pleasure and heat lanced through him. He came first, hard, long. Forever.

He wanted it to be forever.

Rome woke up first, as always. Once his eyes got used to the dark, he focused on the two people toppled on the bed near him. Mia had one hand resting on his arm and another on Grey's chest. Grey was snoring lightly. Rome lay there for a moment more, listening to them. Looking at them. A tendril of Mia's blonde hair was caught between her lips. Grey's face was relaxed in his sleep, the way it never relaxed while he was awake and watchful.

Rome blinked.

Easing his arm away from Mia's hand, he got off the bed. The other two slept, curled together, like the dead -- or people who had fucked themselves to sleep. Rome stood, picking up his boots and clothing en route to the door.

Mia made one muffled sound, almost like a protest and Rome stopped moving until the sound eased back into peaceful breathing. Only then did he open the door and slip outside without looking back.

They were the two people he cared about most in the world. He hoped they'd understand when they woke up and found him gone.

Chapter Seven

Too bad Mia wasn't here -- No. That wasn't what he meant. Too bad he wasn't Mia. She'd have disengaged the damn security system in less than the half hour it took him. But he did it. There was no sound as he slipped through the window.

Time to go hunting.

Once inside, he scented his prey. He'd gotten only the faintest whiff the day of the fire, before the smoke clogged his nostrils. But he knew that smell. That was the one who'd been in the house just before all hell broke loose.

The scent was stronger. Right there. Rome opened the door.

Two men sat there. They turned, as if they had been waiting, to stare at him.

"You think you should be here alone?" The smaller man looked faintly amused when Rome walked in. "Considering what you know we can do?"

Rome froze. He felt cold metal against his ear. There was the distinct click of a safety being unlatched on the gun that rested against his neck.

Hell. So much for caution. And giving warnings.

Another safety clicked.

"Who said he was alone?" That was Dek's voice.

Dad? Double hell.

"Boy, you keep forgetting about the part where even when it looks safe, you keep your eyes open. Makes me wonder sometimes." And Grey. Of course. He'd have to be there to watch Rome fuck up big time.

"And you never knew that you always check for a backup silent alarm. I cut that off first thing."

Mia, too?

Rome fought his emotions and won. He managed to sound measured instead of strangled. "Shit. Bad enough you have to tag along. But you can't keep your mouths shut after you do. Folks, we don't have time for a long chat. Everyone needs to get out. Now."

"Or?" The strange were, the one who had tried to kill them, didn't move while he asked.

"Or you'll blow up along with your fucking house in seven minutes. Did all of you really think I was stupid enough to -- never mind. Get out." Not that he was going to move while that gun was still against his neck. Dying in seven minutes rather than right now seemed like a better idea. "Grey, get Mia the fuck away."

He heard movement and then the sounds of footsteps. Rome almost relaxed. If the strange pack didn't get to them first, Grey would get Mia out.

If.

His temporary captor looked over at the were who hadn't spoken yet. "Hunt? Boss? Dunno if it's true or not but seven minutes -- "

"Six minutes thirty seconds -- " Rome interrupted.

"Why don't we all just put down our weapons, get out, and figure out what else to do later?" Dek said, very calmly. "Rossi, you first, of course. Or I'll blast a hole in your head. I'd rather rip your throat out, but human weapons are faster and we're a little pressed for time."

It had been a long time but he should have known Rossi's smell. Maybe it was all Rossi's sweat and adrenaline that had interfered with Rome recognizing him. Too bad it was Rossi holding the weapon. The idiot might shake too hard and set things off.

"Rossi, if you keep that gun at my head much longer, I'll be close enough to give you a big sloppy kiss good-bye before we head off to hell," Rome said.

"Dunne? What are we gonna do?" Rossi's distinctive whine was the same. And his stupidity. It was all coming back to him now. Even as an adolescent he'd known why the pack was glad to see the last of Rossi.

"If we don't leave, we'll all be done." Damned if he wasn't feeling a little sweaty himself. But charged. Rome had never felt so charged in his life.

"All right." The man who was boss finally spoke. He stared hard at Rome. It wasn't a friendly look, but Rome hadn't expected a buddy. "Let's go."

"Damn, son. Where did you learn how to do that?" Dek looked at the opening that was now in the side of the pack's office building.

Everyone seemed a bit stunned. What did they think he'd meant to do? He wasn't here to play. The bomb had done just what he had intended it to do.

"From you. Well, sort of. Remember the summer we went to Alabama for your job? Folks weren't taking kindly to the takeover there and there were bomb threats and explosive experts all over. I didn't have anything to do except hang out and listen." Rome couldn't help but glance over at Mia and Grey.

They looked all right. Not too happy with him, but safe. Some of the adrenaline humming through his system eased.

"What did you think you'd get from doing this?" The tall, impossibly tall, thin Alpha called Hunt asked.

Icy voice. Icy look.

"Your attention. You seemed to have forgotten weres bite when they're attacked." Rome didn't add that once he'd got the pack outside he'd planned to get a little more one-on-one with the Alpha.

"You got my attention. Maybe too much of it." Hunt's fingers tapped at his suit jacket. Rome wondered what lethal surprise he might have inside. "All we want is the female. Give her up and we can all go home. I might even forget about this. Eventually."

"Give it up, Hunt. Mia is ours. She's pregnant with my child. It's over." Grey's voice was almost gentle.

"Damn it!" Rossi burst out. "You knocked my sister up? You're lying. You couldn't get it up for a woman -- "

"Shut up." Hunt didn't even look over at the other man.

"I figure you're the one who came up with this little plan to grab Mia to start with. You might even have been the one to burn her out." Grey's voice was almost gentle. His face wasn't. "Me, I'm just a beta. I'm not in charge of saying what the pack will do to you next. But could be you'll be getting another visit real soon. I wouldn't sleep too hard for the next lifetime, if I were you, Rossi."

Rossi glanced over to Hunt and Dunne but saw no support.

"Shoo." Grey made a dismissive gesture. "Now."

Rossi backed up. Slowly at first, then faster. A few yards away from them, he turned and ran.

"It's time for us to talk, Hunt." Dek ignored the interlude and jerked his head to indicate a spot further away. "Alpha to Alpha. Anything I say, Lowell will back when he arrives."

"I hate negotiating." Hunt's smile glittered. "I'd rather try other methods."

"Me, too. So let's make it short and sweet before we remember how much we hate this." Before Dek moved, he touched Rome briefly on the shoulder.

Rome watched his father walk away before turning to face the rest of the group. The adrenaline was all gone now, leaving nothing but flat bleakness.

No one said anything but the silence was an accusation in itself. *We almost got killed. Your daddy had to be there to mop up after you. You screwed up.* Damn it, he knew that.

They could have died. All of them. Watching his damned back.

"I can't stand this. I can't be like you." Rome pushed his hair from his eyes. "This just proved it."

"But you needed us," Mia blurted.

"I fucking well did not. Not this time, babe. Not next time, either. I don't need -- I don't want to need anyone."

You'd rather die?

"Maybe I would." Rome glared at her. "Anything is better than having to do what everyone else tells you to do. To breathe when they let you. To second guess what you do."

To never measure up to what they want of you. He hastily tried to banish that thought in case Mia burrowed into his brain and heard it.

"But you're part of us now. You can't -- "

"Mia, sweetheart." Grey put his hand on her shoulder, sort of the way he had when they were in the burning house. It was more than a touch. It was an order.

She didn't say anything more.

Then again, Mia could handle orders much better than Rome could. He felt as choked as when the smoke threatened to kill them. As smothered. He had to get out.

Before he went and blew their lives up.

"I know this is a cliché, but fuck it. It's not you, it's me. All right? Good-bye. Have a nice life. Be safe. Both of you." Grey would take care of her. The whole pack would. And Mia would stick with Grey. Rome was sure of it. She and Grey's baby would do just fine.

* * *

"Do you think he'll be back?" Mia didn't want to ask. Had to ask. Grey knew Rome better than anyone else.

"What if he doesn't return? What then?" Grey held her, but he didn't look down at her.

She would have liked his full attention when she made her announcement but she knew it was already overdue. She shouldn't wait longer for the right time. "I'm pregnant. Did you know you weren't lying when you told everyone?"

Grey's grip tightened for a moment. "You said you weren't."

"I -- I must have been spotting. That's what Leila tells me. It happens sometimes."

"Does that mean something is wrong? With the baby? With you?" He looked down then, frowning.

"No. As long as it stops, everything is fine. I guessed what was going on after the bleeding stopped because I still felt a bit...off. While you and Dek were trailing Rome, I finally let Leila check me out the way I should have before." Mia took a long breath. Let it out. "Anyhow, your duty here is done."

"Looks that way." He kept his hold on her.

"You aren't going to go after Rome? Like last time?"

"I caught him, sure. Could do it again, most likely. But I can't keep him if he won't stay." Grey ran his hand over her hair. "Guess you can't, either."

"No. I'm not good at making people stick around." She was good at being lonely. Well, she'd been before. She could be again.

And she'd have a baby. She could manage. She would.

"I'm not going anywhere, Mia."

"What -- what does that mean?" It couldn't mean what she wanted it to. She tried to keep from hoping.

"I miss Rome. Will miss him for the rest of my life if he's fool enough to stay away that long. But you're here. That's good, because I'd miss you, too."

Mia looked down at her stomach. "You mean because of the baby."

"Because of the baby. And because of you." Grey bent his head to kiss her hair this time. "We belong together."

The two of us isn't like three. But it's a damn sight better than one. Especially when all of us were meant to be together.

Mia swallowed at the echoing of Grey's thoughts. But she had to be sure. "You want me? Even if it's just me?"

"Just you isn't half-bad, little girl."

Mia turned and let her lips graze his. "Show me you want me."

Please. She had to feel. She had to know.

He didn't hesitate. He deepened the kiss, slowly at first, so it was like being petted. His tongue strokes were soft and persuasive, coaxing out her response. Mia slid her hands into his hair and clung. Grey kept the kiss going, made it deeper and hotter.

He touched her breasts as he kept the kiss going. How did he know she was already getting more sensitive there? Just his touch was sending shocks of heat through her -- from nipples down to her clitoris.

She was whirling, falling deeper and deeper into a velvet blackness that promised slow, sensual delights. She'd wondered if she and Grey would ever have sex alone. She'd wondered if it did happen whether she'd have to seduce him.

This was better than anything she had imagined. They weren't just having sex. Grey was making love to her.

Her sigh mingled with his as she stroked the side of his head. He turned to kiss her palm. Then he laved it with his tongue.

"You, Mia. I want you." He was hard against her, rocking slightly against her hips.

"Well, you have me. Now what?"

"Guess we'll find out." He slid his hand under her shirt and unzipped her pants. She tilted her hips up, let him trace the edge of her panties with his finger. He ran them once, twice against her skin. Then he paused. Tease.

She rocked against him this time, rubbing against his erection through his pants. He was hard, so hard. He unzipped his own jeans.

"These are in the way," Grey murmured, and with one lethal swipe, her panties were in tatters and he inched inside her. Perfect. His controlled ferocity was perfect. She clenched his hardness, wanting more, wanting everything, and he shuddered.

He suddenly withdrew.

"Wh -- ?" Mia opened her eyes.

"I like this."

"Driving me insane?"

"Yeah. Tasting. You taste different. You smell different." He licked his lips and Mia sucked in her breath. His eyes looked dazed. "'s good. Real good. I like taking time with you. I like hearing -- " he ran his tongue between her breasts and she bucked -- "you whimper. I like hearing you beg."

"You're horrible."

"Try again, sweetheart."

"You're wonderful. And if you don't keep moving just that way, I'm going to kill you."

"Beg me."

Mia kept her mouth shut. She was good at that. She had self-control. She was the quiet one. The head of Grey's cock tickled her clit, the traitorous clit that swelled and tingled at his touch, sending more waves of need through her. She clenched her teeth to keep from screaming.

"Meeee -- ahhh. *Mi alma.*"

His soul.

"Please. Grey. Oh, please." She spread her legs wider, knowing she was wet and ready and needy. "Please, I want you in me so badly."

He entered her without hesitation, filling her up, making the ache better and worse at the same time. He paused before he moved. She arched her back, still silently begging for more.

"Look at me, *mi alma*. Keep looking."

He kissed her, the stubble of his beard scraping against her skin. His kiss was tender and hungry and close to hurtful. All the ways there were to kiss a woman, all at the same time. And then he fucked her.

Without any more warning his cock was deep within her, pushing inside her, battering her body.

She stared at him. He looked back, the tension in his face matching the tension in her body as he kept up the strokes within her. His eyes were intent on her. He looked at her face and into her soul, memorizing just who he had up against the wall.

Close. She could feel his breath on her, feel his skin against hers, knew the ache of wanting in her, matched the need in him.

She mouthed the words to him, unable to speak as the beautiful pressure mounted.

I. Love. You.

He shuddered and thrust.

Hard enough to make her scream. Deep enough to make her gasp. And long enough to make her body shudder in response once, twice. Three times.

He was sitting, quietly, when she opened her eyes. She crawled, still half-dazed with sleep and sex, and settled into his lap.

"I prob'ly don't smell very good." She was sweaty and come streaked her thighs.

"You smell perfect."

She smiled and let her head rest against Grey's chest. Warm. Safe.

She couldn't ever remembering feeling so good.

In the distance she faintly heard the sound of a wolf howling, all alone, up at the moon.

Oh, God. She couldn't ever remember feeling so sad.

* * *

"The house isn't a total loss." Lowell shook his head. "But it's going to take months to restore."

"The house never was my favorite anyhow. It was too -- too cold. Impersonal." Lin didn't look bothered at all.

Mia hadn't cared about the rest of the house but she'd miss her one refuge. And that was gone forever. Her bedroom would never be the same. Would never feel as safe.

Then again, she was getting used to sleeping in Grey's bed. But how would that work now that everyone was back? She wasn't part of Grey's pack. Lowell had huge respect for Dek, his former Alpha as well his father-in-law, and the packs got along better than two packs ever should, but no one in separate packs ever lived together.

"Dek, how the hell did you keep Hunt from coming back to finish the job after Rome blew their office to hell?" Lowell didn't look bothered, either. In fact her two Alphas looked strangely cheerful.

Mia frowned. Lowell was a good Alpha. Even though he usually kept himself carefully controlled, she'd always figured there was more to him than he showed most of the pack. Lord knows Lin seemed to adore him and swore he was funny and warm -- all things he never revealed to anyone but Lin. But while he might be many things, cheerful had never been his style.

What was going on?

"I promised him something for the future." Dek glanced uneasily at the women. "First choice of the next female we have available."

Mia gulped. So did Lin.

Lowell just shook his head. "Why the hell would he wait on a possibility? And, even if it happens, why allow for something that won't do him or his pack any good for a long time? Even if we have a girl, it will be almost two decades before they can do anything with her."

"Desperation?" Dek shrugged. "There aren't many other packs or were females out there."

My baby. Bargained away before she's even born.

Grey turned and looked at her. Even though they didn't touch, she heard him.

I'll make sure nothing hurts her. Not even something the Boss has promised.

Mia managed a nod back. How a beta was going to do that was beyond her, but it didn't matter. The panic inside subsided. Grey would do what he said. She knew that.

"Lowell, before this goes any further, I need to talk to Mia." Lin touched her mate's hand.

Lowell nodded and Lin turned to Mia.

"Mia, I want you to know first. Before everyone else in the pack." Lin's eyes glittered as she grabbed Mia's wrists, pulling her up and away from the rest.

Mia raced along, trying not to be pulled. Lin was powerful and she was determined. Whatever the Big Talk was, Mia had a feeling she wasn't going to want to hear it. She hadn't liked anything else she'd heard so far.

When Lin stopped at last, Mia braced herself.

"Don't look so worried! It's good news. The best. I'm going to have a baby." Lin's grin spread all over her face. "Given all that's happened I figured you deserved to know before anyone else but Lowell."

"That's wonderful!" Mia smiled back. Then her smile faltered. "Oh."

Lin had done it. Mia wasn't needed for anything now.

What did you do with an Omega's baby when the Alpha was pregnant too? Mia touched her stomach.

Her pack wouldn't turn them out. They wouldn't. The stories about the other packs --

Mia opened her mouth to tell her Alpha her own news and shut it again. Lin would find out soon enough. She'd keep quiet and let Lin shine. She'd --

No.

"So am I." Mia's chin firmed. "I don't know what that means for you, Lin. I'll go if you want. But I'm going to keep my baby. I'm not giving him or her away. And I'm not acting like it was a mistake. Because it wasn't."

This was something she had to stand for. Even if no one stood with her.

Lin shook her head. "Mia, dear, I'd never do that. I know how much having a baby means. Except for Lowell, it's the most important thing ever."

"I have to tell Grey."

"We have to tell everyone!" Lin's laugh bubbled over.

"No, I have to tell Grey first. Because if you can get pregnant, then maybe all those things Rome believed about himself are wrong."

Things like not being a were. Not being able to father a child.

"You worried that I'll step away if the baby might not be mine?" Grey asked behind her back.

Mia jumped. She'd forgotten how quiet Grey could be.

She turned. Grey. He was unshakeable. Steady. Someone to depend on. And so sexy, even when all he did was look at her with that half-smile on his face.

"No. I don't think you would. But I wondered if you'd want to." Mia swallowed down more words. She wanted Rome back. For so many reasons. But a small part of her was thrilled that Grey had chosen and chosen *her*.

But a larger part didn't want to make him choose. She didn't want to choose one or the other herself. All. She wanted it all. Both of them, her pack, her baby. Everything.

"Think again, sweetheart. I always figured it was Rome's baby as much as mine, no matter who provided the sperm. We'd never have gotten here without him. But I'd never leave you now." Grey smiled a little wider. A real smile. ""Course if Rome ever finds out the news, could be he'll finally realize who he is."

"A real were?"

"Hell, he's always been that. I mean he's Alpha. Pure Alpha. Born to the role. He's been fighting it for too long, pretending he couldn't be."

"He's always been way too bossy, if that's what you mean," his loving sister muttered.

"Bossy. Protective. Knows what he wants and will barge in to get it. Alpha." Grey shrugged.

"Do we need yet another Alpha nearby?" Lin asked.

"We don't know yet if we're going to have one."

* * *

The music blared. The yells at the bar were too loud. The lights were too bright.

He had a mother of a hangover. Rome ran his hand over the stubble on his face and ran his tongue over the fur on his teeth. He must look as good as he felt.

"Hi, honey. I bet you could use a friend." The redhead smiled at him a little too blearily and hung over his table, showing a little too much cleavage for so early in the morning.

"Uh, thanks for asking but -- "

"You trying to hit on my woman?" The bruiser who stepped up to them looked like he was ready for a fight.

A week ago Rome would have been happy to oblige both of them.

"Not at all. I'm leaving. I'll tell the bartender to set you up with another round on me on my way out." Rome got up, made sure his balance was all right before he put one foot ahead of the other and left a faintly puzzled, scowling couple behind him.

What had he been thinking? This wasn't his place. These weren't his people.

He had a place.

He was bonded because how the hell else could Mia hear their thoughts? Too bad he couldn't hear hers or Grey's, the way bonded mates were supposed to. Then again it might not be what most weres had, but even a half-assed bonding meant something. Meant everything.

Hell, even more importantly, he felt bonded to them. He wanted them happy. He wanted to comfort them if they were sad. He just wanted to be with them.

Two mates. Two were mates.

Whether he was a were, a human, or just some genetic freak, he had two lovers who cared about him. He'd left them because --

Because he didn't want them to see him as weak? He was an idiot then. They made him strong. They made him better because he was with them.

Better than when he was alone.

Damn it, they needed him, too. Just as much as he did them. What kind of coward ran because things might be too good?

***

"I'm back."

Shit. Grey and Mia stared. The two of them were standing together, staring at him. Looking tight. Looking as if they were together.

Looking like he wasn't a part of them.

"I can tell that." Grey didn't look welcoming.

"Oh?" Mia crossed her arms, everything in her body language shutting him out. "Why are you back?"

He'd rather confess to murder. Rome loosened his shoulders and admitted, "Because I need you two."

"Really. Why do you suddenly need us?"

He'd never believed Mia could look so cold. Instead of her melting at his words the chill was getting worse.

But he wanted this badly enough to try again. "Because we belong."

God, he hoped he still did. How much could change after a few angry words and a day or two away?

"Are you sure?" Mia asked.

"Damned sure."

No response.

She couldn't hear his thoughts any more? Couldn't tell he meant it with all his soul? There were no more words for what he wanted. But he could try again. Keep trying until he convinced them. He had no choice.

Sudden blinding insight hit.

Hell, there were words. It's just they were the ones he'd been terrified to say.

Rome swallowed. "I love you. Both of you."

When Grey smiled, the first tendrils of relief started growing inside Rome. "Welcome home, kid."

Rome tried to hide the sudden weakening emotion inside him with a quick laugh. "What? No 'I told you so'?"

"Naw. I'm too busy thinking 'hallelujah.' All I'll tell you is -- " He reached forward to bear hug Rome. " -- I'll kill you if you ever try to do this again. It'd destroy me to go through this one more time. Hear me?"

"Heard and understood. Don't worry. It won't happen."

Grey bent, rested his face between the palms of Rome's hands. Didn't look up. Were those Grey's tears dripping onto his skin? Rome swallowed as he stared down at Grey's head.

Submission. Trust.

It's stupid not to take what's offered when you finally get what you want, Rome. Took me long enough to figure that out. Hope you're smarter than that. Love.

Rome bent down and bit hard into the sinews of Grey's neck. His. Grey grunted and looked up, eyes glittering with lust and love.

"You better not try. Because after he kills you, I will too." Mia grabbed as much of the two of them as she could gather in. "We missed you so much. We love you, Rome."

One small hand slid between his legs, resting against his cock. Why not? Rome bent and bit her shoulder, not quite as hard, but enough to mark, to claim her.

Love. Submission, trust and love.

He'd given them to Grey and to her once. Now they were giving the same to him.

He held them both, gripping them like a lifeline. All he had to do was tell them and this was his? It was just that easy?

Just that hard.

Rome cleared his throat. Made sure he could say something without bawling first.

"How about a welcome back fuck?"

"Rome, bad dog! No biscuit."

"I'm not looking for a biscuit, exactly."

Mia's clever little fingers had unzipped his pants and were now jerking him off. His pulse hammered down into his cock as she gripped him. He could smell the spice of her arousal. If he touched her -- and oh, he wanted to -- she'd be wet, wanting him. Grey's cock was already poking into his thigh.

"You never change, Rome. But first, I think I'll watch you gentlemen. That will be...fun. And later, much later, we'll tell you our surprise."

For an instant he could almost see Mia pregnant, she was thinking the image so clearly. Rome stared over at his female mate. She smiled.

But you might be the daddy. Honest.

It was the shock of her words that let them do it. The shock and the stunned pleasure. But before he could think anymore, Grey had him pinned.

"Don't think you get off easy tonight, boy," Gray growled in his ear. "I think it's time for pay back."

"Wha -- ?"

Shit. Mia hadn't just been jerking him off. One quick pull and the harness was strapped firmly onto his cock and balls.

"Don't think I forgot what you did to me, Rome." Gray's smile was just a bit menacing.

Mia settled herself, cross-legged, on the rug as Grey rolled him over and spread his legs. When Rome looked at her, her smile was just a bit evil.

"Don't you think you need to be punished, just a little?" Mia asked.

Rome looked at her hand, resting on her thigh but sooo close to that pretty pussy -- and forgot how to talk.

Punished. Grey was already behind him. Rome could smell the arousal and the need and the sex and the first bite of the restraint stung his hardened cock.

Grey's cock pushed the first inch inside him and Rome groaned. So it wasn't going to be all submission on their parts.

He fought a grin as he pondered just what they might have planned. He wouldn't mind. Not at all.

"Sure. Go ahead and punish me."

His ass was going to be sore for days. He knew it. Hell, he wanted it.

"First, you don't get to decide. And, second, when Grey is done, it's not going to be over. I think you might just be tired enough for me to use you next. I'll try to be gentle. For my sake, not yours."

Mia on top of him, teasing the hell out of his tired, sore body. Rubbing his soon to be abused ass on the floor while she enjoyed herself.

Damn it, the pull of the harness as his erection stiffened, hurt. Felt good.

Rough. Gentle. He'd take them any way he could get them.

Rome licked his lips. "Bring it on, baby."

Grey wasn't gentle. Not with his hands and especially not with that monster cock of his. Rome tried not to groan -- at least not until the groans were that of pleasure as well as pain.

"Jesus, Rome. You are a...hell...of a...good...fuck." Grey's voice was as rough as his entry.

It was over with just a few jackhammers of Grey's cock. It had been too long for both of them. If that damned noose hadn't held him back, he would have been shuddering out his seed along with Grey.

As it was, his balls screamed for release. He panted against the floor, humping his hurting, horny cock against its cool, unforgiving strength. Neither the floor nor the cock were going to move doing what he was doing, but he was desperate.

"My turn."

Rome turned his head and blinked the sweat from his eyes. Mia pursed her lips as she crawled forward on her knees. He blinked again and then bit back another groan at the sight of her over him, her breasts just teasing the skin on his back.

Her nipples were hard. She brushed them against him, very deliberately, tiny hard pricks of desire against him. His head sank back down on the floor.

Then she smacked his butt.

"Nice ass. I like yours as much as you say you do mine." She smacked the other cheek for good measure. "Now roll over and let me see the rest of you."

And damned if he didn't obey. When did Mia learn to get so bossy? The thing he thought he'd liked most about her was her sweetness.

She looked his erection over before smiling. Well, he was wrong again. That smile wasn't sweet, but he liked it just fine. He caught his breath when she moved over him. His cock strained to get closer.

Her wet little labial lips teased him with their slick promise before she slid her body away. Then she chuckled.

She ran one finger lightly down his shaft. He growled, his teeth biting into the inside of his mouth. She was going to kill him. He had to take it like a man.

That meant arching his hips up for more, mutely begging, with sweat trickling down his back. How else could a man take torture like that? She meant cold-blooded murder and he was begging for a quick death.

She moved, slid deeper down onto his cock and wiggled.

Whether it was slow or quick, he'd die happy.

"We have to be careful," she warned.

Oh, God. He'd forgotten. The little tease was going to get him too crazy to remember.

"You will be careful, won't you?" she whispered.

He looked into her eyes, alight with laughter and pure, naked lust. She was so beautiful. So precious.

"Of you? Hell, yes."

"That's what I needed to know." She sank down further onto his cock and clenched around it, almost painfully tight. "I'm going to ride you nice and slow and careful. Forever. But put your hands behind your head first. This is my show."

He was in so much damn trouble. How could you be careful when you wanted to rip into someone?

His cock jumped as she twitched above him.

"I love you, Mia." He tried desperately to keep it safe, to slow things down. He shoved his hands under his head, just the way she'd asked. He had to play it her way. He couldn't hurt her. He'd die rather than hurt her.

She was making sure of that. She wouldn't even let him touch her. At least not with his hands. But she sure as hell let him use his cock on that warm pussy.

She rocked against him and sighed.

"That's so nice, Rome. But I knew you loved me already. Now you're going to show me how much you love me."

And he did. For what seemed like the whole damn night, while she moaned and laughed and scratched and bit, her body rising and falling over him again and again.

He could hear the screams of passion in her head as her arousal rose higher and higher.

And when she finally, finally climaxed, her head thrown back and her eyes shut, he could feel every nuance of the white-hot pleasure running through her body. The only thing he couldn't do was come with her.

"For the love of God, Mia!" He moaned at last, a pitiful moan when her body let him go, when she backed off and pulled off him with a contented little sigh.

"Don't you ever, ever leave us again. Hear me?" Her voice was slurred and sated.

He was beyond talking. His balls felt like they were two sizes too big and they ached. Jesus, how they ached.

Before he could even think of what to do next, Mia was curled up, collapsed against him and already asleep, her breath stirring the hair on his chest as she breathed in and out.

Gray touched his shoulder and Rome jumped. Had Grey been watching the whole time? Rome had actually forgotten there was anyone else but Mia. At least until the second Grey's hand was on his body.

It wasn't possible, but Rome could tell he was getting even harder at Grey's touch.

"She does that a lot now. Hungry as a she-cat and then fast asleep when she's done."

Grey was still awake though. Awake and amused and, thank God, still horny.

Rome could smell his other mate's arousal.

"Let me go, Grey. I'll suck you off. I'll do anything. But let my cock out of this damned thing. I've got to --" Rome begging by now. Hell, his voice was hoarse from begging Mia. He was more than willing to plead with Grey. He didn't have any pride left.

Grey knew what it felt like to need and not be able to have. He'd understand.

"Yeah, I know what it's like to have your balls on fire. You showed me, Rome." Grey smiled. His smile was even more evil than Mia's had been. "Suck me off first and then we can talk."

Ah, hell. No relief yet?

Rome cautiously unclasped his hands. They were numb from where he'd gripped them behind his head to keep himself from grabbing Mia and using her the way he wanted.

He flexed his fingers and rolled over yet again, crawling to Grey.

"Motherfucker," Rome croaked out the words.

"Need some water, Rome? You sound a little parched. Might not be the best blow job you've ever given if you're that dry. I'm expecting a hell of a good one before I allow you to come."

Rome glared before he bent his head.

"Fuck you, Grey."

"Fuck me indeed." Grey's cock was already down his throat, thrust down to where Rome could lick Grey's balls, almost before Rome could swallow. "Let yourself go by yourself, idiot. You're the fucking Alpha."

Jesus, he *was* an idiot. Almost before Grey finished the sentence, Rome was free and jerking himself off while he swallowed Grey whole.

Grey's moan of satisfaction came a split second before fireworks exploded in front of Rome's eyes -- and through his body.

Grey's nails biting into his shoulders eased. "Jesus, I forgive you. A fucker with a mouth like yours should be forgiven two or three times a night."

Grey touched Rome's sweaty hair. It felt like a caress, lighter and more delicate than anything either of his mates had done to him all night.

Rome was sore as hell and higher than a kite. Still on his knees, he looked up at Grey and laughed.

Punishment had never felt so good.

But forgiveness was even better.

He woke up first, as always, still sticky from sex, with one hand on Mia's stomach and the other nestled on Grey's chest.

"You never change, Rome."

He had changed. He had a family again.

But the sex and the love, that hadn't changed. It had been there from the first.

Rome mouthed the words, unwilling to wake his partners. "I won't change. And don't you guys ever change on me, either."

Home.

~ * ~

Treva Harte

Treva Harte read far too many romances for far too long. One day the inevitable happened. She started writing her own brand of romance. She claims raising two pre-teens is a full time job itself, but in addition she works as an attorney in a city with many other attorneys. She and her husband both like writing in whatever time they have left, so they often fight over -- sorry, since they are attorneys they NEGOTIATE -- keyboard time.

Visit Treva on the Internet at www.trevaharte.com or email her at fanmail@trevaharte.com.

Printed in the United States
92475LV00003B/1-60/A